Praise for the

"A thoroughly entertaining series debut, with enjoyable yet realistic characters and enough plot twists—and dead ends—to appeal from beginning to end."

—*Booklist*, starred review, on *Booked 4 Murder*

"Filled with clues that make you go 'Huh?' and a list of potential subjects that range from the charming to the witty to the intense. Readers root for Phee as she goes up against a killer who may not stop until Phee is taken out well before her time. Enjoy this laugh-out-loud funny mystery that will make you scream for the authors to get busy on the next one."

—*Suspense Magazine* on *Molded 4 Murder*

"Engaging characters and a stirring mystery kept me captivated from the first page to the last."

—Dollycas, Amazon Vine Voice, on *Divide and Concord*

"Well-crafted sleuth, enjoyable supporting characters. This is a series not to be missed."

—*Cozy Cat Reviews* on *Death, Dismay and Rosé*

"A sparkling addition to the Wine Trail Mystery series. A toast to protagonist Norrie and Two Witches Winery, where the characters shine and the mystery flows. This novel is a perfect blend of suspense and fun!"

—Carlene O'Neil, author of the Cypress Cove Mysteries, on *Chardonnayed to Rest*

Books by J. C. Eaton

The Wine Trail Mysteries

A Riesling to Die
Chardonnayed to Rest
Pinot Red or Dead?
Sauvigone for Good
Divide and Concord
Death, Dismay and Rosé
From Port to Rigor Morte

The Sophie Kimball Mysteries

Booked 4 Murder
Ditched 4 Murder
Staged 4 Murder
Botched 4 Murder
Molded 4 Murder
Dressed Up 4 Murder
Broadcast 4 Murder
Saddled Up 4 Murder

The Marcie Rayner Mysteries

Murder in the Crooked Eye Brewery
Murder at the Mystery Castle
Murder at Classy Kitchens

Saddled Up
4
Murder

J. C. Eaton

BEYOND THE PAGE
PUBLISHING

Saddled Up 4 Murder
J. C. Eaton
Copyright © 2022 J. C. Eaton
Cover design and illustration by Dar Albert, Wicked Smart Designs

Beyond the Page Books
are published by
Beyond the Page Publishing
www.beyondthepagepub.com

ISBN: 978-1-954717-73-2

In memory of Barbara Jordan, friend, confidante, and role model of how life should be lived. We will miss your wit, style, and humor. Nights at the Sun City West Dog Park will never be the same.

ACKNOWLEDGMENTS

Thank you, Gale Leach, Larry Finkelstein (U.S.), and Susan Schwartz (Australia) for all you do to keep us on the straight and narrow. We count our lucky stars you've managed to stay with us so long!

And to Margi (M.J.) Evans for inspiring us with her amazing Riding Colorado equestrian books.

Without our agent, Dawn Dowdle, from Blue Ridge Literary Agency, none of this would be possible. You continue to amaze us every day.

And to Bill Harris, our editor at Beyond the Page, all we can say is Wow! Your encouragement and support put smiles on our faces every day.

Finally, we thank you, our readers, for embracing our looney characters and welcoming them into your lives!

CHAPTER 1

Bagels 'n More
Sun City West, Arizona

"It's only a matter of time," Myrna Mittleson announced, "before someone loses it altogether and shoves that deli-witch from the library bell tower." She patted her brunette curls and gave her head a shake. "And why that woman insists on running up and down those steep stairs is beyond me."

My mother reached across the table for the salt shaker and proceeded to add salt to the lox on her bagel. "It's her exercise routine. She made a big deal of it when someone asked her about it at the deli."

I was used to my mother's book club ladies and conversations that came out of nowhere, but this time, I was totally lost. "Deli-witch? Library tower? Will someone fill me in?"

The ladies and I were seated at Bagels 'n More, their favorite haunt across the road from their retirement community in Sun City West, Arizona. It was early April, and while the weeds had begun to take over, the snowbirds were slowly departing for points north and east.

Myrna took a deep breath, clasped her hands, and sighed. "The deli-witch is Billie C. That's what her name tag from the supermarket says. Don't know what the *C* stands for but everyone we know refers to her as the deli-witch."

"Try curmudgeon, cranky, crass, callous—"

"We get the idea, Lucinda," my mother said. "The woman's a veritable nightmare."

I moved my head from left to right, making eye contact with Shirley Johnson, Lucinda Espinoza, Cecilia Flanagan, Louise Munson, and Myrna Mittleson, before looking directly at my mother. "If she's so unbearable, then why do all of you use that deli? There are a zillion supermarkets around here and all of them have delis."

"Oh, honey," Shirley replied, "it's a matter of convenience. At our age we want to keep things as easy as possible. Once you figure out where everything is located, the last thing you want to do is switch markets. I've got those aisles memorized to the point where I could walk down them blindfolded."

I nodded. "I suppose you're right."

Louise reached across the table and grabbed three sugar packets.

"Forget about the deli. I have to deal with that misery of a woman every time I do my cardio exercises on those stairs."

Lucinda gave her a funny look. "Why don't you use one of the fitness centers? You've got a Rec card. You're entitled to make the most of it."

"My doctor wants me to walk up and down stairs. Something about belly fat. Forget the stairs at Palm Ridge. Not many steps. Anyway, Billie takes over that tower as if it were hers alone. Last week she sideswiped me out of the way as she flew up the stairs. I was so incensed I called her every name in the book and then some."

She reached for another sugar packet and my mother handed her the small tray. "I hope no one heard you, Louise."

"Everyone heard me. Herb Garrett was in the computer room and he told me my voice carried all the way in there. It doesn't matter. That she-witch deserved a tongue-lashing."

Myrna propped her elbow on the table and leaned her head into her fist. "Like I said before, one of these days someone's going to give her a shove and send her flying. We'll know because the bells will be ringing something other than the Westminster Chimes."

"Oh, that reminds me," my mother said, "Herb was supposed to stop by and join us. I wonder what's keeping him."

Common sense.

"You don't suppose he called that pinochle crew of his and invited them, do you?"

Judging from the pained expressions on the ladies' faces, I hoped that wasn't the case. There's only so much grousing and complaining I could take in one sitting.

My mother looked around the room and continued. "He probably spotted some good-looking woman in the parking lot and he's out there ogling her." Then, she stretched her neck and pivoted in Shirley's direction. "Have you told Phee about our idea for Streetman's special wedding outfit?"

At the mention of the words *wedding outfit*, I felt a sudden knot in my stomach. That instant, I wanted to talk about the deli-witch and every other witch from Salem to the latest Stephen King novel, but once the subject of my upcoming nuptial came up, there was no turning back.

In less than two months, I'd be tying the knot with Marshall Gregory, my boss's partner at Williams Investigations in Glendale, Arizona. This would be my second marriage, having failed miserably at my first with one exception—my daughter Kalese, who just began her teaching career in Minnesota, where I'm from.

I'm Sophie Kimball, better known as Phee, and I'm the bookkeeper/accountant for Nate Williams, who, along with my fiancé, retired from the

Mankato Police Department to start an investigative business in a state where snow is optional. I joined him on a temporary basis when he made me an offer that was too good to pass up, and before I knew it, I sold my house in Mankato and took up permanent residence in Peoria, a stone's throw from my mother. Heaven help me.

Once every month or so, when I'm not working on a Saturday morning, I have brunch with my mother and her friends at Bagels 'n More or the Homey Hut. If I'm lucky, I get to leave without indigestion or a headache.

"Go on, Shirley, tell her," my mother said.

"I don't believe in upstaging the bride, so I'm keeping it simple."

Oh, believe me, wedding outfit or no outfit, that neurotic little chiweenie dog of my mother's will upstage everyone in the Glendale City Hall. And why I agreed to let him do a doggie dance is anyone's guess.

I swallowed a large gulp of coffee and bit my lower lip. "Okay, what's Streetman going to wear?"

Shirley steepled her hands and smiled. It was impossible not to notice how the lovely shade of iridescent aqua accented her dark skin. Meanwhile, I was content with a French manicure once in a while, since it never involved selecting a color that would or wouldn't work for me.

"Your mother and I thought perhaps the dog would wear a version of a cummerbund that matched Marshall's tie, and in addition, we'd add matching ankle booties that wouldn't interfere with his paws."

The last time I had to worry about matching cummerbunds was for my senior prom. Even Kalese's date, if I recall correctly, didn't bother to do that.

"A cummerbund, huh? Okay. That sounds simple enough."

"Good," Cecilia said. She looked down at her white cardigan and adjusted the buttons so that the white blouse beneath it was completely covered up. At least she wasn't wearing black. Maybe because we were approaching summer. "If you must know, I found a way to avoid getting waited on by Billie. If she calls my number, I tell her I'm still thinking and she can go to the next person. Then, I get the other person at the deli, whoever that is."

"I still think you ladies should shop elsewhere, or at the very least, complain to the management."

"Complaining to management takes way too much time," my mother said. "And it wouldn't do us any good. We've got better things to do with our time, like figure out who's going to man our Booked 4 Murder book club booth at the Bye Bye Birdie event at the end of the month."

Oh, no. Not another event. Please don't tell me there's another event.

My mother went on. "I've got to juggle the Broadcast club booth and the clay club. Plus, I'm on the event committee."

"I'll fit it in somehow," Shirley said. "But I'm stretched as it is with the Rip 'n Sew and the Creative Stickers. Maybe Cecilia can add another slot."

"I've got the Rhythm Tappers, remember? You were the ones who insisted I join. What about Myrna?"

"Hey, I've got the bocce club and the clay club."

"Don't look at me," Lucinda said, "I'm in charge of the clay club's booth. What about you, Louise?"

Louise Munson shook her head. "I've got the Sunshine Animal club. The bird group, to be precise."

Then, everyone looked my way and I felt like the proverbial deer in the headlights. "Oh, no. Absolutely not. I don't even live in this community. I'm only in my forties."

Shirley gave me a pat on the wrist. "Phee's right. The poor girl has enough on her plate as it is. We'll figure out a schedule and go from there."

Without thinking, the words slipped from my mouth. "What's the Bye Bye Birdie event? I don't seem to remember it."

"That's because you were too busy with your aunt Ina's wedding the last time they held it," my mother said. "Which reminds me, everyone, Ina says to give you her regards. She and Louis are at some cockamamie meditation retreat in the Catalina Mountains near Tucson."

I tried not to laugh. My aunt Ina was a hippie long before the word was even invented. I suppose "free-spirited" might be a better way to describe her, but my mother's label of "artsy-fartsy" was the one most family members used, including her own son, my cousin Kirk from Boston.

"Oh, yes. What did you say, Phee? Something about the Bye Bye Birdie event?"

"She wants to know what it is, Harriet," Lucinda said before glopping more cream cheese on her bagel.

My mother turned to me, and without pausing to catch a breath, gave me the complete rundown on the "end of the snowbird season" in Sun City West. "It's a giant send-off," she said. "Think of it as a Bon Voyage party where all the partygoers are happy to see the guests leave."

I chuckled. For the past couple of years all I heard were complaints about overcrowded restaurants, congested roads, and drivers who didn't know how to use turn signals.

"Yes," Louise added. "All of the clubs have booths and sell their handmade items in case the snowbirds want to bring something back to their home states. The other clubs sell foods and treats, so it's a real moneymaker. Each year a different club performs. Cecilia's off the hook since the Rhythm Tappers performed last time. I think the Westernaires singing group is on for this celebration."

Then, a chorus of "tell her about the send-off" followed.

Louise gave a nod and continued. "The event begins at two in the afternoon and concludes at dusk, at which time giant balloons are released from the top of the library bell tower. The snowbirds purchase the balloons in advance and write their names and home states on them. Very touching."

Myrna motioned for the waitress and pointed to her empty coffee cup. "Too bad someone couldn't release the deli-witch. There's one send-off I wouldn't mind seeing."

I watched as the waitress went around the table topping off everyone's coffee. "She can't be that bad, can she?" I asked.

Just then, the waitress spoke. "Sorry, but I couldn't help overhear you. And yes, if it's the same woman, Billie C., she can and *is* that bad. Yesterday after my shift, I went to the supermarket for cold cuts. They've got a new system there with numbers that indicate how you want your meat sliced. One is for shaved and five is for thick. You get the idea. Well, this poor man kept asking for a half pound of low-salt ham, when that miserable woman kept yelling at him, 'What number? What number?' The man, obviously flustered, kept replying 'a half pound.' So, what did she do? Screamed even louder. I pulled the man aside and explained to him that the chart on the deli counter had numbers to indicate the thickness. After that, he said 'three,' and she stormed off to get his ham. Can you imagine? I'm surprised they still have customers."

I gulped. "Whoa. Remind me to stick with salads."

The waitress chuckled and walked over to another table. "Seriously," I said, "someone needs to register a complaint."

"Don't worry, honey," Shirley replied. "She'll get what's coming to her. I'm a strong believer in what goes around, comes around."

Myrna gave her a nudge. "If you must know, I'm a strong believer in putting marbles on that library stairwell. That'll teach her."

"Marbles? How about if someone lets a few bats loose in there?" Lucinda asked.

"Bats? What about . . ."

And for the next five minutes, the Booked 4 Murder book club wrote its own script for murder. I did at least four mental eye rolls before thanking my lucky stars I shopped in Peoria and Glendale.

"Well, as much as I enjoyed getting together with all of you," I said, "I really need to get home and defrost something for dinner. We ate out last night so I promised Marshall a home-cooked meal, even if it was prepared eons ago."

"Ask him what color tie he plans to wear for the ceremony," my mother said. "Two months is not that far off and Streetman needs to be prepared."

God forbid I upset the dog's social calendar.

"I have a better idea," Myrna said.

My mother turned to her. "About Phee's civil ceremony in Glendale?"

"No, about that deli-witch. Someone should dress as Quasimodo and stand at the top of the tower by the bells. That would teach her a lesson."

I shoved my chair into the table and took off. Then, I spun around and winked. "It wouldn't work. She'd just get on her broomstick and take off. Like I'm about to do."

With that, I figured I'd heard enough about the deli-witch, but boy, was I ever wrong.

CHAPTER 2

No sooner had I left the table and arrived at the register than Herb walked in. "Hey, cutie, don't tell me I missed all the fun."

"Trust me. The ladies are just getting started."

He sucked in his stomach and stood straight up. "Quick. Fill me in so I can catch up."

I sighed. "The deli-witch, the Bye Bye Birdie event, and the dog's outfit for my wedding. Don't ask."

"Billie C.? That deli-witch?"

"How many are there?"

"Oh, it's her, all right. If you want my opinion, what that woman needs is a—"

Please tell me a good swift kick in the butt and not something obscene.

"I know. I know. Don't say a word. I already got the lowdown on her. Anyway, I should be going."

"Sure you don't want to stick around for another cup of coffee? I just got an email from the Broadcast club. They've chosen the announcers for the Bye Bye Birdie send-off. Last year my pinochle crew had the honors. This year it will be your mother along with Myrna Mittleson and Paul Schmidt. Their combination murder mystery/fishing show is a big hit. Go figure."

Go figure indeed. It's a disaster if anyone asks me.

My mother, along with Myrna, host a murder mystery radio show once a week on KSCW, the voice of Sun City West. She figured if Herb could have his own pinochle pointers show, she and Myrna could discuss cozy mysteries. Guess the radio station management agreed. And then Paul Schmidt came along with his own show—*Lake Fishing with Paul.* Apparently Minnesota wasn't the only state with lots of lakes. Arizona was on the list, too. Unfortunately, sometime last year they got the schedule wrong and the three of them showed up to do their shows at the same time.

The result was a hodgepodge of fishing and bait tips coupled with recent murder mysteries because neither was willing to give up the spot to the other person. Anyway, the radio audience, including Williams Investigations secretary Augusta Hatch, loved it. From that point on, my mother and Myrna got to do a combined show with Paul a couple of times a month.

"Um, I'm sure my mother will give me all the details." *And a whole lot more . . .*

I paid my bill and headed for the door. "Nice seeing you," I said. "Enjoy your brunch." Then I bolted for my car.

The remainder of the weekend was everything I loved about living in Arizona—a late afternoon swim with my friend Lyndy, an early Sunday morning hike with Marshall, who endured another recap of my conversation with the book club ladies, and warm, balmy weather that wouldn't turn into an inferno for a few more weeks. Too bad it was short-lived. The easygoing weekend pace had shifted to the Monday morning rush before I realized it. As usual, Marshall and I took our own cars to the office since he was constantly on the move with his cases.

According to Augusta, who kept me apprised of Nate and Marshall's caseloads, usually before they were aware of them, nothing looked to be out of the ordinary that morning. But everything changed when their nine thirty appointment arrived. Even the static in the air, according to Augusta. I had just left my office to grab another cup of coffee out front when Augusta ran her thumb across her neck and said, "Got a bad feeling about this one."

"Is the client in Nate's office or Marshall's? And what does he look like? It's a he, isn't it? I thought I heard a man's voice. Older guy? Younger guy?" I leaned over Augusta's desk and kept my voice low.

"You're getting as bad as those book club ladies. Middle-aged. I'm guessing early fifties. Tall, lean, salt-and-pepper hair, clean-shaven, cleft chin. No visible tattoos but he does have a scar that runs from his right elbow to the wrist. Did I cover all the bases, Miss Marple?"

"Uh-huh."

"Good. Then now maybe you'll let me get back to work."

I walked to the Keurig and popped in a cup of McCafé medium roast. "Did he give you his name or the reason for the appointment?"

"It wasn't an appointment we had on the schedule. The client left a message last night insisting he meet with both detectives this morning. Said he contacted the sheriff's office but wasn't satisfied."

I rolled my eyes. *No surprise there if he wound up talking with Deputy Bowman or Ranston.* "Who's the client? Did he leave a name?"

"Perry Gaynes from Wickenburg. Owner of the Dancing Caballeros Stable."

"The Dancing Caballeros? I've been dying for a weekend at that posh dude ranch. They've been featured in *Phoenix* magazine and there was a segment about them on HGTV not too long ago. It's a five-star resort with every possible amenity imaginable."

Augusta patted her high bouffant hairdo and went back to her computer. "Five-star or no star, a horse is a horse and your butt's going to smell like one when you're done riding. No amenity in the world's going to change that."

"Shh. I think I hear chairs moving. The meeting must be over. I don't want to appear like a busybody."

"Too late for that."

I immediately removed my coffee cup from the machine and busied myself with the creamer.

"You're not fooling anyone, "Augusta whispered.

Sure enough, Augusta's description of Perry Gaynes was right on the money. As was her thumb-across-the-neck gesture. Given the expression on Perry's face and the somber looks on Nate and Marshall's, it didn't take a soothsayer to figure out this wasn't the usual fare for us.

Nate walked Perry to the door and told him Augusta would fax a contract to him within the hour. Marshall, who stood a few feet back, gave the guy a wave and a nod. Not a happy smiley nod, but more like the kind I'd seen funeral directors use at viewings.

The minute the door closed behind Perry, I walked toward Nate and Marshall. "What was that about? It's as if the temperature dropped by twenty degrees in here."

The men looked at each other before Nate spoke. "The client is Perry Gaynes, owner of the Dancing Caballeros Stable in Wickenburg, but I'm sure Augusta provided you with those salient details." He crinkled his nose at Augusta, who in turn shrugged. Then he continued. "Sometime yesterday afternoon, three horses were stolen from one of their stables—two were quarter horse geldings and the other a sorrel Arabian mare."

Augusta sat bolt upright in her chair. "I knew it was only a matter of time before our office wound up investigating horse thieves. Too bad they don't hang them anymore in this state."

"Too bad they don't have the resources," Marshall said. "That's why the client came to us."

I took a sip of coffee and eyeballed both men. "What about the sheriff's office? Augusta mentioned—"

Nate tried not to laugh. "Good grief. What hasn't Augusta mentioned?" Then he went on. "Perry called the Maricopa Sheriff's Office and after a grueling conversation with one of their deputies, *his* words, not mine, the deputy referred him to the Arizona Department of Agriculture since horse theft comes under their jurisdiction."

I bit my lip. "Uh-oh. I can see where this is going."

Marshall walked toward me and gave my shoulder a squeeze. "You've got that right. That's when he knew he was in trouble and left a message with our agency last night. Still, he did contact the Department of Agriculture first thing this morning and was referred to their livestock field office."

"Moving him further down the dungeon, Mr. Gregory," Augusta said.

"No wonder the guy looked like a corpse when he walked in."

Marshall sighed. "The livestock field office is the one responsible for investigating horse theft, which, by the way, is considered to be a property crime."

I put my coffee cup on the edge of Augusta's desk and widened my eyes. "A property crime? How can it be a property crime? Horses are live animals."

"Hurrump." Augusta crossed her arms and leaned back in her chair. "That's the same thing my uncle Roscoe said when his prize bovine got snatched during the Wisconsin State Fair back in 1978. They caught the thief, but let me tell you, it was one hell of a night."

"Good to know," Marshall said to Augusta before turning his attention back my way. "That's just how it is. Horse theft is deemed a property crime and the factors that determine the value of the animal are mind-boggling. Was the horse a racing horse? A breeding horse? Age and condition? Then there are the circumstances surrounding the theft. Was a weapon used? Was there any sign of forced entry? I could go on but you get the idea."

I swallowed. "I get it, all right. You and Nate are the guy's last chance to ever see those horses again."

"You know what the awful thing is?" Nate asked. "No one can remember prosecuting a horse theft in this county for at least fifty years. But right now, all I'm concerned with is finding those horses before they wind up in another state."

Augusta edged her chair closer to where Nate stood. "Do you want me to reschedule your appointments today, Mr. Williams? And Mr. Gregory's?"

"The cases on our docket aren't time-sensitive, with one exception— the cheating wife. So, yeah, go ahead but keep her appointment with me. It's not until forty thirty so Marshall and I can get started."

"What about the contract?"

"Oh," Nate replied, "I think Perry Gaynes is good for his word. Right now, we're on our way to Wickenburg to review his surveillance tapes and interview the employees. From there, we'll see if anyone from the neighboring ranches noticed anything unusual."

Marshall gave me a peck on the cheek and mumbled something about cold cut sandwiches for dinner.

Five minutes later they were out the door and I was back at my desk. I never really pictured our office handling horse theft, but then again, it was surprising the kinds of cases that wafted our way. I thanked my lucky stars it wasn't another murder case, but in retrospect, I should have held off.

At a little past ten, Augusta and I were both hankering for a donut so I volunteered for a quick run to the nearest Dunkin'. When I got back and handed her the two French crullers she'd requested, she pointed to the bag and winced. "You might want to eat your donut now before you return your mother's call. I've got to admit, her messages rival the Navajo Code Talkers."

"Why? What did she say?"

"And I quote, 'Tell Phee the witch is dead and the tower is off limits.' Guess that beats 'The crow flies at midnight.' Please don't tell me your mother is trying out for a local production of *The Wizard of Oz*."

"No, but horse theft may wind up taking a second seat to whatever nightmare is about to unfold in Sun City West. Geez, I hope I'm wrong."

CHAPTER 3

I never demolished a donut so fast in my life. Less than a minute later, I dialed my mother and prayed the witch in question had died of natural causes, like too much sodium from all that deli meat.

My mother's voice was strained and scratchy. "Oh, good. You called. Augusta said you were out on an errand. I just got off the phone with Shirley, who's stuck at the library because they've got the place on lockdown. Someone found the deli-witch at the bottom of the tower stairwell. Dead. It must be foul play or they wouldn't have locked the library to speak with the patrons. Same deal with the computer room. Shirley said she'd call me back as soon as she hears anything."

"Maybe the woman had a stroke or heart attack and the deputies are merely covering their bases."

"I don't think so. About an hour before Shirley called, I was on the phone with Gloria Wong and she stopped in mid-sentence because she heard the tower chimes ringing like crazy. I immediately thought about what Myrna said on Saturday but didn't say a word to Gloria. Is that what you think it was? Someone murdered that witch and her body got shoved into the bells before the killer rolled it down the stairwell?"

"Whoa. Slow down. You don't know she was murdered. For all anyone knows, someone from maintenance might have been up there and accidently bumped into the bell. It wouldn't be the first time according to Herb."

"Herb? What does he know? Oh, never mind. That man's got his nose into everything. Anyway, I thought you should know about Billie C.'s body being found so you can give your boss and your fiancé a heads-up."

"A heads-up? They're not investigating her death."

"Not at the moment, no, but give it time. Listen, I'm going to call Louise and see if she knows anything about it. Louise does her cardio step run every morning. Maybe she saw the killer lurking around before Billie got there."

"Good grief. You're not Lee Child. Let it go. The poor woman probably suffered some sort of medical emergency, lost her balance and fell to her death. Not pleasant, but not exactly screaming murder."

"We'll see about that."

I got off the phone and rubbed my temples for what seemed like ages before returning to the spreadsheet I had been working on. Later on, when I told Augusta about the call, she didn't seem too surprised. We were in the break room munching on tacos that Door Dash delivered because neither of us felt like sandwiches from Qwik Stop.

"You know," she said, "if that woman was as bad as what your mother described, it wouldn't surprise me if someone did her in. All sorts of unsettling road rage cases around the valley."

"This wasn't road rage. And there's no such thing as tower rage."

Augusta ripped open a packet of hot sauce and doused her taco. "True, but someone might have had a seething rage building up inside them and took advantage of a situation to make it look like an accident."

"Oh, brother. Please don't tell me you landed on the mystery writer home page along with my mother's looney book club."

"Don't be ridiculous. I'm quantifying the evidence and proposing a theory, that's all."

"What evidence?"

"The dead body."

I washed down my taco with a Coke and laughed. "If it turns out you're right, I'll buy your tacos for the next month."

"Start hoarding your pocket change."

It was a good thing I had a dollar eighty-eight at the bottom of my bag because, if Augusta's words held true, I'd need it. At a little past four, my mother called again and I had to hold the receiver a good five or six inches from my ear.

"Phee! I finally reached Louise Munson. Poor woman got a surprise visit from that deputy who resembles a desert toad—Ranston. He was by himself and told her he was following up on some information. Turns out, someone in the computer room, which is adjacent to the bell tower entrance, spotted Louise leaving the tower a few minutes before Billie's body was found. Louise told me Billie arrived shortly after she did and shoved her out of the way just before she reached the first landing. Said Billie called her an old fossil on her way up the stairs."

"What was Ranston's reaction?"

"He kept asking her if that's the only thing that happened. Louise got the idea he didn't believe her. Not about the fossil comment, but the fact that Louise told him nothing else happened."

"Heavens. All he had to do was take one look at Louise and he'd realize there's no way she could have gotten to the top of the tower with the strength and stamina to give Billie a hearty shove down the stairs."

"Well, one thing for sure," my mother said. "The murder had to have happened once Louise left. Face it, she'd have noticed if a body went sailing down those steps while she was doing her cardio thing."

"Not a murder. It's an incident. An unfortunate incident."

"Call it what you want, Phee, but a mangled body at the base of a tower is not an unfortunate incident. It's a crime scene."

"Why don't we wait until a further determination can be made? And let me clarify, a *further, substantiated determination* by law enforcement."

"If you're referring to Deputy Ranston and his obnoxious partner, it'll be a long wait."

"Uh-huh. And what did you mean by *mangled body*? Who said anything about a mangled body?"

"The woman fell from the tower to the ground. It goes without saying the body would be mangled."

I shuddered and took a deep breath. "Fine. Mangled. Did Louise say anything else?"

"No, but Deputy Ranston did. He told her not to leave town. You know what that means, don't you?"

"Yeah. Ranston's now reciting the lines from the late-night TV crime shows."

"For your information, Louise was quite shaken up. But I told her not to worry. I reassured her that if anything came of that little talk with the deputy, your boss and your boyfriend would step in and set things straight."

"What? How could you make such a statement? What were you thinking?"

"I had to say something that would put her mind at ease."

Terrific. Louise Munson's mind is now at ease while mine is twisting and contorting all over the place.

"Don't make any promises or commitments to anyone, Mom. Nate and Marshall have enough on their plate. For your information, they're dealing with a highly sensitive equine matter."

"You mean a horse theft?"

"Yeah, a horse theft."

"Hmm, that's a first. I mean, this is the southwest and all, but I haven't heard of any horse thefts and I've been living in the valley for ages."

"You've been living in a senior community. Cars and golf carts."

"And a pending murder."

"Arragh."

My head was spinning when I got off the phone, and once again, I rubbed my temples. This time because I knew what was coming—endless phone calls back and forth among the book club ladies. Each call embellishing the incident. And while Louise was questioned by Deputy Ranston, I had no reason to believe she'd be a suspect. Getting elbowed in a stairwell was hardly a motive for murder. *If* it was murder.

I began to relax. There was no justifiable reason for the book club ladies to insist I snoop around to find out who could have had it in for Billie C. No reason whatsoever. Or so I thought.

Marshall phoned me at quarter to five explaining that he and Nate were still in Wickenburg and Nate's prior appointment had to be rescheduled. They had reviewed the footage from the barn's security camera and had completed preliminary interviews with the staff. Now they were headed to the neighbors' houses and weren't sure what time they'd be back.

"Get yourself something to eat, hon," Marshall said. "Nate and I will fend for ourselves on the way home, whenever that'll be. Tell Augusta to lock up and we'll see her in the morning."

I knew that the first forty-eight hours following a crime were the most important. Especially when it came to kidnapping, or horse-napping in this case. I gave Augusta the message and went back to my spreadsheets. Thankfully the only phone calls our office received for the remainder of the day were ones associated with our business. Too bad that little piece of Nirvana didn't last in the week ahead.

Marshall arrived home at a little past seven. Tired, headachy, and thirsty.

"That'll teach me for ordering spicy nachos at a local cantina in Wickenburg," he said. "I should have played it safe and ordered a salad." He poured himself a glass of filtered water from the fridge and sank into the closest kitchen chair. "There were only two neighbors spread out over twenty acres but it took forever."

"Any leads?"

"Not really. We've got a few more people to chat with tomorrow so it looks like another hectic day. I'll stick around the office in the morning to handle our current cases while Nate heads back to Wickenburg. I suppose you had a quiet day at the office, huh?"

"The office, yes. Sun City West, no."

Marshall took another gulp of water before putting the glass on the table. "Do I dare ask?"

"Only if you want to add heartburn to your other ailments."

Chapter 4

The nightly news confirmed everything I told Marshall. Only instead of half-baked theories from my mother's friends, it was the news anchors who had their own take on the matter. No sooner did they relay the facts that "the body of a woman who appeared to be in her fifties was found at the base of the Sun City West's tower stairwell," when they immediately launched into the usual banter, leaving the viewers to reach their own conclusions regarding the cause of death.

"Until next of kin can be notified," the female anchor explained, "the name is being withheld. We will keep our audience apprised of the situation as we learn more. Be sure to stay tuned to KPHO for all the latest news."

"Forgot KPHO," I announced. "I have Harriet Plunkett, the voice of Greater Phoenix and beyond." Granted, I was being a tad sardonic, but I never, in my wildest imagination, thought for one iota of a second that my mother not only honored that position but would do everything in her power to retain that reputation, even if it meant suckering me into finding out who killed the deli-witch.

• • •

It was Thursday when the preliminary cause of death was made public—a fall as a result of an altercation. Terms like *defensive wounds* combined with a graphic depiction of what happens to someone when their body falls from four or five stories aboveground were all over the news channels. Not to mention the local radio stations and social media. And while the death hadn't been deemed a homicide, it certainly met the bill for manslaughter. As for the degree, it was anyone's guess.

Billie C.'s full name and marital status became public knowledge as well. Willameena Addison Churl, single. With a name like that, it was no wonder people said she was in a perpetual bad mood. It would be weeks before a full toxicology report was available but the sheriff's office was fairly certain she died as the result of trauma and not something she ingested. As part of the ongoing investigation, they kept the library tower off limits and the crime scene tape was still plastered across the entryway.

"How long does it take for that forensic crew to gather up whatever they need and reopen the tower?" my mother exclaimed when she phoned me on Thursday. I had finished sending out some invoices and was about to tackle a few more from the pile when Augusta had bellowed, "Your mother is on the line," and transferred the call to my office.

"Uh, hi, Mom. I guess as long as it takes to complete the investigation. Why? You don't exercise on those steps and Louise can always use Palm Ridge."

"It's not about the exercise. Louise can buy a mini-stool and go up and down those steps. It's about the Bye Bye Birdie event. If they don't open that tower, we won't be able to have our grand send-off with the balloons and Myrna, Paul, and I won't be able to announce the festivities from the tower."

Why didn't I see this coming?

"The event is what? About three or four weeks from now? Give or take a day or so? That's plenty of time."

Oh, who am I kidding?

My mother screeched, "In what world? In what world will that suspicious death be solved in three weeks? Give or take a few days."

I knew she was right but the last thing I needed was to get involved. Especially since the past week had been so stressful for Nate and Marshall.

"Can't you make the announcements from the radio station or a makeshift table in front of the library?"

"It's not the same thing. No other community has a bell tower and no other community hosts an event of this magnitude. It'll be on the evening news, the nightly news, and the next day early-bird morning news. In fact, Gloria Wong told me the *Sonoran Living* show might do a segment about it. She heard that from her hairdresser."

Oh, yeah. Another reliable source . . .

"It hasn't even been a week. Perhaps—"

"I knew you'd offer to help. Thank goodness."

Huh? What? Since when is the word perhaps *considered an offer?*

"I think you should begin with Cindy Dolton at the dog park. She'll know who was gunning for that deli-witch. Streetman will be overjoyed. He loves getting to the park at dawn."

Good for him. I don't exactly love getting to the park at dawn.

"Look, I've got a really busy schedule, so—"

"I'll have him ready by six. That way you'll have plenty of time to drop him off and get to work when you're done. I bought some to-go cups so I can even give you a cup of coffee to take with you to the park. I'll reheat what's left in the pot."

"Uh, no. That won't be necessary. Not at all. I'll get coffee on the way over."

I could have slapped myself the second those words came out of my mouth. It wasn't the first time my mother got me so flustered that I agreed to take the dog to the park, and sadly, I knew it wouldn't be the last.

"Fine. Six o'clock. Is he off probation? I need to be sure. People ask."

"Yes. He's been off his second probation for over a month. It's not his fault he likes other dogs."

Streetman gave new meaning to the term "public displays of affection." And a new adjective to go along with it—"unwanted."

"Is Aunt Ina back from her meditation retreat or whatever the heck that was?"

"She and your uncle Louis should be home by the weekend. They must not have Wi-Fi where she is because I haven't heard a word from her. Just as well. She'd be pestering me with all sorts of questions. You can't imagine how annoying that is."

If it were possible to grimace and roll my eyes at the same time, I would have done so. Instead, I muttered "Uh-huh" and told her I'd see her and the dog in the morning.

As it turned out, Marshall had an early start to the next day as well. After canvassing the neighboring ranches, he and Nate learned that the three horses stolen from the Dancing Caballeros weren't the only ones. Two trail horses, which were more pets than horses, were taken from one ranch, leaving a six-year-old boy and his younger sister devastated according to the parents. Like Perry, they, too, had called the Arizona Department of Agriculture. And like Perry, they also notified their insurance agent of the loss. It was hard to wrap my head around the fact horses were property and were part of the owner's insurance package, but with values that could exceed thirty thousand dollars, I suppose it made sense. Still, it wouldn't compensate for the loss of a pet.

"Was that it?" I asked as he hurried to get dressed. "Five horses?"

Marshall shook his head. "Seven. The neighboring ranchette, for lack of a better word, had one of their geldings taken as well. Also a young quarter horse. The owner told us the horse was one of their best trail riding horses that didn't spook easily. He reported the theft to the sheriff's office and was referred to the livestock services field staff. When he learned Perry hired us to investigate, he asked about retaining our services as well."

"How valuable are these horses? Do you think they're being traded on a black market somewhere?"

"Quite possible. But why all of sudden? And why trail horses? Sure, they're valuable, but certainly not the same caliber as racing horses or horses used for dressage. Then again, I've learned not to dismiss anything when it's early on in an investigation. And this one's turning out to be a doozy. The case ballooned overnight."

We headed to the kitchen, where Marshall opened the fridge and swallowed a V8. "Got to run. Augusta agreed to do some of the preliminary research on our easier cases in order for Nate and me to concentrate on this one. We're off to Wickenburg again. Let's face it, seven stolen horses all in the same time frame . . . it has to be connected."

He gave me a hug and a soft kiss on my cheek before grabbing his cell phone and charging to the garage. "I'll keep you posted, hon. At least our investigative work doesn't involve a persnickety little chiweenie. Look on the bright side, any intel you pick up may help the sheriff's office with their investigation."

"Forget the sheriff's office. It'll get my mother off my back. And one step closer to a guest appearance on *Sonoran Living*."

"Huh?"

"Long story. I'll tell you tonight. I'm making a healthy chicken salad for dinner so don't fill up."

Next thing I knew, I heard the garage door open and close. It was five ten and a hazy sunrise crept over the horizon in shades of mauve and yellow. I got dressed quickly and was behind the wheel of my car in less than twenty minutes. No sense fussing in the kitchen with Dunkin' and Starbucks in every plaza between Vistancia and Sun City West.

My mother's porch light and the overhead garage door motion-sensor light were both on when I pulled into her driveway. She'd either gone out to retrieve the morning paper or a coyote had skirted past the house. Seconds later, the motion light went out.

I walked to the security door, rang the bell, and all but jumped when she flung open the front door. "Have you been standing guard at the door?"

"Streetman was getting antsy."

Looking down at the little chiweenie, I realized he had wrapped his leash around his legs. I went to unravel it when my mother stopped me. "Whatever you do, don't touch his paws. He goes ballistic."

"Then you do it."

"Honestly, Phee."

My mother bent down, waved one hand in front of the dog and used the other to unwind the leash. "It's much easier when he's distracted." Then, she furrowed her brow and looked at me. "Do you suppose that's what happened to Billie in the tower? Someone distracted her and then tossed her down the stairs?"

"The news anchors all said 'a fall resulting from an altercation.' Look, either way, she probably knew her assailant."

"And hopefully today, you'll find out who that was."

"Mom, Cindy Dolton may be a wealth of information"—*or rumor and hearsay*—"but I doubt she's clairvoyant."

"She's not the only source of information in that park. Noodle around. I'd do it myself, but every time I go in there, all I get are complaints about the dog."

No kidding.

Then she gave the dog a pat on his head and told him what a good boy he was. I all but gagged.

CHAPTER 5

Streetman jumped into the passenger seat, curled into a ball, and proceeded to enjoy a seven-minute nap while I drove to the dog park. For a city where barely a soul can be spotted on the streets after seven thirty at night, the opposite held true at six fifteen a.m.

The pickleball courts were packed, the bowling alley appeared to be doing a brisk business, and folks were elbow to elbow at the outdoor track. The parking lot in front of the pool resembled a concert night at the state fair and the benches at the bocce court were filled to capacity.

I gave the library bell tower a cursory glance when I pulled into the Rec Center's sprawling parking lot. It was odd that no one had noticed any commotion at the top of the tower on the day of Billie's fall to death. The bell tower was open on all four sides with arched columns and a ledge surrounding it. If there was a struggle, as the postmortem indicated, wouldn't a passerby have noticed something? Then again, who looks at the top of the bell tower? Too much else going on below.

As I rounded the corner of the lot, a silver KIA Sorento pulled out and I immediately nabbed the parking space. "Come on, Streetman," I said. "Time for your grand entrance. And whatever you do, behave!"

The dog yanked so hard on his leash I all but fell forward on my way into the dog park. Like the morning hotspots, this was SRO as well. Once unleashed, Streetman made a mad dive for the nearest tree and proceeded to water it.

"Is that Harriet Plunkett's dog?" a lady in light blue capris and a floral top shouted.

Oh, crap. We haven't even been here one full minute.

"Yes, it's Streetman. I'm Harriet's daughter." *Heaven help me.*

The woman walked toward me. "I thought that was him. He looked absolutely adorable in that leprechaun outfit last March. You wouldn't happen to know who sewed it?"

The last thing I wanted to do was pile more work on Shirley's plate. She had such a kind heart, she'd never turn anyone down, even if it meant turning her own schedule inside out.

"One of my mother's friends, I think. You can always ask her next time you see her in the park."

Just then, the brief eight-bell chime from the library tower rang out, signifying the half hour. The woman glanced at the tower and shuddered. "Horrible thing what happened a few days ago. Although I can't say I'm all broken up over the loss. I suppose you've heard all about it. Everyone has. I really shouldn't speak ill of the dead but that woman could destroy someone's good mood in a matter of seconds."

"Uh, did you know her?"

"I had the misfortune of being waited on by her at the deli. Talk about rude. I once placed my order, and when she was done, I remembered that I had forgotten something. I asked her to please give me a quarter pound of olive loaf. She sighed as if I'd told her to climb Mount Rushmore. Then, when she finished, she slapped it down in front of me and asked, "Did you forget anything else?"

"Too bad I was running late for my canasta game or I would have gone to the manager."

I nodded. "Yeah, I've heard she wasn't the most pleasant employee."

"That's an understatement. If she was that insufferable at her place of employment, I hate to think what she was like elsewhere. Being rude to customers isn't a motive for murder, so I figure she had to have done something really horrific to wind up like a plate of cooked squash at the base of the tower stairs."

I recoiled at the image and glanced behind me to see what the dog was up to. So far so good. Sniffing and lifting his leg.

"Other than the deli, did you know anything else about her?"

"She was in the Boomers club. That much I *do* know. My friend Julia Ornstern is in that club and knew her. She said Billie, that's the woman's name, had no patience for anyone who moved slower than she did. According to Julia, Billie nearly drowned someone during a water volleyball game. Said she shoved the person out of the way to get to the ball and the poor woman lost her balance and went under."

"Holy cow."

"I know, right? Oh, you'll have to excuse me. Kugel, that's my dog, is at the gate. He's ready to go. Nice chatting with you."

I was about to ask her name but she was gone in a split second. Streetman was still moseying around the park and thankfully no one registered any complaints. There were at least fifteen people seated at the benches or strolling around. I eyeballed the place for a short, stocky gray-haired lady, but no luck. Usually Cindy plants herself by the fence adjacent to the tennis courts, but maybe I had arrived too early. Or, heaven forbid, too late. I figured I'd wait a few minutes to see if she'd show.

There was an empty seat next to a heavyset man who looked as if he hadn't seen his razor in a week. I said hi and plopped myself down. Thirty seconds later the gate flung open and a closely shaved white dog charged inside. It took me another five seconds to realize it was Bundles, Cindy's dog. She must have gotten him clipped for the summer.

Sure enough, Cindy came through the gate, saw me, and waved. I immediately walked toward her. "Good morning. I almost didn't recognize Bundles without all that fluffy white hair."

"I know," she said. "I had to get him groomed before the heat kicks in. I use Dapper Doggie Groomer. Where does Harriet take Streetman?"

I laughed. "She doesn't. Unless she wants a lawsuit from the groomer. He turns into Cujo the minute anyone goes near him with a pair of clippers. So, she figured out how to trim him herself using pet scissors and bribing him with deli meats. Trust me, you don't want to know."

"If she uses the same supermarket I do, buying the deli meats was probably worse than trimming the dog. Of course, that's not an issue now. Wow. I can't believe I'm being so catty. Especially since the woman who worked there was found dead. Oh, my goodness. Is that why you came to the park? To ask me if I know anything about it?"

"Well, yes, as a matter of fact. My mother's pitching a fit because the sheriff's office has sealed off the library tower for their investigation and she's afraid it won't be opened in time for the Bye Bye Birdie event."

Cindy moved closer to her usual spot by the fence and I followed. Once we were out of earshot from the other dog owners, she spoke. "I figured it had to be something but I seriously doubted your mother was concerned about Billie Churl's death. Not like the other times."

"I know. It was understandable when my mom's name was found on a piece of paper in a murder victim's hand, and that other time when her friend from the Rhythm Tappers was accused of committing murder. I can even rationalize her furor to find the killer at the Stardust Theater because the cast members were convinced the victim's ghost was haunting the place. But this? This is purely self-serving."

Cindy tilted her head slightly and looked directly at me. "What do you mean?"

"She's going to MC the event, along with Myrna and Paul from their radio show."

"The mystery fishing hour? I love that show. It's a hoot. Especially the time Paul wouldn't stop talking about the difference between filleting a flounder and filleting a halibut while your mother and Myrna went on a long spiel about fish-themed cozies."

"Don't remind me. Anyway, *Sonoran Living* plans to cover the event since the balloon launch from the tower is such a spectacle, and if the tower is off-limits, then—"

"I get the idea. No *Sonoran Living* and your mother's chances of appearing on their show will literally evaporate."

"Yep. That's about it. So, do you have any idea who Billie's assailant could have been? Have you heard any rumoring around the park?"

Terrific. I've now resorted to gathering information via rumor-mongering.

"Not rumors, exactly, but something interesting. Face it, Billie worked at the deli because she needed the money. For whatever reason, she must have retired early to relocate out here. She drove a 1996 Oldsmobile that looked as if it had seen better days. Then, about a month ago, she was behind the wheel of a 2022 Hyundai Sonata. Makes you wonder, huh?"

"Maybe she saved up for the car."

"I'd believe that if it was only the car. But I was at Spencers checking out washing machines two weeks ago and guess what? There she was, completing the purchase of a fifty-five-inch Samsung TV. If that's not fishy, I don't know what is."

"Gambling maybe?"

"Not that I know of. Lots of us go casino cruising and she hasn't been spotted in a single one. No. If you ask me, she was involved in something else. It would make sense if she turned seventy-two and cashed in an IRA, but Billie was in her fifties. A regular Boomer."

"I see what you mean. Hmm, I don't suppose there's anyone else who would know more about her?"

"Have you spoken with Adelaide Sasher at the library? She's the book recommendation lady. Knows everything from romance to thrillers. She's got a special table in there on Tuesday afternoons from two to five and Saturdays from ten to one. If anyone can tell you anything about Billie, it would be Adelaide. I'd try her before you waste your time with hearsay."

"Thanks, Cindy. I really appreciate it." Before I could say another word, someone from across the park shouted, "Poop alert! Small brownish dog. Poop alert!" Since Streetman was the only brown dog in the park, I pulled the blue plastic bag my mother had given me and raced to the far end of the park.

"They do that, you know," Cindy said. "No matter where their owners stand, the dogs do their business the farthest point away. Anyhow, it was nice talking with you, Phee. Keep me posted."

"You got it. Tuesdays and Saturdays, huh? Guess I'd better add Adelaide to my to-do list."

As soon as I deposited Streetman's gift in the receptacle, I reattached his leash to the collar and scurried him out of the dog park. No sense tempting fate. We were back at my mother's house in less than ten minutes and I still had a good forty-five minutes or so before I had to be at the office.

"I've got to make it quick, Mom," I said. "No guarantee about the traffic."

"Did you find out anything?"

"Yeah. We'd be better off hunting for the one person who didn't have anything against Billie Churl."

"What was Cindy able to tell you? Was Billie blackmailing anyone? Was it an affair gone bad? What? What?"

"She didn't know, but she did tell me to have a chat with someone named Adelaide Sasher at the library."

"You asked Cindy for a book recommendation?"

"No. She seemed to think Adelaide knew something about Billie."

"Only one way to find out. You *will* find out, won't you?"

I looked at the dog, who had now made himself comfortable on the couch. "As long as I don't have to take Streetman, I'll pay Adelaide a visit next week."

"Don't wait too long. Herb has to order the balloons."

"And I have to get to work. Have a good day, Mom!"

CHAPTER 6

Fortunately, my mother wasn't familiar with Adelaide's schedule at the library or she would have insisted I rework *my* every-other-Saturday-morning at the office in order to accost the poor book-recommendation woman first thing tomorrow. Still, it wasn't out of the question. I figured there'd be plenty of time for a chitchat with her if I left Glendale at noon and drove straight to Sun City West.

When I got to the office, Augusta was in a flurry shuffling papers around on her desk. "Mr. Williams just called from Wickenburg. I've got to reschedule all of his and Mr. Gregory's appointments today. That horse case mushroomed overnight."

No sooner did she say "mushroomed" than a text message from Marshall came in on my cell phone.

Heading to Phoenix to meet w/ field rep from gov't. Late night. Sorry, hon. Augusta has details.

I starred at the small screen, then looked at Augusta. "That was Marshall. He said you'd know what's going on."

"I'm not so sure I know what's going on, but I do know that three more geldings were taken from a ranch near Congress. That's a few miles up from Wickenburg."

"Yeah, I've seen it on the map."

"Mr. Williams got on the horn with the field agent at the Department of Agriculture and he and Mr. Gregory are on their way downtown to meet with the man. Some bureaucrat by the name of Martin Winston-Featherly. If that's not a moniker for a pencil pusher, I don't know what is."

"Wow. This doesn't sound like ordinary equine property theft. Did Nate say if they were thoroughbreds?"

"Trail horses. Like the others. And whoever stole them didn't have breeding in mind unless they were a total jerk. Then again, I've seen a lot of that back on the dairy farm in Wisconsin."

"Uh-huh. Any luck with video cameras in that barn?"

Augusta shook her head. "They had them, all right. *Had* being the pivotal word. They were shot up according to the ranch owner who discovered the missing horses around four in the morning. He reached out to Perry Gaynes since he knew Perry and knew about the theft of his horses. In fact, when the rancher from Congress first found out, he made sure his cameras were working and running a live feed. Then, boom. Sometime last night, someone used a BB gun on them. That was all Mr. Williams said."

"That was certainly enough. How'd Nate manage to reach someone in the field office so early in the morning. Did he say?"

"Yeah. Martin Winston-Featherly gave Perry his cell number when Perry first contacted the Department of Agriculture."

"Lucky for Nate and Marshall."

Augusta chucked. "I'm not so sure about that. Got a feeling this Martin character isn't going to be much help."

"You're probably right, but now that the first horse theft escalated, the department may be willing to offer up more resources."

"I wouldn't hold my breath if I were you. And I told Mr. Williams not to hold his either. That's why he asked me to phone Rolo Barnes. No time to wait. Although Mr. Williams did say to call after nine thirty. Something about Rolo needing digestive time for his new plant-based diet."

"I'm going to need a cup of coffee before we continue this conversation." I walked to the Keurig, put in a McCafé and moseyed back to Augusta's desk. Rolo Barnes was the cyber-sleuth our office used when we needed information that was unobtainable anywhere else. Frankly, cyber-sleuth didn't even come close to describing Rolo. He used to work for the Mankato Police Department in their IT department before turning fifty and deciding to branch out on his own.

Rolo was a master hacker and an absolute genius when it came to algorithms. Codes and encryptions didn't stand a chance against him. The guy could hack into anyone's bank accounts from Cincinnati to the Cayman Islands and they'd never know. Same deal with tracking down info from the dark web. That's why he was on speed dial, even if it meant we had to pay him in kitchen gadgetry. Yep, kitchen gadgetry. Mainly because his needs changed with every new diet he tried.

I had to admit, as looney as he was, Rolo exuded a certain charm and was never at a loss when it came to his social life. I always thought he resembled a black Jerry Garcia sans the guitar. And the entourage.

"What's Nate having Rolo do?" I asked. "It's not as if there are bank routing numbers that need to be uncovered."

"Actually, there may be. Nate and Marshall are pretty convinced that the number of stolen horses equates to a boatload of money somewhere. They need Rolo to look for transactions emanating from other dude ranches or entertainment venues where trained trail horses would be used."

"That makes sense. So, what's the agricultural department doing?"

"According to your boss, not much. Looks like Rolo may be the one to track down horse trailer rentals in Maricopa and its surrounding counties as well. Could be a rogue operation."

"You may be right. Hmm, it's uncanny you mentioned Rolo. I know this has nothing to do with Williams Investigations but I wanted to give

Rolo a call myself to see if he would be willing to look into Billie Churl's bank accounts for me and find out where her windfall came from."

"What windfall are you talking about? Honestly, Phee, sometimes it's like walking into a movie theater halfway through. Start at the beginning."

"Sorry. My mind is skipping all over the place. I was at the dog park this morning to placate my mother by having a conversation with Sun City West's gossip source."

"Cindy Dolton, right? I didn't think that much would change."

"Yeah. Cindy. Anyway, she told me Billie rid herself of the twenty-five-year-old Oldsmobile she drove and was behind the wheel of a new Hyundai. And that's not all. She was seen buying a large flat-screen TV. Naturally, I'm curious where all that money came from. Face it, if she had such a large stash, she wouldn't be working behind the counter of a supermarket delicatessen."

Augusta shuffled a few more papers around on her desk and nodded. "If you plan to call Rolo, take a number and get in line."

"I'm not calling him. I said I *wanted* to give him a call but not now. Not under these circumstances. He's about to be up to his neck hacking into all sorts of unsavory places in order to help Nate and Marshall find those stolen horses. Whether my mother likes it or not, Billie Churl's death will have to take a backseat."

"Some backseat. I know you and you're not about to let it rest. But why all the bother? It's not as if someone's life is resting on the line."

"No, but my nerves are. That bell tower is now off-limits to anyone other than the sheriff's office. And who knows how long it will stay cordoned off. That means the gala Bye Bye Birdie balloon drop may fizzle completely along with my mother's chances to be on *Sonoran Living*. Don't ask."

Augusta leaned her neck back, giving the appearance of three or four chins. "I knew it had to be something like that. But goodness. That event isn't for a few weeks. Surely the forensic team will have gathered all their evidence by then. Heck, back home, the rinky-dink sheriff's office in my county would've had the job done in two days. Three tops."

I looked around even though I knew we were the only ones in the office. "I don't think it's a matter of finding and securing evidence."

"Then what?"

"Okay, fine. I have this unsettling feeling that the sheriff's office may have reached a totally different conclusion. What if Billie's assailant wasn't someone she knew? What if it was a deranged killer who had his or her sights on assaulting someone at the top of the tower? That might explain why they're keeping the tower door locked."

"Either that, or, like I said, they're really poky when it comes to gathering evidence."

"I hope you're right. Billie Churl wasn't the only person who used that stairwell for exercise. Yeesh. Think of the timing. It could have been Louise Munson at the base of the stairs and not the deli-witch."

"Whatever you do, keep those thoughts to yourself and don't breathe a word to your mother."

"I'm not crazy. But that's why Rolo Barnes sprang to mind. If he could pinpoint how Billie's cash flow suddenly changed, then maybe it would point to premeditated murder and not some lunatic in the tower. Anyway, I'm certainly not about to call him. Not with that major horse theft going on. Nate and Marshall need his resources more than I do at this point. Besides, I have another lead."

"Another lead? Who are you? Stephanie Plum?"

"I might as well be. I'm doing as much running around as she does. Anyway, Cindy told me about a lady in the library who gives book recommendations to patrons. She gets to know readers' tastes and preferences so she can direct them to books they might enjoy."

"Again, you've lost me."

I sighed. "This lady, Adelaide Sasher, may know more about Billie than anyone else. After work tomorrow I'll stop by the library and see what she's willing to share with me. Nate always said the best results are gleaned through old-fashioned detective work."

The taut lines around Augusta's lips broadened into a smile. "And here I thought you were satisfied with bookkeeping and accounting."

"I'm also satisfied when I'm not being nagged to death by my mother."

"Not to be a glutton for punishment, but you said 'another lead.' What other leads *do* you have?"

"All right, maybe it's not a lead in the definitive sense of the word, but a lady at the dog park told me that Billie belonged to the Sun City West Boomers club and wasn't exactly what you'd call a model club member."

"Boomers, huh? What do they do?"

"Everything. Hiking, camping, water sports, kayaking, horseback riding, rock climbing, you name it. It's one of those clubs with lots of spinoffs. And I'm keeping my fingers crossed my mother doesn't find out. The last time she and her crew looked into a murder, they came up with this loosely thought out scheme they called Operation Agatha."

"I remember Operation Agatha. They infiltrated the Rhythm Tappers and that railroad club to see if they could track down the killer."

"Yeah, and they dragged me into it. Last thing I need is to find myself kayaking, or worse yet, rock climbing, in order to eke out some information."

"I hate to say it, but you'll find yourself doing those very things, or worse, if your so-called lead with Adelaide in the library doesn't pan out."

"Bite your tongue."

CHAPTER 7

I f I thought Marshall looked like hell the night before when he came home from Wickenburg, he looked worse when he came through the door at a little past eight. He had called me around four to let me know he and Nate met with Martin earlier in the day and returned to the Wickenburg area to track down more clues. He also told me not to wait on dinner, but that's exactly what I did.

"I made us chicken salad and bought those flakey croissants you like from the Wildflower Bread Company," I said. "You must be famished. I know I am."

"You mean you haven't eaten?"

I threw my arms around his neck and gave him a few snuggling kisses at the nape. "I really didn't get my appetite until you walked in the door. Get comfortable and we can share horror stories. But only after the first few mouthfuls. Like I said, I'm starving."

It was only after we had devoured enough forkfuls of food that we began to talk. Marshall gritted his teeth and had a sheepish look on his face. "Good thing Augusta got Rolo up to snuff because we're going to need him. It hasn't even been six hours but the guy already uncovered some shady entertainment venues that were buying horses at bargain basement prices."

"What about the field rep from the Department of Agriculture?"

"About as useful as a toad on an iceberg."

"Yeesh."

"Well, maybe not quite that bad. He did give Nate and me the information his office garnered, but with scant resources that's about all we expect. Which brings me to the next topic of conversation. Sorry, hon, but Nate and I both agree these cases are only the starting point for something more sinister. And before it reaches that point, we need to take the leads we have and get on the road."

I tore off a piece of my croissant, and before I knew it, I had shredded it on my plate. "On the road where? How long?"

"Southeast of Tucson. We plan to get an early start in the morning and go from there. It shouldn't be more than a few days, but as new information emerges, that may change. These things always have tentacles."

"I know I'm sounding like a nervous Nellie but don't do anything reckless."

Marshall chuckled. "Me? Look who's talking. I'm surprised I don't have any more gray hairs from some of the situations you've gotten into."

"You don't have *any* gray hairs."

"And I intend to keep it that way. Relax, Nate and I will exercise the appropriate amount of caution. And I'll keep you posted best as I can via text or voicemail if I can't reach you."

"Thanks. I know it's your job but worrying is now part of mine. Um, speaking of tentacles, I had an enlightening little chat with a lady at the dog park this morning. She said Billie was active in the Boomers club and—"

"Oh, no. Please don't tell me we have to worry about Operation Agatha Part Two from the book club ladies."

"Not if I can help it. That Boomers club is enormous. I plan to start slow. With a woman who volunteers at the library. Cindy said the woman knew Billie. After work tomorrow I'll swing by there and see what I can find out."

Marshall let out a slow breath and the tight lines around his eyes loosened. "Good. The library. A nice, safe place with lots of people."

"And a bell tower that's now a crime scene. Tell me, do you really believe the sheriff's office is still gathering evidence?"

Marshall shook his head. "Nope. I think they may be worried about a copycat murder. Or, in this case, *accident*, as a result of an altercation."

"And here I thought I was the only one who reached that conclusion."

• • •

The sound of rustling noises woke me before dawn. I sat up in bed and watched as Marshall moved about in our walk-in closet. The dim light seemed to brighten as my eyes got used to the semidarkness.

"Are you packing already?" I asked. "I'll make us some coffee."

"No need to do that. Get back to sleep. I'll be fine. I'm meeting Nate at the office and from there we'll head south."

"Whose car?"

"His. It's bigger and more comfortable according to him. Although we'll both take turns at the wheel."

"I'm up already. Might as well have that first cup here."

If there was one word to describe Marshall's idea of packing, it was *light*. He threw a few shirts and a change of pants into a carry-on bag along with socks, underwear, and an old ratty T-shirt that he sometimes slept in. The toiletries barely took up any space and he wore his sweatshirt since mornings were still cool by Arizona standards.

Less than twenty minutes later he was out the door and I was way too wired to go back to bed. Instead, I picked up around the house and plunked myself in front of the computer to do some internet searching of my own.

Beginning with Billie Churl's Facebook page.

Talk about a total bust. With the exception of extreme sports photos, the Facebook page didn't offer much. Of course, there was the opportunity to connect with her as a friend, but unless I wanted to contact a medium, all bets were off. Instagram, LinkedIn, and Twitter weren't even on Billie's map.

Resigning myself to the fact I'd have to resort to old-fashioned gumshoeing, I took a shower, got dressed, and headed to the office. An early start meant an early getaway, and if I was lucky, maybe Adelaide Sasher could fill in the blanks. Or, in this case, paint the entire canvas.

It was one of those rare days when I beat Augusta to the office. Even if it was only by four or five minutes.

"Couldn't get back to sleep with Marshall leaving so soon, huh?" she asked the second she opened the door. "It's a sign you're meant to be an old married couple."

"Gee, thanks. For your information, I wanted an early start. I don't want to miss Adelaide at the library. She and this other woman, Julia something, from the Boomers club are the only leads I have. Good thing I wrote her full name down and stuffed it in the car's console."

Augusta laughed. "You would have made Sam Spade proud."

"Very funny. By the way, social media was a total waste. I tried tracking Billie down on Facebook and every other reasonable site known, but came up empty. Now I'm resorting to gossip media. Hey, did Nate or Marshall ever mention DNA evidence from Billie's body? I meant to ask them but they were both so preoccupied with those stolen horses. I thought perhaps in their conversations with Ranston and Bowman something might have come up."

"Mention those names and the only thing coming up is some unsettled food in my stomach. No, neither of them said anything."

"I supposed if there was DNA evidence or even trace DNA, it would leak out to the press. So far nothing. According to the TV stations, Billie's assailant hasn't been identified. Anyway, I've got a stack of invoices to deal with, so off I go. As soon as I make myself the second cup of coffee for the morning."

The phone rang a few times and with my door ajar, I could hear Augusta conversing with a few potential clients. Then another call came in and this time it was for me.

"Phee, it's a lady by the name of Louise Munson on the line. Is that the book club lady with the African gray parrot? Hers can't be as bad as the one Mr. Williams is babysitting."

"According to Nate, nothing's as bad as having Mr. Fluffypants as a roommate. Go ahead, transfer the call in here."

"Phee! It's Louise. Louise Munson. From the book club. I tried you at home but there was no answer and then I remembered you work every other Saturday morning."

Since Louise was most likely the last person to see Billie Churl alive, other than the person who made sure she wasn't, I hoped she didn't call to tell me she needed bail money and couldn't reach my mother.

"Uh, hi, Louise. Is everything okay?"

"I don't know. That's why I'm calling you. You work for that detective agency. Maybe you can help."

"I, um, er . . ."

"That horrid deputy called me first thing in the morning and wanted to speak with me again. Asked if I could meet him at the posse station today."

"What did you tell him?"

"I didn't. I sort of hung up on him and unplugged my landline. Then I left the house and spent most of the morning at Costco."

Oh, geez. If that's not an admission of guilt, I don't know what is.

"Where are you calling from now?"

"I'm back home. I had to put the groceries away."

"Okay. Fine. Call the sheriff's office, ask for Deputy Ranston, and when you get him on the line, tell him you had some phone trouble and then had to leave for an appointment. Don't elaborate. Ask if he'd be willing to chat with you at the library after two p.m. I've got to be there on some other business and I'd be happy to sit in while he speaks with you. Does that sound all right?"

"Phee, you don't think I need a lawyer, do you? What if he arrests me?"

"There's no evidence pointing to an arrest." *Unless that forensic crew did find DNA and it belongs to Louise.* "Try to relax. Make yourself a cup of tea and call my office back once you reach the deputy. Fair enough?"

"Yes. Thank you. Thank you *so* much."

I walked to the outer office and plopped myself in the chair next to Augusta's desk. "I think I may have signed on to offer legal services but I'm not sure."

"What? Snooping around and playing detective isn't enough? Now you want to go all Janet Reno on us?"

"Deputy Ranston wanted to bring in Louise Munson for more questioning and she panicked. I told her I'd sit in with her today. That *is*, if Deputy Ranston agrees to talk with her at the library. I have to be there anyway. You know, to—"

"I know. I know. To pry every single drop of information you can from some poor lady who gives book recommendations."

"That poor lady may very well turn out to be the one person who can nail this case."

Augusta rolled her eyes and went back to her computer monitor. "I'd have a plan B if I were you."

As it turned out, not only did I need a plan B, but a plan C and D wouldn't have hurt.

CHAPTER 8

A delaide Sasher was seated at a round table adjacent to the library counter when I arrived at twenty to one. Stacks of books were piled everywhere and a few were fanned out. An elderly petite woman with tight bluish curls thanked her and walked past me. I smiled and made a beeline for the table, hoping my grumbling stomach wasn't audible.

I'd planned on forgoing lunch in order to make it to the library before Adelaide left knowing I could hit a fast-food place on the way home. But now, since I added the Louise Munson–Deputy Ranston tête-à-tête to my early afternoon to-do list, my stomach would rival one of those F-32s from Luke Airforce Base.

"Hi!" I said the minute I approached Adelaide. With her perfectly styled chin-length hair and a matching pink sweater and skirt ensemble, she reminded me of my fourth-grade teacher, only a few decades older. "I'm hoping you can help me out. Do you mind if I take a seat?"

"Please do. Take that comfortable chair on the left. I'm delighted to help folks with their book selections but I must say, you look young to be living in Sun City West."

Whew.

"My mother lives here. Harriet Plunkett. I'm—"

"Harriet Plunkett! I listen to her radio show whenever I can. Murder mysteries are my favorite genre. So, what brings you here?"

"That very thing. Only not in the form of entertainment. I'm Sophie Kimball, but everyone calls me Phee and I work for Williams Investigations in Glendale. As their bookkeeper and accountant. But I'm not here because of Williams Investigations." *I've got to stop rambling. It's quarter to one already.* "I'm here on my mother's behalf to help figure out who could have been responsible for causing Billie Churl to fall to her death in the library tower."

Adelaide turned her head in the direction of the tower and then looked back. "Shocking thing. Of all places. Were you close to Billie?"

"I didn't even know her. Gee, this is sounding more and more bizarre so I'd better explain. Right now, the library tower is cordoned off and it may remain that way for quite a while. Investigations emanating from the sheriff's office tend to take a long time. That means the annual snowbird send-off won't come with its usual panache."

"The balloon launch?"

"Uh-huh."

36

"I love that balloon launch. It's better than watching the ball drop on Times Square. But I'm not sure how I can help you. I wasn't here at the time of the incident."

"Oh, I'm not looking into the incident, I'm trying to find out who might have had a motive to assault Billie in the tower. I was told that if anyone knew anything about her, it would be you, since you're so familiar with the library clienteles' reading habits."

Adelaide leaned forward and repositioned the fanned books. "I was certainly familiar with Billie's." She motioned me closer, and when our heads all but touched, she whispered, "I think that woman was a witch."

I straightened my back. "Oh, yeah. I've heard that from lots of sources. Including her nickname, the deli-witch, because she was so abrasive to the customers."

Adelaide shook her head. "Not that kind of a witch. A witch-witch."

"You mean one of those practicing Wiccans who sanctify nature?"

Again Adelaide shook her head. "Nope. I mean a self-serving woman who may have dabbled in the dark arts. At least according to her book selections and requests. All nonfiction. And many from interlibrary loan from universities."

"Please don't tell me she was interested in casting spells and making potions."

"Honestly, I have no idea. From time to time she'd ask for recommendations about other topics such as knot tying, leather working, money laundering, hedge funds, and nontraditional investments. Go figure."

"Wow. That's a bit unnerving. I don't suppose you have any idea who she tangled with in the tower?"

"Not a clue. I wish I could be more help. I'd like to see things get back to normal around here, too, but it's hard with crime scene tape plastered a few yards from the romance section of the library."

I chuckled to myself. "It's daunting, all right. Anyway, thank you so much for your time, and if you think of anything, please call me." I handed her my Williams Investigations card, and unlike other times in the past, I didn't cover up the words *bookkeeper* and *accountant*.

It was now ten after one. Enough time for me to grab a bite from the Subway shop across the parking lot and get back in time for Louise and Deputy Ranston. That is, if Deputy Ranston agreed to meet with her. I figured if he was anxious to press her for further information, he would be at the library within the hour.

No sooner did the sliding glass doors open than I nearly collided with him.

"Miss Kimball. Please tell me you're checking out a book for your mother and not engaging the patrons in one of your unsanctioned investigations."

"Nice to see you, too. In fact, I'll be seeing more of you. Louise Munson asked if I'd be willing to sit in for moral support during her conversation with you. I figured I'd have time to grab a bite for lunch first."

"You still didn't answer my first statement. Please don't tell me you've got your nose in Billie Churl's unfortunate demise."

My nose and every other part of me apparently.

We skirted away from the sliding entrance doors and positioned ourselves against the outside of the building. "Look," I said, "you know as well as I do that whenever a body crops up within a fifty-mile radius of my mother and her book club friends, I'm going to be coerced into doing some serious sleuthing. My mother can be very convincing."

Deputy Ranston let out a slow, loud sigh. "I give up. Just don't get in the way. That woman's fall has led to more speculation than anything I've seen in the past year. And being one of those Boomers, she was into everything. Darn it all. Why couldn't she have just belonged to the knitting club and called it a day? Too bad your boss and your fiancé are unavailable to assist with this one. The interviews alone are going to kill us. Do you have any idea how many people we need to speak with?"

"We as in Deputy Bowman?"

"Unless MCSO decides to hire additional staff, it's Bowman and me on this one."

"Tell me, you don't really think Louise Munson had anything to do with Billie's death, do you? I mean, I could understand if it was, say, Myrna Mittleson, on those stairs doing cardio exercises. She's built like a Russian tank. But Louise? Honestly."

"I really shouldn't be offering up information like this, but I know it won't go any further. Louise is not a suspect. However, she may know more than she realizes. Sometimes when things like this happen, witnesses don't recall all the specifics of a situation until hours or sometimes days later."

"But Louise left the library tower before the incident happened."

"That doesn't mean she didn't hear anything or even smell anything."

For a brief second I remembered an odor I smelled a while back and it was instrumental in solving a murder case. "Hmm, I suppose you're right. Were you thinking perhaps it might have been a delicatessen odor? From someone who worked with Billie?"

"Our office interviewed everyone from that deli and all the employees had ironclad alibis for the time in question. That leads us to believe Billie Churl's assailant was either someone she knew from her activities in Sun City West or—"

"My God! Don't say it—some poor psychotic person off of his or her meds. The West Valley has seen an uptick of homeless people on the streets and many of them refuse to get help."

"We're not ruling out anything but we do have to start somewhere."

"Well, you can start by telling Louise she's not a suspect. The poor woman is one step away from cashing in her IRA to hire an attorney."

"It's not my fault your mother's friends are, shall we say, a bit prone to overreacting."

"Just tell her. Meanwhile, I intend to dart out for something to eat. I'll be back in a little bit. By then, Louise should be here."

I gobbled down my half roast beef sub and washed it down with Coke before racing back from Subway to the library. Louise and Deputy Ranston were already seated at a round table across from the DVD section. The adjacent tables were unoccupied but a few patrons milled about.

Deputy Ranston kept his voice low but it was audible as I approached their table. "As I was saying, Ms. Munson, you were most likely the last person to see Billie alive. That's why I need you to think back and recall every single detail you noticed. Even if it seems irrelevant."

"I already told you, I was partially up the stairs when that wretched woman, may she rest in peace, elbowed past me and called me an old fossil."

"Prior to her arrival, did you notice anything that seemed strange? Perhaps directly above you on the base of the tower bell."

"I wasn't looking up at the tower bell. I'm not an owl."

"What about odors? Did you notice an unfamiliar odor?"

I pulled out a chair, smiled at Louise and motioned for her to continue.

"The bell tower always has a musty odor. Not terribly bad but stale air. Hmm, come to think of it, there *was* something else. Like overdone campfire smell."

"Overdone?" he asked.

"It was cloying. That's the word—cloying. Definitely a mix of smoke and ash, but with something sickening sweet mixed in. I didn't really give it any thought at the time. Those maintenance guys are always checking out that bell. Oiling it, dusting it, whatever they have to do. I just assumed the odor came from one of them. Maybe it was an aftershave. Or something they used to cover up smoking. Smoking's not allowed on the premises but I've seen them behind the Dumpster next to the fitness center. They think no one's looking, but we are."

Deputy Ranston reached in his pocket, pulled out a pen and small pad, and proceeded to jot down something. "That's been very helpful, Ms. Munson. Very helpful indeed. If you can think of anything else, you have my card."

"Um, *I* thought of something," I said. "Video surveillance. Doesn't this library have video surveillance?"

The deputy looked around, clasped his hands, and shook his head. "The only camera they have is outside by the computer room entrance. We checked the footage and accounted for everyone who used that entrance that morning. There are no cameras by the front entrance and nothing inside, although I imagine that will change due to recent circumstances. Now, if you ladies will excuse me, I need to be on my way."

He stood and started for the door before walking back to the table. "One more thing," he said. "Until this matter is resolved, please leave the investigative work to the sheriff's office."

I did a mental eye roll and widened my eyes. *Like that's going to happen.*

CHAPTER 9

"I'm sorry I dragged you away from whatever it was you were doing," Louise said, "but I was really sure I was going to be read my rights."

"No problem. Given your second round of questioning, my take is that you're not the only one the deputies will be interviewing again. I don't think the forensic crew was able to pull enough evidence from the scene of the crime. Trace DNA is a tricky thing."

"But those TV reporters said it appeared as if Billie had defensive wounds."

"Yeah, it was the same party line on all the networks. But it wasn't definitive. It was speculation. They're careful to use words like *appeared*. Anyway, if those deputies had anything, they wouldn't be re-interviewing the library patrons."

"I don't know about anyone else, but this place is beginning to give me the willies. What if there's some nutcase out there stalking unsuspecting seniors?"

"I think you'll be fine, Louise, if you stay in visible areas with lots of people around. Besides, everyone's on the alert now."

"I suppose you're right. Thanks again for helping me out. I might as well check out a book while I'm here. A pleasant domestic murder for a change. Like one of Libby Klein's or Debra Goldstein's books. I like the food ones especially but I gained ten pounds after reading Debra Sennefelder's food blogger series. Still, I ordered her next release."

I laughed and pushed my chair into the table. "Call me any time. I mean it."

If nothing else, past experience taught me that if my mother knew about one of my reconnaissance missions, like the chat with Adelaide Sasher, she'd plague me to death until I coughed up every last detail. Since Marshall and Nate were on their own mission and I didn't have any plans for the afternoon, I phoned her from the car and asked if she'd be home for a while.

"You found out something, didn't you?" she bellowed in my ear. "Those library volunteers are notorious for gathering information. So, what was it? What did you find out? Should I be worried about my Streetman?"

I'd be worried about your Streetman with or without a recent assault leading to death.

"Look, I'm a few blocks away. I'll swing over and we can talk."

"Good. I'll take something out of the freezer."

"No! I mean, no, don't go to any trouble. I already ate. See you in a few minutes."

My mother's freezer was like a meat locker from another century. And one that should come with a warning, "Defrost at your own risk." The coffee was iffy, too. It could be fresh or, heaven forbid, reheated from the day before. I didn't take any chances. I swung by Bashas and grabbed a bottle of Coke before proceeding to my mother's place.

Streetman greeted me at the door with a quick sniff before darting under the coffee table.

"See," my mother said, "he's getting much better. Sit down and tell me what Adelaide dished out."

I moved to one of the floral chairs, Coke bottle in hand, and sat. "She certainly knows the clientele, that's for sure."

My mother took the other floral chair and leaned in my direction. "What does she know about that deli-witch?"

"Basically, Adelaide is familiar with the reading choices Billie made. Eclectic topics, if you ask me."

"Like what?"

I took a swallow of Coke and caught a breath. "Um, things like, well, money laundering, hedge funds, knot tying, the dark arts, leather working, unconventional investments—"

"Witchcraft!" my mother screamed. "The woman was into witchcraft!"

"That's what you took away from that list? And I didn't say witchcraft. I said she read books about the dark arts. Among other things."

"What do you think the dark arts are? Witchcraft! I've got to call Shirley and Lucinda to let them know. And Louise. Poor Louise. Someone has to prepare her."

"Prepare her for what? And by the way, I saw her a few minutes ago before I drove over here. She was at the library. Chatting with Deputy Ranston. And before you get all worked up, he was only following through with the original interview. The sheriff's office is hoping someone will remember something relevant."

My mother furrowed her brow and stared at me before speaking. "Did Louise call you and ask you to meet her at the library? How did she know you were there?"

Once I explained how worried Louise was, given the fact she was the last person to see Billie alive, my mother seemed to relax. "At least she's not a suspect. That's the last thing she or our book club needs. So, getting back to Billie. You don't suppose she was in one of those covens, do you? Your aunt Ina seems to know a few women who belong to one. What was the name? Circle of the Rising Crescent? Or maybe Desert Crescent or Desert Moon. She told me once but it blew past me like most of the things she says."

I shrugged. "Look, evidently Billie had lots of interests outside of the deli at the supermarket. And no, I do not believe she was in a coven." *My God, I can't believe we're having this conversation.* "If anything, her interests in money laundering and nontraditional investments would have seemed more likely to stir up trouble for her. And if that's the case, I'm sure the sheriff's office will look into it. They've got the means and the authority to go through her computer and cell phone. I don't."

"But you've got the wherewithal to infiltrate that Boomers club and find out more. Remember when we did that with the model railroad club and the Rhythm Tappers?"

"Impossible to forget."

"Unfortunately, none of us have the energy level those Boomers have. Did you pass that group of them on their bicycles? Talk about extreme sports."

"They were riding single file down Limousine Drive. Nothing extreme about that."

"Like all Sun City West clubs, they always welcome new members. Take my guest card and tell them you're thinking of purchasing a home but want to be sure the activities in our community will be challenging and exciting for you. Then, get entrenched in whatever Billie did and find out who she could have ticked off to the point where it got physical."

"I know this means a great deal to you, so I'll do what I can. However, you need to promise me that you and the book club ladies will keep your distance on this one."

My mother stood, walked over to the small counter in the kitchen and opened a drawer. She returned with a guest card in her hand and thrust it at me. "I'd start by finding out which activities Billie participated in with the Boomers. Ask for the membership director's phone number. They're like salespeople. They'll tell you what you want to know in order to convince you to buy something, or in this case, to join their group."

"No problem." *I'm one step ahead of you. Thanks to the lady in the dog park with that cute little black dog named Kugel, I know Billie didn't make too many friends in water volleyball. Thank goodness I can swim.*

I hadn't noticed the heat when I left the house in the morning but now, the early afternoon temps were making it known it was the start of summer. When I got home, I peeled off my clothes, threw on a swimsuit and called my friend Lyndy to see if she was interested in a quick dip in our community pool.

"Great timing," she said. "I got back a few minutes ago from Target and the sweat is literally pouring off me. See you in fifteen minutes, okay? I'm dying to know what you know about that tower death in Sun City West.

I figured if anyone had the inside information on it, you would. All I got was my aunt's hysteria. She's convinced a crazed lunatic is out to murder senior citizens."

"She can join the club. I'll tell you all about it. See you in a bit."

If I didn't have Lyndy Ellsworth to bounce things off of, I would have lost my mind a few years ago when I moved out here. Not that I didn't enjoy or appreciate the camaraderie of my mother's friends, but it was a relief to be with someone my own age.

Lyndy and I met at the community pool in Vistancia and have been fast friends ever since. Widowed at a young age, she moved to Arizona to get out of the brutal weather back East and to keep an eye on her looney aunt who lived in Sun City West. Her employment at a medical insurance company was "tedious but paid well." The retirement benefits were pretty good, too. Although neither of us wanted to think past the next decade, we had to be realistic about our pensions and annuities.

Lyndy was already in the water when I approached the pool. At least six or seven other folks were in the shallow end, but since Lyndy and I were good swimmers, we hung out in the deep-water section, away from the crowd.

"Hey, stranger!" she shouted. "Water temp's about eighty-four. You'll love it."

I stashed my bag on a nearby lounge chair and climbed in. "Ah, relief at last. The past few days have been brutal."

Lyndy shook the water from her dark curly hair and swam toward me. "Tell me all the details and don't spare a thing."

I began from the moment Billie was found dead at the base of the library bell tower and backtracked to her physical and character descriptions, as told to me by the book club ladies and the patrons at the dog park. From there, I moved to the horse theft case Nate and Marshall took on and then zigzagged back to Deputy Ranston's second interview with Louise Munson, pausing now and then to catch my breath and tread water.

"Good grief," Lyndy said. "It's like trying to follow a Fellini movie and giving up at the end."

I laughed. "It's worse. Your aunt isn't the only one who thinks a deranged killer is loose. Billie, aka the deli-witch, according to my mother, was despised by everyone she came in contact with. Hence, the moniker from her job at the supermarket deli. Apparently she was more than a little abrasive with the customers."

"Yeesh. Glad I shop on Happy Valley Road in Vistancia. Please don't tell me you're going to poke your nose into this one. It's not as if the victim was a friend of your mom's, or worse yet, one of her friends is a suspect."

"No, nothing like that. It's something entirely different." I went on to tell Lyndy about the Bye Bye Birdie event and my mother's obsession with making an appearance on *Sonoran Living*.

"It's hard to explain, but my mother's life at this point is comfortable. Lots of friends, volunteer work at the food bank from time to time, a steady routine, and, heaven help me—that dog of hers."

"So what's the problem?"

"It's too comfortable. Without these little sparks, for lack of a better word, my mother's world would be flat. She needs something to look forward to. Something exciting and different. That's why she was in that play, and now on the radio station with those bizarre mystery shows of hers. Without those sparks, it's just one day after another. The Bye Bye Birdie event is her next big spark."

"Gee, I never thought of it like that. I mean, I've got things I'm looking forward to, like owning my own home before I turn fifty, and visiting Santorini before it sinks. I understand. The Bye Bye Birdie event is her Santorini. At least for this year. All right, what's the game plan for this one?"

"I need to track down a woman by the name of Julia Ornstern from the Boomers club. I got *her* name from a nice lady at the dog park whose dog's name is Kugel. I never did get the woman's name but she told me Julia would have information about Billie."

"That shouldn't be too hard to do. My aunt is always giving me copies of the Rec Center bulletin hoping I'll move to Sun City West. All of the club contacts are listed. If you call the membership person, I'm sure they'll give you Julia's phone number or email."

"That's exactly what my mother said earlier today."

"Oh, no. It's scary when I start to think like your mother."

Thankfully, Lyndy was a long way off from thinking like my mother. If she did, she would have bounced from the Boomers club straight into the Wiccans.

CHAPTER 10

T he moment I got home I noticed the red light flashing on the landline's answering machine and immediately pressed the button hoping it was Marshall. Instead, it was my aunt Ina.

"Phee! Louis and I walked into the house a few minutes ago. The tranquility of our meditation retreat was blown to smithereens the second I played back the phone message your mother left. She asked if I was still friendly with, and I quote, 'those witches who don't use broomsticks.' Honestly, I have a few Wiccan friends and they are the most delightful ladies. I couldn't figure out what my sister wanted until she finally got to the point about some horrid woman who fell, or was pushed, to her death at the library tower. Thinks she might have been a Wiccan. I doubt it. Said you were looking into the matter. Are you doing investigative work at your detective agency now? Call me."

I exhaled for what seemed like five minutes before traipsing off to the bathroom to hang up my swimsuit. One of the things I loved about our community pool was its air-conditioned locker room and shiny new showers. Saved all the squeegee work at home.

Once I settled in with a glass of cranberry juice and a few chocolate chip cookies, I picked up the phone and dialed my aunt. At least my mother had laid the groundwork so my aunt was pretty conversant with the salient details regarding Billie's demise.

"As I told your mother," she said, "simply because someone decides to broaden their horizons by reading about the dark arts, or *any* arts for that matter, doesn't make them a dabbler in witchcraft."

No kidding. "That's exactly what I explained."

"Still," my aunt went on, "she does make a point. Who knows what that woman may have been into that led to her untimely death? Every contact she had might have been the very one who caused it."

"Um, I'm not really sure what you're saying."

"If this Billie woman had any dealings with the Solstice of the Desert Sands—that's a highly sought-after coven in the West Valley—then I'm sure my friends Serena and Tersee would know. They're high priestesses in that order and naturally they shun causing harm to anyone. But they might know if Billie was involved with less harmonious people. I'll call them and see what I can find out."

"Uh, sure. I appreciate it, Aunt Ina."

"Not at all. Your mother will be beside herself if that Bye Bye Birdie

46

balloon send-off is canceled. I got an earful from her. All I needed. Now I plan to make myself a nice soothing cup of rose hip and chamomile teas. I need to restore the tranquil state of mind I was in when Louis and I returned from Tucson."

"Good idea. And, uh, thanks again."

"I'll call you and let you know what I learn."

When I got off the phone, I was doing so many mental eye rolls, I thought I'd get dizzy. Meanwhile, no word from Marshall. Rather than allow myself to get edgy, I did what I always do when I wind up attempting to solve someone's murder, or in this case, *untimely death*. I create a murder map.

Rather than deal with poster board and construction paper, I took the easy way out. I had a stack of new spiral notebooks in my desk and pulled one out. In the middle of the first page, I drew a stick figure of Billie and used it as the focal point for creating an information web. With spikes emanating from my drawing, I drew "suspect hubs," since I really didn't have any actual suspects in mind. The hubs included: supermarket deli employees, even though Deputy Ranston ruled those employees out, supermarket customers, Boomers club water volleyball group, possible affiliations with leather crafters club and, heaven help me, local Wiccans. Since I didn't know of any club that focused on knot tying, I left it alone.

Then, I drew a second web. Same stick figure but this time with a time line and note to myself to find out who was in the library that morning, in addition to Louise. Usually Nate and Marshall wind up as consultants on some of the high-profile cases in Sun City West since the Maricopa Sheriff's Office is bogged down with its usual fare—assaults, carjacking, kidnapping, drugs, murder, and anything else under the Phoenix sun.

Without having an in with my boss and my fiancé, I felt like a castaway as I stared at my recent notebook entry. Tapping my fingers on the table, I thought perhaps I'd begin with the Boomers. Especially since there was no way Deputy Ranston was going to tell me who was in the library around the time of the incident.

On a hunch, I pulled up Julia Ornstern's Facebook page and sure enough, a striking photo of a water volleyball match took up most of her banner with the options to "Add Friend" or "Send Message" at the bottom of the screen. No need for a Rec Center directory or a phone book when Facebook had me covered. I immediately sent Julia a message that sounded strikingly similar to the one Madonna's boyfriend penned in *Desperately Seeking Susan*. Yeah, I was showing my age.

Amateur sleuth seeking Billie's assailant. PM me so we can talk. Got your name from Kugel's owner.

Once I pushed the blue Send arrow, I shut down the computer and nuked a Lean Cuisine dinner. It was a little past seven and I debated whether or not to phone Marshall. The last thing I wanted to do was disrupt his investigation, and that included any surveillance he and Nate were up to. I decided to wait until at least nine, and if I didn't hear from him by then, I'd make the call.

As much as I hated to admit it, the house felt empty and even a tad creepy. I turned on the Weather Channel so I could hear voices as I ate my chicken and mixed vegetables. Cleanup took all but three minutes and nine p.m. was still a good hour and a half away. Too wired to sit around, and too uninspired to do any cleaning or laundry, I did the next best thing. I grabbed my bag and headed for the supermarket on Happy Valley Road. Usually I hate food shopping, but I wasn't in the mood for clothes shopping or worse yet, trying on shoes.

I'd gotten as far as the exit from our development when a thought occurred to me in such a flash that I switched directional signals and turned in time for me to hear the guy in the car behind me shout, "Make up your mind!" Talk about ironic. Usually I was the one offering up not-so-kind comments to the drivers in my mother's community. Comments like, "You're making a three-point turn, not putting the *Queen Mary* in dry dock!"

It hit me in that momentary flash that if I was about to do food shopping, why not do it at the deli-witch's supermarket in Sun City West? True, Deputy Ranston told me all of her coworkers had solid alibis, but I've learned people have been known to lie.

The sun had set by the time I left the house but the glorious red and gold waves on the horizon lingered as I pulled into the supermarket parking lot off of RH Johnson and Meeker Boulevards. Squeezing past a few SUVs and luxury sedans from the late 1990s, I managed to find a decent spot near the cart return.

I clicked the lock button on my key fob and marched into the store like I meant business. Since I really didn't have a shopping list, anything was fair game. Especially the conversation I was about to have at the deli counter.

Two young men were at the slicing machines and an older woman was in the back washing something. Only one person was in front of me—a man seated in a power shopping cart who appeared to be in his eighties or maybe even older.

"Do you have those pre-orders ready, Tyler?" the woman at the sink asked one of the men at the slicer.

"Yeah, almost."

"Good. I'll take them to the quick-pick-up fridge when you're done."

At that moment, the other man handed the order to the customer in front of me and told him to have a nice night. Then, tossing off the food prep gloves he wore and putting on another pair, he looked at me. I gauged him to be somewhere between sixteen and twenty. Longish blond hair with a net over it, a few tattoos on his arms and one pierced ear. According to his ID badge, his name was Neal W. "What can I get you?" he asked.

I thought fast. "A quarter pound of honey-glazed ham sliced thin."

"Anything else?"

"Um, sure. Give me a quarter pound of the roast turkey. Also sliced thin. Very thin." Then I paused and hoped my next question would get the response I needed. "That's not a problem, is it? Slicing the meat thin, I mean. I heard there are sometimes issues with that."

"Oh, man," Neal sighed. "Thanks to one of our former employees, we're never going to live down our reputation. No, it isn't a problem. Not at all."

He reached below the counter, pulled out an open ham and started for the slicer.

I raised my voice. "Wait! Are you talking about Billie Churl? The lady who was found dead at the library bell tower?"

"Yep, we used to call her Billie Hurl behind her back because that's what she made us feel like doing. The woman was a real—geez, I shouldn't be talking like that. It could get me fired."

I leaned over the counter. "I won't say a word."

Just then, Tyler spoke up. "No one got along with her. At least old Eddie Krome had the good sense to transfer to the Vistancia store a month or so ago. She was in his face all the time. Then again, he was no prize either."

Hmm, Vistancia . . . my neck of the woods.

"Did other employees leave as well?"

Suddenly, the woman from the sink spoke up. "No. None of us were that lucky. At least Eddie left while he still had all ten fingers. He and Billie were always going at it. I swore the man would lose one of his digits if she got any closer to the slicer when he was on it."

"Yikes. How awful. Did you know what they were fussing over?"

The woman wiped her hands on a towel and walked toward the counter while Neal proceeded to slice my ham.

"Rumor had it that witch was going to file a sexual harassment complaint with HR. That would have cost Eddie his job. By the way, I'm Rashida and I've worked here for at least six years. Unfortunately, the last few were with Billie. I tried to get on different shifts but it didn't always work out."

"Um, if you don't mind my asking, why did everyone put up with her if she was so miserable?"

Rashida turned to the two men and then looked back at me. "We were terrified about what she might do."

"I'm not sure I understand," I said.

There was no one else at the deli counter but Rashida still looked around before she answered. "Lots of people make comments like, 'I'd watch it if I were you,' or 'Hope you've got a good insurance policy,' but when Billie did, it scared the hell out of us. *That*, and the goings-on at break time when she went to the smoking area around back."

"Billie smoked?"

"No, but she had some friends who did. Well, maybe not friends, but contacts. And none of them worked for our supermarket. They'd show up on foot, in cars, or sometimes on bicycles. And the only reason I know is because I watched her. Only good thing to come out of it was the fact I quit smoking about two weeks before she died and I don't intend to go near a cigarette again."

"Wow. And, uh, congratulations for quitting."

Just then Neal handed me the two plastic bags of cold cuts. "Would you like anything else?" I needed Rashida to keep talking so I ordered a quarter pound of roast beef and told him to slice it a tad thicker than the ham and turkey. At this rate, I'd be buying out the entire deli meat section.

"Rashida," I went on, "what do you suppose she was up to? Could she have been buying or selling drugs?"

"If so, she wouldn't have been stupid enough to have that stuff here. No, whatever she was doing, I think the break area was her office. In fact, I tried telling one of the deputies what I thought when all of us were questioned, but all he was interested in was finding out what *I* was doing at the time of her death. Thank goodness I was at work."

"Yeah," Tyler called out. "And I was sitting in a boring psych class."

Neal shrugged as he sliced the roast beef. "My alibi beats all of yours. Got a speeding ticket on Grand. Hell. Now they're raising the speed limit. Why couldn't they have done that a week ago?"

I laughed and turned my attention back to Rashida. "Uh, these so-called contacts of Billie's . . . how many were there?"

"I always saw the same three men. Middle age, average build, dressed well but stubble on their faces. Oh, and one of them had a tattoo of a Gila monster on his arm. Whatever it is they were up to, it didn't leave too much time for shaving. Shady if you ask me. The regulars don't suddenly stop their conversations when people walk past, but these guys did. Funny, but the only time I saw them was with her. Never in the store."

At that moment, a harried woman rushed over to the counter and shouted, "Can someone slice me a pound and a half of low-sodium ham? My husband was supposed to get it in time for me to make sandwiches for our Mexican Train group but he forgot. They'll be over to the house in a half hour, so hurry."

Darn that Mexican Train game. I was about to find out more about Eddie Krome.

I put my cold cuts in the shopping cart and stepped aside. "Thanks, everyone. Maybe the deputies will catch a break and find out what really happened to your former employee."

"Whatever it was," Tyler said, "she deserved it."

"Shush," Rashida whispered. Then she gave me a wave as I headed to the fruit and vegetable section.

CHAPTER 11

I couldn't wait to get back to my murder map and add Eddie Krome to the list of possible suspects, along with "three shady unidentified male smokers." Usually I take my time in the fruit and vegetable aisles, but that evening I tossed cantaloupes, honeydew melons and grapes into my cart without a second glance. Then I moved quickly through the store, adding cereal, English muffins, salad dressing and air-popped popcorn to the mix before heading to the checkout line. That's when I heard an unmistakable voice at customer service.

"Smell this cottage cheese! It's spoiled! I sat down to enjoy some nice sliced pineapple pieces in the cottage cheese and when I opened the container, I all but gagged."

Then, the employee from customer service, "No problem. We'll give you a refund."

"A refund? You need to smell this so you know exactly what I faced."

The voice belonged to none other than my mother and the last thing I felt like doing was getting entangled with one of her grocery returns. From where I stood, it would have been impossible to walk to the checkout line without being seen. I had to think fast. Any movement to the left would take her in the direction of the milk, eggs, and cheeses. With few choices available, I raced to the one place in the store I'd never been before—the wine bar.

Yep, the wine bar. Evidently wine bars are quite popular in supermarkets that are housed in senior communities. I grabbed a seat at the end and slouched down on the bar stool hoping my mother wouldn't pass anywhere near that area.

"What would you care to try?" the man behind the bar asked.

Getting out of here. That's what I'd care to try.

"Um, uh, I'm not sure. I just need a few minutes to think."

Having a glass of wine in the middle of a supermarket on a Saturday evening was about as appealing as eating filet mignon at a laundromat.

"Are you trying to get away from someone? I can call security if you'd like."

"Uh, no. I mean yes. But it's my mother. No need to call security. I simply don't feel like dealing with her right now. A minute ago she was at customer service. Some issue over the cottage cheese she bought. She doesn't know I'm here."

The server tried not to laugh but couldn't keep a straight face. "Sorry.

But this takes the cake. Funniest thing that's happened to me since I got to work. Want me to keep an eye out for you?"

"That would be wonderful."

I gave him a complete description of Harriet Plunkett, and when she skirted by the frozen fish section, he gave me the all-clear and I raced my shopping cart to the cashier in record time.

It was nine twenty-nine when I pulled into the garage and still no word from Marshall on my cell phone. Unless he used the landline. I slipped my left hand through the four grocery bag handles and with my right unlocked the utility room door and went inside. No flashing red light on the answer machine. Drat. I was about to put the groceries away and call Marshall's cell when the landline rang.

Please don't let this be Aunt Ina, or worse yet, my mother.

Without hesitating, I picked up the receiver. At the sound of Marshall's voice, the tension that had built up in my body began to dissipate.

"It's me and I hope you haven't been too worried. Nate and I just checked into a motel in Willcox."

"Willcox? Isn't that like the end of the state?"

"Not quite but close enough. We picked up a decent lead and met with a deputy from Cochise County. Seems they had a few horse thefts a while back as well. Same scenario. Same kind of horses. The cases got tossed to the Department of Agriculture, where they're sitting in a pile somewhere. There's more but I can't really get into it right now."

"That's fine as long as you and Nate are okay."

I hugged the receiver to my ear and used my free hand to put away the cold cuts.

"How'd it go with the book lady today? Any revelations?" he asked.

"She was certainly conversant with Billie's reading habits. And some weird interests."

"How weird?"

"From laundering money to tying knots. Oh, and don't let me forget witchcraft. Adelaide, the book lady, thought Billie may have dabbled in the dark arts. Or wanted to."

"You'd better keep that last part to yourself. If those book club ladies find out, who knows what lunacy will come of it."

"Don't worry. I'll nosey around with safe leads and even safer meeting places."

"Good!"

We spent the rest of the phone conversation with those sweet little musings about missing each other and all that stuff. Marshall promised to call when he could and reminded me again to steer clear of anything that smacked of the dark arts. I didn't dare tell him about Aunt Ina's Wiccan friends, although, from what she told me, they kept a safe distance from the dark arts as well.

When the phone call ended, I returned to the kitchen and put away the groceries. By the time I was done, I was too exhausted to add names and notes to my murder book so I plunked myself on the couch, turned on the TV, and sat back to catch the ten o'clock news.

The usually calm and delightful Linda Williams from Channel Ten, who definitely reminded me of Shirley Johnson, had an edge to her voice that made me take notice. "A new twist in the mysterious assault leading to the death of a Sun City West woman. Stay tuned."

Oh, I'm staying tuned, all right.

Following all sorts of reports about vehicle accidents in the East Valley and one wrong way driver in the west, Linda finally got around to the latest development in the Billie Churl investigation.

She took a breath, turned to her cute blond co-anchor, Rob Moon, and then back to the camera. "A detailed autopsy report on the woman who was found dead at the base of the library tower in Sun City West indicated that the wounds found on the woman's hands and wrists were not defensive wounds. Well, at least not defensive wounds from any human assailant."

"That's right, Linda," Rob said. "We had originally speculated the wounds came from someone who attacked her at the top of the tower, but according to the information our station received, the wounds appear to have come from an animal. We don't have any other details at this juncture in time, but as soon as we hear anything, we will certainly keep our viewers informed. The good news is that the sheriff's office is working with a new lead—a possible witness who may have recognized a distinct smell in the tower that could point to the assailant. And now, on to the new playground progress in Goodyear."

I knew there was no way Deputy Ranston was about to share that autopsy report with me but if I played my cards right, using Eddie Krome as leverage, maybe Ranston would be willing to make a trade. If I was right, Eddie slipped through the cracks when those deputies interviewed the employees who worked with Billie. All I needed to do was have a conversation with Eddie and then another one with Deputy Ranston.

Given what the news anchors said, Billie must have had some sort of run-in with an animal. A cat maybe? They leave scratches. Or a dog? They definitely could do some damage. Whatever it was, I was certain that animal wasn't at the top of the tower stairs hanging out by the bell. This was Sun City West, not Paris. And Billie's death was hardly *The Murders in the Rue Morgue*. Whatever animal she tangled with, the incident had to have happened shortly before she arrived for her daily workout. Otherwise, the preliminary autopsy would have said "old wounds," and that wasn't the impression I got from Linda and Rob.

It didn't matter. Those wounds were inconsequential as far as I was concerned, but chatting with Eddie Krome was a priority. I made up my mind to pay a visit to the supermarket in my neighborhood first thing in the morning. If nothing else, I could find out when Eddie would be working, and hopefully, get him to talk with me.

I half-heartedly watched the remainder of the news but shut off the TV when they got to sports. Then, I made sure the house was locked up tight before turning down the lightweight sheet and getting into bed.

A beam of sunlight woke me at a little past six and I stumbled into the kitchen to make myself a cup of coffee. Without Marshall moving about, every single noise from the hum of the refrigerator to the fan from the air conditioner seemed to have intensified. I turned the TV to a national news station and let the drone of the usual banter fill the silence. Then I gave the house a quick dusting with the Swiffer and opened my murder book to add Eddie Krome and the three unidentified smokers to the mix.

Taking a chance that Eddie wouldn't be at work until after nine, *if* he was working at all that Sunday, I grabbed a quick swim at the pool before visiting the second deli counter in two days. If I kept this up, my sodium levels would be off the charts.

It was a little past ten when I sauntered up to the deli counter and kept my fingers crossed that one of the two middle-aged men was Eddie. Both were helping other customers but I was the next in line. As soon as the barrel-chested worker with a receding hairline approached, I eyeballed his name tag and tried not to look disappointed.

"Excuse me," I said. "Is that Eddie Krome behind you?"

The man shook his head. "Eddie's on break. Probably out for a smoke around back. Anything I can help you with?"

"Um, no. I needed to see him about something."

"Break area is to the left of the entrance by the coffee shop. Next!"

A zaftig woman in a floral housedress nudged past me and shouted out her order as I left the deli counter. A few seconds later, I was out the door and fast approaching the break area.

Terrific. There's enough cigarette smoke here to saturate my clothing for the next decade.

Two pencil-thin women were chatting away at a table in the rear, both of them with cigarettes in their hands. There was only one man puffing away while scrolling through his phone and it had to be Eddie.

I walked over to where he was seated and cleared my throat. "Excuse me. Are you Eddie Krome?"

The man looked up and squinted. "In the flesh. What can I do for you?"

"Mind if I sit down?"

I didn't feel like leaning in and thought I'd be less likely to inhale secondhand smoke and that awful aftershave of his if I sat across the table rather than right next to him. Eddie might have sensed my apprehension about the cigarette so he snuffed it out in the ashtray and motioned for me to take a seat. "Please don't tell me you're from HR and someone filed a complaint."

"No. I'm Phee Kimball and I work for Williams Investigations. I'm not an investigator but I do help with some of the ground work."

Oh, my God! I can't even listen to myself lie so shamelessly.

"If it's about the pilfering from the deli's cash drawer, the worker who did it confessed a few days ago and was let go."

"No, not that. I wanted to speak with you about Billie Churl."

Eddie's ruddy complexion turned a shade lighter. "Might need another cigarette for that, but I can hold off. What is it you want to know? I saw the same news everyone else did."

"Um, yes. About that . . . I understand you and Billie weren't on the best terms when you worked together in the Sun City West store."

Eddie rolled his eyes. "No one was on good terms with that shrew. But if you want to know if I had anything to do with her death, the answer is no. Billie didn't ruffle people's feathers, she plucked them out one by one."

"Ew."

"Yeah, she was a piece of work, all right. Probably pushed someone over the edge, but it wasn't me. Say, how'd you find out about me? The county deputies haven't even questioned me."

"I think you slipped under the radar when you transferred stores, but our investigation firm is very thorough. Listen, is there anything you might know that would help in determining who might have had an altercation with her in the library tower?"

"I'll tell you what I do know." Eddie took a breath, crossed his arms over his chest, and plopped his elbows on the table. "Billie was a grifter. Always swindling someone. Always looking to make a quick buck."

"Did she swindle you?"

"What do you think?"

I shrugged and didn't say a word. Eddie rubbed his chin and stared directly at me. "If I were you, I'd talk with the employees in Sun City West. Then again, I doubt anyone will give up anything because they don't want people to know they've been played."

"Anyone in particular?"

"Try everyone. No one wanted to get on her bad side. That's all I know. That's the honest truth. Anyway, I'd better get back inside. Don't want to get docked for taking too long a break."

I thanked Eddie and headed straight for my car. I drove home with the windows down so the car wouldn't smell like an ashtray, but secondhand smoke lingered on my clothing and in my hair. I figured it was a small price to pay for information I could hopefully barter.

CHAPTER 12

A s much as I was eager to trade information with Deputy Ranston, I knew enough not to bother him on a Sunday. Besides, I needed to throw my clothing in the wash and either take a shower or go for a quick dip in the pool and use their shower so I wouldn't have to clean it afterward. I considered my options when I pulled into the garage and was leaning toward the pool when I heard the phone ring.

My immediate reaction was that it was Marshall. I dropped my bag on the floor and charged to the phone, only to hear my aunt Ina's voice.

"Phee! I completely forgot that today is the Gittlestein anniversary in Fountain Hills. Fifty years together."

Who the heck are the Gittlesteins? And please don't tell me they're our relatives.

"Do I know them?"

"I doubt it. Why would you know them? Louis is playing the saxophone for their anniversary party. He had that event on the calendar for months. He and that little band of his are very popular with retirees. He'll be leaving around three and I don't expect him back until seven or eight."

I had no idea where this conversation was going but I played along. I had lots of practice with this sort of fill-in-the-blanks with my mother and her friends.

"That's nice, Aunt Ina. Good for Uncle Louis."

"Oh, goodness. That's not why I called. With Louis out of the way for the afternoon, I figured we could have a chat with Serena or Tersee. I called both of them and Tersee's free today. Serena has a luncheon with her knitting group."

"She's in a knitting group? Like knitting sweaters and scarves? That kind of knitting?"

"What other kind is there? Just because she's a practicing Wiccan doesn't mean she can't enjoy everyday pastimes like the rest of us."

"No, it's just that—"

"Honestly, Phee. For someone as open-minded as you are, you can be downright phobic when it comes to witches."

Much as I didn't want to admit it, my aunt hit home with that remark. I had a stereotypical image of Wiccans in my mind, but I had the feeling Tersee was going to change all that.

"Only because I haven't met any."

"Well, you can meet Tersee this afternoon. I told her I'd call back. She lives in Glendale and I thought we could have a nice late lunch or early dinner at the Spicery in Caitlin Court."

I'd been to the Spicery once before with my mother and the book club ladies. It was a quaint little restaurant housed in a tiny cottage smack-dab in the city's historical district. Vintage décor, cutesy tablecloths, old-fashioned spindle chairs, and savory sandwiches.

"Um, yeah. Sure. That would be fine."

"I'll find out what time and call you back. I can drive us or Louis can drop me off at your house and you can drive us there. Naturally you'd have to take me home."

"Yes. That. Have Louis drop you off here. No problem." The last time my aunt drove us anywhere, she wore her reading glasses instead of her distance ones. I still jump whenever I hear a car horn. "See you later. And thanks, Aunt Ina."

At twenty minutes to four, my aunt Ina arrived and heaved a large satchel into the nearest chair. Unlike similar experiences with my mother, I didn't have to worry that Streetman was inside the tote.

"Why did you bring such a large bag?" I asked, eyeing the maroon and white caftan she wore.

"Tersee's giving me dried herbs for bathing and medicinal purposes. And before you say anything, it's not marijuana."

"I wasn't going to say anything. Besides, that stuff is sold everywhere now. All I see are signs for CBC oil. Even for pets."

"Tersee's herbs are more refined. Anyway, we should get going. I don't want to keep her waiting."

"I probably should have asked this before, but did she know Billie? I mean, I'd hate for us to make a wasted trip."

"As my Louis always says, no trip is ever wasted if it results in a good dining experience. And yes, she was acquainted with Billie. That's all she'd tell me over the phone."

My aunt retrieved her satchel, tossed her long braids from her buxom chest to her shoulders and walked to the front door. "I'm glad you and I are the ones meeting with Tersee and not your mother. Harriet has an uncanny knack of saying things that could be embarrassing."

Really? I'd no idea.

It was a fairly quick drive from Peoria to Glendale and we were in the historical district before I knew it. Tiny cottages, street parking only, and lots of tourists milling about. I parked a few yards from the Spicery and walked alongside my aunt on the narrow sidewalk, occasionally stepping down onto the street so we'd have room.

"Look!" my aunt shouted. "Tersee's across the street. Getting out of her car."

The spotless silver metallic Buick gleamed in the afternoon sun. It was too large to be an Encore so I figured it had to be one of the pricier larger cars, like the Enclave. I was glad we were parked down the block since I hadn't washed my car since the last rain.

"Ina!" a tall svelte woman called out. From a distance she appeared to be in her late fifties or maybe even sixties. Her shoulder-length dark hair was offset by dangling silver earrings with an abstract design. She wore dark capris and a blue-green color-block tunic. And the satchel she carried made my aunt's look like a mini-purse.

"You must be Phee," Tersee said as she approached us. "Nice to meet you."

"You as well."

No doubt, my aunt's friend exuded a certain warmth that was contagious.

"Come on," she said. "We'd better get a seat before it fills up. Sunday evenings can be very busy."

The three of us nabbed a corner table in one of the small sitting rooms and ordered a pot of Queen Elizabeth tea and finger sandwiches. Tersee wasted no time getting to the point. "I understand you wanted to know about Billie Churl's involvement with our coven."

"I'm trying to get as much information as I can about her. Until the county deputies find out who assaulted her in that library tower, the place is off-limits. That means the annual community send-off for winter visitors will take place without the usual fanfare. And that's causing lots of consternation for the residents, especially my mother. Who thrives on that sort of stuff."

"The balloon launch. I know. It's always on the news. When your aunt called me, I was taken aback that anyone, other than the authorities, would be looking into Billie's death. But now I understand your interest. But before I continue, I need to make something very clear—Billie was not a member of our coven and would not have been accepted into our coven had she shown an interest."

I widened my eyes as Tersee continued. "We have a clear sense of ethics and our rituals and practices are for good, not evil. We have a hierarchy and we adhere to certain rules. There's guidance, friendship, and support. But Billie wasn't interested in any of that. She approached Serena, along with Laurel, who's another Wiccan in our coven, and me, because she wanted to 'get her hands on some spells to remove obstacles.'"

"Obstacles? What kind of obstacles?"

"All she would tell us was that she needed to get something done and didn't have much time."

My aunt inhaled one of the mini sandwiches and chuckled. "If that was my sister, it would have been housework."

Tersee and I both laughed. "Unfortunately," Tersee said, "that's not how we work. When we tried explaining that to Billie, she became extremely rude and left."

"How long ago was this?" I asked.

"About a week before she was found dead. She looked us up on the Meetup Group for the West Valley and showed up to our pagan pride event in North Phoenix. We never turn anyone away. We're the only coven in the West Valley. Most are in the Tucson area and there are a few in the East Valley."

"Do you remember anything else about your conversation with her?"

"Not the conversation, but her mannerisms. While we were talking, she kept tying knots on the pull-string of her bag. She'd tie one, then untie it and tie it again. Serena told me the knots were all different but I didn't pay as close attention as she did. Sorry, I wish there was more I could tell you."

"No, that's fine. The more I learn about Billie and her habits, the closer I'll get to figuring out who her assailant could have been."

"I'll do my best to direct positive energy your way."

Much to my astonishment, Tersee was nothing like the stereotype I imagined and I chastised myself for being so judgmental. The three of us enjoyed our finger sandwiches and went on to order chocolate mousse and mini cakes for dessert. She even invited my aunt and me to join her coven for their annual Beltane Festival at the end of the month. According to the lunar calendar date, it was a few days before my mother's gala community event. *If* they managed to pull it together.

"We're joining with another two larger covens south of Tucson in the Ramsey Canyon Preserve in Nicksville," Tersee said. "The celebration honors the joy and ecstasy of life. As the sun frees itself from winter bondage, we rejoice in our own awakening. We'll be camping out, so don't worry about accommodations."

I gave my aunt one of those *don't you dare* stares and thanked Tersee for her generosity. When we left the Spicery, I reiterated how much I enjoyed making her acquaintance. She and my aunt gave each other a quick hug before Tersee crossed the street back to her car and we proceeded down the block to where I had parked.

"Thanks for not getting us into that Beltane Festival," I said to my aunt once we were in the car.

She adjusted her seat belt and scoffed. "Don't become like your mother. You need to widen your horizons."

"Oh, trust me. They're wide enough."

"Hmm, getting back to Billie, what do you suppose the knot tying was all about?"

"Not sure, but according to Adelaide, the book recommendation lady at the Sun City West library, one of Billie's interests included knot tying."

"Harrumph. Not much use for knot tying unless you're a Boy Scout or in the Navy. Or maybe one of those serial killers you see on *Criminal Minds.*"

"I think we can forget about the last option. But it *is* rather perplexing, isn't it? I mean, the woman had some strange interests, but according to what Tersee said, Billie had a motive. She needed to get something done and needed to do it in a hurry. Maybe the 'something' was what got her killed. Geez, so many weird little clues going nowhere."

"I'm sure you'll be able to piece it together. But I wouldn't mention our lunch with Tersee today when you speak with your mother."

"Don't worry. I'm not going down that road."

"If I think of anything, I'll let you know."

"Thanks, Aunt Ina."

I dropped my aunt at her house in Sun City Grand and started back to Vistancia. The sun had already set and waves of turquoise and pink layered the sky like a woven blanket. I thought about my conversations with Eddie Krome and Tersee as I turned onto Route 303. It was surprising that my amateur sleuthing had taken such a different path from the official investigation that Deputies Ranston and Bowman pursued. My mind drifted back to the scene of Billie's death and something occurred to me.

Without wasting a second, I took the first exit off of the 303 and doubled back to Sun City West. If I was lucky, there'd still be a good deal of daylight left.

CHAPTER 13

Snooping around at dusk isn't exactly the best time to study a crime scene, let alone look for evidence. Especially since the sheriff's office had already combed the place over the past week. I wasn't sure what I might find, but I had a nagging feeling whoever tangled with Billie at the top of the tower didn't exit the building right away, or they would have risked being seen. That meant one thing—they took the side tower door and climbed onto the ledge, where they remained out of view. Then, once the commotion began, they could have easily escaped into the crowd.

The parking lot in front of the library was empty. Same thing with the one by the pickleball courts and the main one by the bowling alley. I surmised that Sunday evenings weren't a popular time for club activities.

There was plenty of daylight left and I had to take advantage of it before I lost my nerve completely. I parked the car adjacent to the pickleball court so as not to arouse suspicion should someone stroll by with their dog. Then, I walked to the side entrance of the library and hoisted myself onto the book receptacle that hugged the side of the building. I had no intention of climbing up on the ledge, only having a look-see. But when I realized how easy it was to make the two-foot jaunt, I took the chance. Something I never would have done two years ago. But then again, I never would have climbed into Dumpsters, wrestled with stone-faced killers, or traipsed around in the high desert, where anything could have happened.

That old saying curiosity killed the cat floated around in my head but I didn't realize how relevant it was until I made a soft landing on all fours. A sudden hiss and I was face-to-face with a well-fed bobcat that eyed me as if I was his or her next meal.

"Good kitty. Nice kitty."

And the stupidity award of the year goes to Sophie Vera Kimball . . .

I edged backward slowly, my hands trembling and my feet moving like lead sinkers.

Okay. So maybe I'll stick to paper and pencil investigations and murder notebooks tucked safely in my desk.

Without warning, the bobcat leapt off the ledge and darted behind the library in the direction of the Men's club. I stood motionless and watched as the graceful predator disappeared from sight. My heart pounded and my feet felt like Jell-O. It took me a few seconds to recall why I was even on the ledge, but it was only when I spotted a teal green pack of cigarettes next to the wall that my brain kicked into gear.

Maybe my hunch is right, after all.

I knew enough not to pick them up in case Billie's assailant left fingerprints on them. But since I had left my bag in the car and wasn't in the habit of carrying plastic bags in my pockets—unless I had to take Streetman somewhere—I had two options: go back to the car and get a tissue or kick the pack of cigarettes over the ledge and then pick it up with a tissue.

There was, of course, a third option. I could leave the box right where it was and tell Deputy Ranston to retrieve it, but I needed as much leverage as I could get. I eyeballed the soft pack of Newport cigarettes with the plastic wrap pulled partially down and sighed.

Terrific. I'll kick this sucker and cigarettes will fly everywhere.

The sky darkened and I took my chance with a series of short kicks that finally resulted in me being able to get the tip of my toe under the bottom of the box and give it enough thrust to send it over the edge and onto the driveway by the large metal book return. Worst-case scenario was that I'd find cigarettes strewn everywhere, but that didn't happen. Instead, something much worse did.

Herb Garrett pulled up alongside the library, got out of his car, and looked up at me.

"Hey, cutie, I thought that was you. I'm on my way over to the bowling alley. Sunday night leagues begin at eight. I like to get here early."

I was so occupied with the bobcat and the pack of cigarettes, I hadn't paid attention to what was going on in the large parking lot.

Herb stepped closer to the building. "Don't tell me Harriet sent you on one of her wild-goose chases for who-knows-what."

No. Apparently I can do that on my own.

"Um, not exactly. And whatever you do, don't touch that pack of cigarettes off to your left."

"Huh?"

"Hold on, I'll be right down."

"I'll give you a hand."

The last thing I wanted was for Herb to eyeball my rear end as I backed down from the ledge and stepped onto the book return.

"Move off to the side and hold out your hand."

Herb did as I asked, making it easier for me to reach the top of the receptacle and jump to the ground.

"Um, I suppose you're wondering what this is all about. It's really quite simple. I think whoever assaulted Billie at the top of the tower exited from the side door and got onto the ledge the same way I did. Or, they could have climbed on those giant boulders near the other side. I thought maybe I could find some evidence to prove my theory."

"The pack of cigarettes?"

"Uh-huh."

"I've got tissues in my car so I won't get prints on them."

Before Herb could say anything, I opened the driver's side of the car, reached into the console, and grabbed a handful of tissues. I figured I'd put the cigarette pack in a plastic bag when I got home.

"Working for that detective agency is rubbing off on you. Next thing you know you'll be getting a gun permit."

"Not likely. Listen, whatever you do, don't breathe a word about this to my mother. Last thing I need is a lecture about heights and accidents."

"No problem. Boy, that Churl woman was something else, huh? From what the pinochle crew told me, more than one person was gunning for her. Heard she owed people money."

"What people? What money?"

"I didn't ask. She didn't owe *me* anything so I didn't pay a heck of a lot of attention to Kenny and Wayne when they mentioned it."

"Good grief, Herb. Pay attention now! I mean, could you please revisit that conversation with the guys and get back to me. If the Rec Center doesn't get that tower opened in time for the Bye Bye Birdie event, my mother can kiss *Sonoran Living* and her dream of getting on the show goodbye."

"Trust me. No one wants to see that happen. And I mean no one. Especially me. I live across the street from her. She'll be moaning about it for weeks. Not to mention the fact I'm supposed to order the damn balloons. And it's not like balloons for a birthday party. It's hundreds of them. I'm on a tight deadline as it is. But shouldn't the county deputies be dealing with the investigation?"

"They are. They're just not dealing with it the way I am."

My God. Like mother, like daughter.

"I'm having drinks with the guys at Curley's after bowling. I'll see what I can dredge up."

"Thanks, Herb. And remember, not a word to my mother."

Herb saluted me as if he was taking orders from a staff sergeant. "No worries, cutie. Got to run."

I watched as he got into his car and headed directly up the driveway to the bowling alley. The clues were coming at me fast and furious regarding Billie and her shenanigans, but nothing would be as substantial as a solid piece of evidence. Maybe I'd luck out and that opened pack of Newports would do the trick.

The first thing I did when I pulled into our garage was to find a plastic shopping bag and put the pack of cigarettes in it before returning them to the front seat of my car.

Although the finger sandwiches at the Spicery were tasty and filling at the time, I was still hungry when I got home. I grabbed an apple from the fridge, along with a handful of pretzels. At least half my snack was healthy.

No blinking lights on the answering machine and no call yet from Marshall. I supposed I'd better get used to this situation since it seemed as if he and Nate would be on the road for a few more days. What started out as a simple horse theft was beginning to take on ramifications that were troublesome, to say the least.

Given the information I gleaned from Tersee and Herb, I went back to my murder book and added more details. The words *swindler* and *grifter* played over and over in my mind. Whatever Billie was up to, it had to be what got her killed. And those animal wounds on her hands and arms . . . what on earth was that about?

I knew I'd have to play it carefully when I called Deputy Ranston in the morning. Carefully and convincingly. The way I saw it, I had more to give him in terms of information than the other way around. But oddly enough, it didn't feel that way.

CHAPTER 14

A ugusta was monkeying around with the printer when I walked into the office the next morning.

"It's the thickness of the paper," she grumbled. "Don't know where Mr. Williams bought the last batch but it's too thin. The paper sticks."

"I can check the invoices if you're that curious."

"Not *that* curious. But I'll tell you one thing—I'm buying the next carton from Staples or Office Max. None of this cheapy-deepy stuff anymore. Have you heard from your fiancé? Mr. Williams called a few minutes ago. Said a team of spiders couldn't weave a web as tricky as the one he and Mr. Gregory are in."

"I know. I spoke to Marshall late last night. More leads but lots of dead ends. It's very frustrating. The same could be said for Billie's death. I should know. I spent the weekend talking with a real witch, going eye to eye with a bobcat on a ledge, and oh, lest I forget, tracking down the one deli employee who escaped Ranston and Bowman's scrutiny."

Augusta stopped fussing with the printer and looked directly at me. "I'm going to need a strong cup of coffee for this. Good thing we don't open for another fifteen minutes. Start talking."

For the next four or five minutes, while Augusta made our coffees, I babbled on nonstop, giving new meaning to William James's definition of "stream of consciousness." Augusta took it all in with a deadpan expression that didn't change.

"I'm not sure if what you want to do is called leverage or quid pro quo, but trust me, it didn't work for politicians and I'm not so sure it will work for you," she said.

"All I want is to find out what animal gave Billie those wounds. It could be the answer to her death."

"I doubt the animal was the one she wrestled with at the top of the tower."

"No, but it might be the reason for the altercation. The way I see it, I'm in possession of evidence *and* I tracked down a suspect the deputies completely ignored."

"You're lucky Ranston and Bowman don't arrest you for interfering with a crime investigation. Unless of course you intend to have your newfound acquaintance cast a spell on them."

"Very funny. What I *do* intend to do is call Deputy Ranston as soon as I get into my office. He wants to expedite this investigation as much as I do."

"Soon as I'm done with the printer, I'll look up Mr. Williams's list of criminal defense attorneys. In case you need one."

"All I need is the creamer. And if you're looking for lawyers, find one that works pro bono."

Augusta laughed as I opened the door to my office. A few minutes later, once I had booted up the computer and made myself comfortable at my desk, I phoned Deputy Ranston. Unfortunately, his partner took the call.

"Sorry, Miss Kimball, but Deputy Ranston has the day off. What's so pressing that you needed to speak with him?"

If I thought Ranston was annoying and irritating, his partner was worse. Deputy Bowman had all the physical and personality traits of a grizzly bear just out of hibernation. Not only that, but he was obstinate and oftentimes myopic. Still, he hung on to an investigation like a Doberman with a bone. A quality, I suppose, that was respected and appreciated in his office.

"I was hoping we could trade information on the Billie Churl case."

"I beg your pardon?"

"Trade. You know, swap, exchange, that sort of thing."

"Miss Kimball, if you're holding back information on an official investigation, I need to inform you it's against the law and you could be—"

"For your information, I have a vested interest in this case. So vested, in fact, that I risked being attacked by a bobcat, *and* I had to endure a luncheon with a professed Wiccan friend of my aunt Ina's."

"Please, do not tell me your aunt is somehow involved."

"Good grief, no! My aunt happens to have lots of contacts in the valley, and they, in turn, gather information like bees do with pollen."

The next sound I heard was some sort of a groan. "What is it you have, and what is it you want to know?"

"Billie's autopsy report. The news said the recent wounds on her hands and arms weren't caused by a human, but rather, by an animal. I need to know what kind of animal."

"That's it?"

"Yes. And I, in turn, will provide you with tangible evidence that may or may not belong to Billie's assailant. And before you say anything, I was very careful not to get my fingerprints on it."

"Miss Kimball, it's too early in the day to have you talking in circles. Simply tell me what you have and what you know."

"If you do the same."

Good Lord. The last time I had a conversation like this I was in the third grade.

"Fine. The lab is still conducting tests. It appears as if those were bite marks but not from a domestic animal."

"What about a parrot? Those things bite."

"Not a bird, either. And before you start with twenty questions, like, 'Was it a rodent?' the answer is plain and clear—we do not know at this time."

"I see. And will you inform me once you find out? I don't want to wait and hear it on the news."

"Hmm, I suppose there won't be any harm in that. You've kept things under wraps before. Now, before I rescind my offer, please let me know what you're holding back."

When I mentioned Eddie Krome, Deputy Bowman asked me to hold on for a minute. In the background, I heard him yell, "Who stamped the interview sheet complete? It's not complete!" Then he returned to the phone. "Forgive me, Miss Kimball. It appears as if there's been an oversight in my office."

"Eddie's working at the Vistancia store. Plan on airing out your car once you talk with him. And the tangible evidence I have may or may not be his. It's an open pack of Newport cigarettes that I found on the lowest outside ledge of the library. Incidentally, that's where the bobcat was."

"What bobcat?"

"The one I first mentioned."

"My apologies. I must not have been paying attention. All I heard was something about your aunt and witches."

"Well, *that*, too, but they're not involved."

Again, a moan. "Do you have the cigarette pack with you?"

"It's in my car."

"Good. I'll have someone in the vicinity swing around to your office to get it. Any word when your boss and fiancé will be back?"

"I wish I knew."

"I must admit, haven't seen a horse theft in years and now, all of a sudden, it's become a thing. It's probably best they're working the case. The Arizona Department of Agriculture moves at its own speed."

"That's what I've heard."

"Expect someone before noon. And I'd appreciate it if you don't mention Eddie Krome to anyone. By the way, why *is* this case so important for you?"

"If your office doesn't solve the case and open the library tower, my mother will not get her day of fame on *Sonoran Living*. And believe me, your office will be hearing about it well into the next century."

"Aargh. Good day, Miss Kimball."

True to his word, a neophyte deputy arrived at a little before eleven to secure "the evidence." He took the plastic bag from me as if it contained a highly sensitive explosive and placed it in a cardboard box. As if that wasn't enough, he had a preprinted seal that went on the box to secure it.

Augusta had all she could do to keep from laughing. When the deputy left, she shook her head and announced, "Our tax dollars hard at work."

"He's following protocol."

"That's the trouble with these government offices. Too much protocol and not enough common sense."

"Hey, I almost forgot to ask. Have you heard anything from Rolo Barnes?"

"*I* haven't, but Mr. Williams did. Rolo's information is what they're using to track down those horses."

"I hope they work fast. I have a funny feeling they're going to be needed on this case."

It wasn't just a funny feeling. It was a desperate feeling. Shortly after the deputy left with the pack of Newports, my mother called. This time demanding to know why I haven't contacted the membership director from the Boomers club so I could infiltrate the activities Billie was involved with.

"I'm not Wonder Woman, for crying out loud, Mom. There's only so much I can do at one time. Between Aunt Ina's Wiccans and snooping around delis, I've been pretty darn busy. Not to mention I have to work. I have an actual job as a bookkeeper/accountant."

"Witches? That sister of mine dragged you off to meet witches?"

I was so rattled by my mother's demands that I accidently let the visit with Tersee slip out of my mouth. At least I didn't mention the encounter with the bobcat and Herb. And here I thought *he* was going to be the blabbermouth.

"It was a nice afternoon lunch. And the woman was a Wiccan, not Grizelda from every fairy tale you've heard."

"So when will you contact the Boomers?"

"Soon. Very soon."

Yep. Like it or not, looks like the Sun City West Boomers Water Volleyball is going to get a new player. Thank goodness they keep the water temperature at eighty-seven.

I was about to look up the club contact numbers on the Sun City West website when I remembered I'd sent a private message to Julia Ornstern via Facebook. I hadn't checked my Facebook page in the last twenty-four hours and didn't sign up for notifications on my phone. Too annoying. With my fingers crossed, I logged into Facebook hoping Julia had responded.

Sure enough, she'd sent me a message.

What else did Martha say about me? I'm curious. PM me.

If nothing else, I got the first name of Kugel's owner. I wrote back, *"Nothing really. Said you knew Billie Churl. Can we meet to talk?"*

I logged out of Facebook and pulled up the accounting spreadsheet I had been working on last week. I thought I'd seen the last of this what-did-she-tell-you-about-me stuff when my daughter was in junior high, but evidently it has a whole new following—the senior citizen set.

CHAPTER 15

I could hear Augusta taking calls throughout the morning but other than that, it was pretty quiet. Until one of those calls turned out to be for me.

"It's a Julia Ornstern," Augusta called out. "Want me to transfer it to your office or take a message?"

"Transfer it. It's about Billie."

Two seconds later, Julia was on the line.

"You'll have to forgive the tone of my message, but honestly, everyone talks about everyone else around here and you never know what they're saying. Martha is the biggest gossip of them all but her dog is adorable. Love that Kugel. So, what can I do for you?"

"I work for Williams Investigations in Glendale but I'm not an investigator. I, um, have a personal interest in this case."

"Were you a friend of Billie's?"

"No. I'm looking into the matter for my mother, who lives in Sun City West."

"Oh. Was she a friend of Billie's? And the only reason I'm asking is because Billie didn't strike me as someone who had many friends. Or any, for that matter."

"Uh, no. My mother's interest in the case is . . . well, a bit more self-serving. She wants the library tower reopened in time for that Bye Bye Birdie balloon launch. She's on the committee."

Julia laughed so loud I could hear her gasping for breath. "That's hilarious. But I don't know how I can help you."

"The more information I can get on Billie, the better able I'll be to find out who might have attacked her that morning. Would you mind meeting me for coffee one evening this week? I get off work at five but it's in Glendale. And I live in Vistancia."

"How about tomorrow night at six at the Bell Road Starbucks in Sun City? The baristas at that Starbucks are the best."

"Great. I'm not sure what I'll be wearing but I'm average height and weight, in my forties, and my hair is highlighted."

"I haven't seen my forties in years and I'm overweight according to my doctor, but I can still get into a decent pair of jeans so I'm not obsessing over losing any pounds. Also average height with short salt-and-pepper hair."

"Wonderful. No need for one of us to stick a flower behind our ear, or worse yet, walk in holding one. Only Meg Ryan could've gotten away with that."

"Loved that movie! I look forward to meeting you."

"Me, too. Thanks."

The second I got off the phone I raced into the outer office. "Augusta! Julia Ornstern's meeting me for coffee after work tomorrow. She's the person who the lady with that Kugel dog told me about from the Boomers club. Julia's bound to know who Billie irked, swindled, or ticked off. Wow. It's exhilarating, isn't it?"

"What? Irritating someone?"

"No, tracking down a lead. No wonder Nate and Marshall enjoy what they're doing. Not that I can consider what I'm doing in the same league, but still, it's exciting."

"As long as the lead you're tracking down isn't some gun-toting lunatic, or worse yet, someone who's giving you a run for your money all over the state. Good thing Mr. Williams's neighbor likes that parrot he's watching and agreed to feed and visit with the thing while he and Mr. Gregory are off chasing horses."

"Yeah, last thing I'd want to do is get stuck with Mr. Fluffypants."

"Yep, surprising what we do for relatives."

Especially if it's your mother.

The rest of the day moved along at a steady clip and I was home before I knew it. Late afternoon/early evening was the hottest part of the day so I took advantage of it with a quick swim before dinner. I wolfed down a chicken salad sandwich and turned on the TV to catch the seven o'clock news on Fox 10. I figured I'd see what the other channels had to offer during the late-night news.

It was the usual stuff about car accidents and near drownings in swimming pools, followed by reminders to parents to watch their children at all times around water. Then, Linda Williams introduced a human-interest segment "in the hopes that viewers might be able to shed some light on the heartbreaking theft of some family horses."

The instant I heard the words *family horses*, I stopped fiddling around with my iPhone and turned up the volume. It was the Marionette family from Wickenburg, neighbors, albeit a few acres away, of Perry Gaynes, and the horses were the beloved pets of their six-year-old son, Brandon, and his four-year-old sister, Robyn. The Marionettes had also contracted with Nate and Marshall to find their trail horses.

As Linda spoke, I could feel my throat tighten. It *was* heartbreaking. She had clips of Brandon and Robyn crying as well as Mrs. Marionette trying to speak but choking up every few minutes. The segment ended with Linda asking viewers to contact the Arizona Department of Agriculture if they knew anything about this unthinkable theft.

I knew Nate and Marshall were topnotch investigators and Rolo Barnes had intel no other agencies could get close to, but unless they were able to work fast, I feared those horses would be sold and shipped to God-knows-where for whatever nefarious purposes.

At a little past nine, Marshall's phone call echoed my concerns. "Seems we had a money trail, hon, but it went nowhere. Rolo's been able to follow some chatter on the dark web and we've been pursuing his leads. As far as the state is concerned, they've got zilch."

"I watched a human interest spot tonight about the Marionette family. It was gut-wrenching."

"I know. The same segment aired in Willcox. Geez, I hope this thing doesn't take us out of state. We're not that far from El Paso. What gets me is the fact that no monetary transactions have showed up. And I'm talking the illegal ones that Rolo's able to track. You'd think whoever's selling those horses would have made the sale by now."

"Maybe it was a trade for something else. Drugs?"

"The horses are valuable, but not the kind of money that would interest drug cartels. Funny, but this is one of those cases that sticks in your craw. What gets me is that the thefts are growing. Good news, if you can call it that, is the fact that each new situation gives us additional clues."

"Well, I hope one of them pays off. I miss you like crazy."

"Same here. Any news on your sleuthing project?"

"I think I'm gaining ground. Either that, or I've found a way to expand my social circle. I'm meeting with one of the Boomers tomorrow to see what else I can find out about Billie. Oh, and I traded information with Deputy Bowman."

"Huh?"

Marshall couldn't believe how confident I'd become when I gave him the details. "Be careful how you handle Bowman and Ranston. Remember, they still have the authority to arrest you."

"Yikes, you're sounding like Augusta."

"I knew I liked that woman. Listen, don't take any chances. I'll try to check in with you tomorrow. Love you, hon."

"Double back at you."

Knowing that Marshall and Nate were safe, at least for the time being, I was able to get a decent night's sleep. Unfortunately, a morning wake-up call from my mother foiled any chance of me pressing the snooze alarm for a few more minutes.

"Phee! We have a crisis over here. I tried to call you last night but the line was busy and that cell phone of yours went to voicemail."

"What crisis?"

And please don't let this be about the dog.

"Louise Munson can't stay alone in her house. That deputy didn't say as much, but Louise figured it out. She was in the library tower the same time Billie's assailant was there. He or she could have easily looked down to the bottom of the stairwell and seen her. She's a marked woman. She could be next on the list."

"What list?"

"Shh, let me finish. Louise and that parrot of hers need to move in with someone temporarily. It's for her own safety. I'd offer to let them stay here but you know how Streetman is. I'd be afraid we'd wake up and find feathers everywhere."

"Don't look at me. Louise and that African gray parrot aren't staying here. Nate's watching the same kind of bird for his aunt and he says they're impossible. Equated it to living with a two-year-old."

"I wasn't thinking of asking you. Besides, Louise wants to stay in Sun City West. The book club ladies and I will be meeting at Bagels 'n More to figure this out today. Any chance you could drive over here during your lunch hour?"

"No. No chance whatsoever. By the time I get there, it will be time to turn around. And don't insist I stay late at work because I made plans. On your behalf, mind you. I'm meeting with Julia Ornstern from the Boomers club."

My mother must have been so taken back that for a few seconds she didn't say a word. Finally, she spoke. "Well, I suppose I can't fault you for that. Talk to this Julia woman and see how you can infiltrate the club activities Billie was in."

"Already thought of it, but don't get your hopes up if she was in the kayaking club, or worse yet, the spelunking club."

"I'll let you know how we work out Louise's situation. Maybe she can stay with one of the girls each night."

"Or maybe she can keep her door and windows locked. Perhaps even invest in an alarm system."

"Up until now she's been relying on the parrot."

I rolled my eyes and tossed the cover off of me. "Look, as much as I'd like to continue this conversation, I'm going to be late if we keep talking. I'll catch you later."

"Call me."

I stumbled into the shower and let the hot water relax all the muscles that had tightened up during my phone conversation with my mother. I was positive Louise was overreacting, but then again, she may have been right. Whoever was at the top of those stairs was either there deliberately to confront Billie or, as the rumormongering suggested, was there because he or she happened to be a dangerous lunatic.

My vote was for option one, but I was beginning to think I was in the minority.

CHAPTER 16

"If my mother phones the office, tell her I moved to Idaho and didn't leave a forwarding address."

Augusta looked up from a stack of mail she was sorting. "Usually most people say good morning when they get to work."

"Good morning, Augusta! And whatever you do, don't transfer any calls from my mother into my office."

"That bad?"

"Let's just say I don't want to get stuck babysitting Louise Munson and that bird of hers."

"Oh, brother. Seems you can't go twenty-four hours without something wacky happening. What is it this time?"

I explained about Louise's fear but I really couldn't call it irrational. Overreacting maybe, but not irrational. "I don't want to say it, but the woman may have a point. Whoever was at the top of the tower was most likely there on purpose. The purpose being to confront Billie. And who knows if he or she didn't look down and see poor Louise doing her cardio steps before Billie arrived. Then again, it could have been a certifiable nutcase, which gets Louise off the hook, but—"

"Strikes terror in the heart of the community? Sorry, I couldn't resist the comic book exaggeration. Anyway, maybe you'll find out something worthwhile when you meet with that Julia woman after work."

"I hope so. But I hate these little charades. Pretending to enjoy water volleyball is bad enough. What if Billie liked rock climbing? The Boomers do that, you know."

"Maybe you'll luck out and find that Billie had a passion for bird watching."

Sadly, she didn't. When I finally met Julia at Starbucks after work, I found out exactly what Billie was into and it scared the living daylights out of me.

Julia was seated in the outdoor area of Starbucks under a canopy of mesquite trees. She had a tall lemonade in her hand and her gaze met mine just as she was about to take a sip. "You must be Phee. Grab a seat. Unless you want to get a drink first."

"It can wait. And thanks so much for agreeing to see me."

I plunked myself down and tucked the chair close to the table. "Like I said over the phone, in order for me to find out who Billie's assailant was, I need to know which activities she frequented and go from there."

"If you mean participating in them, good luck. That woman was nuts.

77

No other word for it. The water volleyball was her relaxation sport. She preferred climbing, but on the extreme side. Ever hear of Direct Line Down?"

I froze as Julia continued. "It's a cliff on the west side of Camelback Mountain. So dangerous that most seasoned climbers steer clear of it. Billie wasn't one of them. That's why it's so ironic she fell to her death on a stairwell."

I gulped. "I think I'll get that cup of coffee right now. I'll be right back."

"Take your time. It's a pleasant evening and this spot is delightful."

I returned a few minutes later with a double shot of espresso. "Climbing, huh? I suppose she had to be well-versed in knot tying."

"I'll tell you one thing. She was well-versed in finagling money out of people. Maybe she needed it to buy the equipment for all those treks. Mountain climbing gear doesn't come cheap, and I know for a fact the club doesn't pay for individual supplies. Like birding. You have to bring your own binoculars."

"Hmm. You mentioned finagling money. How'd she do that?"

"Oh, she had her act down, all right. She'd approach people, one to one, and give them some sob story about being late for her electric bill or needing money to buy food for her dog. And get this! She didn't even *have* a dog! People would fall for it and hand her a few bucks. Mainly to get her off their backs."

"That's terrible."

"That wasn't the worst. She always had some sort of quick money scheme going on. Like bogus tickets for some fake raffle."

"And no one outed her?"

"People were afraid of her. Better to lose ten or twenty bucks than whatever they thought she'd do to them."

The more I heard about Billie, the more convinced I became that her death was deliberate and not an "unfortunate fall as the result of an altercation."

"Julia, if you were to wager a guess as to who she might have stiffed to the point where they sought revenge, do any names come to mind?"

"None of the people I know in the Boomers club strike me as the kind who would do something like that." Julia took a sip of her lemonade and widened her eyes. "Say, we've got a general meeting coming up tomorrow. I know it's short notice, but you might be able to pick up some information at the meeting. You can come as my guest. Have you ever snooped around during one of those things? Surprising what you can overhear."

Oh, my gosh. It's embarrassing to admit it, but I'm the queen of snooping around. At least this meeting is in a public place.

"Where? What time?"

"Seven thirty at Palm Ridge, Summit Hall A. I should have mentioned that the first part of the meeting is deadly with all the committee reports. Then, the group breaks up into smaller activity segments. People just drag their chairs into clusters. Very casual. We don't do refreshments at these huge meetings. Too cumbersome. If you were to arrive, say, at eight fifteen, I'd point you in the direction of the rock climbers and the volleyball players. How does that sound?"

"Like a great plan to me. Thanks."

• • •

Much as I hated to admit it, if it wasn't for my mother insisting I visit the dog park, I never would have gotten Julia's name from Kugel's owner, Martha. Word of mouth in Sun City West was faster than any high-speed internet on record. And, I never would have seen Eddie Krome's coworker at the Boomers club the following night.

He wasn't the barrel-chested guy with the receding hairline, but the other man who stood behind him at the Vistancia store's deli. Tall, well-built, middle-aged with a short scruffy beard and deep-set wrinkles on his forehead.

Julia's timing was right on the money, and when I slipped into the meeting at eight twenty, it had just concluded. She immediately pulled me over and whispered, "The rock climbers tend to leave early, so I'd start with them." Then, before I could say a word, she hustled me to the corner where they gathered and introduced me.

"This is Phee. She's a friend of mine and she may be interested in joining us. Go easy on her, will you?"

The group of eight or nine men and women laughed and I took a seat. "She'll only be with you for a few minutes," Julia continued, "I want her to check out the water volleyball, too."

The second Julia left, the woman sitting next to me asked, "Are you an experienced climber?"

Only if library ledges count.

"Hardly. I'm curious, that's all."

"No problem," someone else added. "We've got lots of trained climbers who can get you started."

"Speaking of started," another person quipped, "let's get going. I have to be up early tomorrow. Are we still on for the climb in Sedona?"

With that, the group discussed its plans for a weekend climb on the red rocks, and without any prompting on my part, Billie's name came up. It was a flurry of fast-hurled comments and I felt like an owl turning my head this way and that to see who said what.

"Finally! I won't have to worry about getting nudged by Billie."

"Nudged? Try shoved or pushed."

"Lucky one of us didn't wind up the way she did."

"At least it wasn't on one of our excursions. Bad press for the club."

"Guess her office is closed for business, huh?"

I turned to the woman next to me and whispered, "Office? What are they talking about?"

She bent her head down and motioned for me to do the same. Then she said, "Billie used the top of the tower stairs as her personal office. The woman had a screw loose, that's for sure."

"I'm not sure I understand."

"In case you weren't aware, she was into all sorts of stuff. Not drugs or anything of that nature, but make-a-quick-buck kinds of thing. You know, grifting people."

That was at least the second or third time I'd heard similar references to Billie, but it was the first time I found out where she met her clientele, in addition to the break area behind the supermarket deli. And that was the moment I realized something—maybe *Billie* was the assailant and things went wrong. If I was right, then that premise changed everything.

Just then, Julia reappeared and ushered me to the water volleyball group. I muttered a quick thank-you to the rock climbers, making a mental note to never, under any circumstances, join their group.

"Remember," one of the ladies said as I approached the water volleyball group with Julia, "the B team is bringing the lemonade and cookies tomorrow night. The A team is next week."

A chorus of "uh-huhs" followed.

"This is Phee, everyone," Julia announced. "I'm shuffling her from group to group hoping she'll connect with us."

"Then you have to try out the volleyball tomorrow night," one of the ladies shouted.

"Seven o'clock at the RH Johnson pool. Clothing optional."

"Very funny, Harold," the woman said. "You'll have to get used to us, we always kid around."

"Enjoy," Julia said. "See you in a bit."

I took a seat between Harold and the lady who first spoke, but no sooner had I sat down than a man a few seats away stood and gave the group a wave. "Sorry, guys. I've got to hit the road. I'll catch up with you next week. Business out of town. Some of us have to work, you know."

A few smirks and some laughter could be heard as he walked past me. That's when I got a good look at his right arm and froze. Between his wrist and his elbow was the most detailed tattoo of a Gila monster I've ever seen. I swore the thing almost looked three-dimensional.

CHAPTER 17

Suddenly my mind flashed back to the conversation I had with Rashida last Saturday in the deli. She mentioned three men who met with Billie outside the deli in the break area. Three middle-aged men with stubble on their faces, one of whom had a tattoo of a Gila monster on his arm. Maybe I jumped to conclusions, but I was certain the man who slipped past me had to be one of them.

Drat. I couldn't very well go chase after the guy, but I wasn't about to let a possible suspect disappear out of sight. It was a ten-second decision and I bolted. "Sorry. Be right back."

The man had already left Summit Hall A and was nowhere to be seen in the corridor. Either he made a mad dash for his car or took a detour in the men's room. I paused for a moment and saw another man exiting the restroom. "Is anyone else in there?" I asked him.

The man's jaw dropped. "It's vacant. Feel free to go in. Everything's fair game these days."

"Oh, that's okay. Only checking."

The man couldn't get out of my way fast enough. I chuckled as I raced to the front entrance to eyeball the parking lot, but it was useless. Whoever the man with the Gila monster tattoo was, he was long gone. And so was my chance for a quick conversation with him. On the bright side, everyone around here seemed to know each other and I figured for certain someone would give me his name.

Boy, was I ever wrong. I waited until the volleyballers finished up with their meeting but no one knew the guy's name.

"I've seen him play a few times," a robust guy with a goatee said, "but I didn't catch his name."

"I think it was Doug something," the lady who sat next to me said.

"Not Doug, I think he goes by Dayton," someone else said.

"Like Ohio?" a woman asked. "Who names their child after a state?"

Then another voice. "Not a state, Dayton is a city."

I began to feel as if I was back at Bagels 'n More listening to my mother's book club friends.

"It doesn't matter," I told the group. "I was curious, that's all."

"Will you be joining us tomorrow night?" Harold asked. "We can squeeze you in on my team."

"Um, maybe next week. I'll let Julia know."

"Good," Harold said. "And ask her to get you a copy of the membership

81

list. Maybe you'll find out that guy's name." Then, he gave me a wink and I could feel the heat rushing to my cheeks. Talk about embarrassing.

Julia had no idea who the man with the Gila monster tattoo was, either, but said it would make a great title along the lines of *The Girl with the Dragon Tattoo*. I thanked her for the invite and told her I'd keep in touch. It felt as if every possible clue slipped out of reach before I could get a solid grasp on it. Shaking my head as I unlocked my car door, I resigned myself to the fact that this was a small community and someone was bound to know who the guy was.

No sooner did I start the engine than my phone rang. I immediately turned off the car and took the call, figuring it had to be Marshall. However, the loud shriek on the line was none other than my mother. "Phee! The most horrible thing happened. Someone tried to murder Louise! They probably found out she was the one who told those deputies about that odor in the library tower. I left a message on your real phone and took a chance that you might answer this one. Dear Lord! Someone tried to kill Louise!"

"Okay. Calm down. Where is she?"

"At my house. Can't you see the return number on that phone of yours?"

"Not while I'm talking. What happened? What's going on?"

"The Rec Center moved bingo night to Wednesday and Louise went. As she was leaving, someone shoved her from behind and she fell into the parking lot right in front of a stream of cars. She was lucky no one ran her over. Got scraped up a bit but that's all."

"Did she see who it was? Did anyone see?"

"No. It was too dark. All they have are those silly decorative lights by the trees. Louise is certain it was deliberate. She called the posse and they took down the information but there's not much they can do. Shirley and Lucinda are on their way over here. Louise is going to stay with Shirley tonight once they pick up the parrot."

"Chances are it was an accident, Mom. You know how crowded and crazy it gets during those bingo games. People are pushing and shoving all the time."

"Yes. To get in. But not out. Once the game is over, the losers take their sweet time getting home."

It pained me to admit it, but she was right. Who shoves someone out of the way after the bingo game is over? *Unless of course Louise was the grand prize winner . . . then again, my mother would have started off the conversation with that. And she did mention Louise cooperating with the sheriff's office.*

"Well, I guess there's not much I can do at this point. Sounds as if you've got everything under con—"

"What? You need to get right over here and help us figure out a plan to catch this lunatic before it's not safe for any of us to leave our houses. Whatever it is you're doing is taking too long. Louise is positive it's the same person who was responsible for Billie's fall and now he or she is stalking her."

"All right. Fine. I'll head over. I'm at Palm Ridge. I was at the Boomers meeting. At *your* request." I ended the call and groaned. Then I took off for my mother's place.

It looked as if every light was on at the house when I turned onto her block. Not only that, but a lineup of cars graced the street as well. Buick, Buick, really ancient Buick, and a Toyota.

I expected my mother to answer the doorbell, but instead I was greeted by Herb Garrett. "Hey, cutie! I was on my way back from pinochle when I saw the string of cars in front of your mother's house. Naturally I came by to check it out. The women are in the kitchen with Louise. She's the one sniffling. I think they used up a whole box of tissues."

"Is that you, Phee?" my mother shouted. "I told Herb to get the door."

"Yes, it's me."

"Good. I made a fresh pot of coffee. Help yourself."

Tins of cookies, brownies and Mandelbrot lined the kitchen counter. If that wasn't enough, someone brought over a large selection of Trader Joe's chocolate-covered pretzels.

The book club ladies were clustered around Louise, who was seated at the kitchen table. Streetman was underneath it, foraging for cookie crumbs.

"Lordy, this is terrible," Shirley said. "We're like sitting ducks."

I took a pretzel and bit into it. "It could simply be a coincidence. Whoever shoved Louise may not be the same person who did the same to Billie."

"Or they could. They very well could," Cecilia said. She pulled her black cardigan sweater tighter across her chest and sighed. "I'm afraid your mother is right, Phee. We need to come up with a plan."

A dizzying sense of fear came over me and I shuddered. Thoughts of previous plans like Operation Agatha and Cleaning Service Impersonation immediately sprang to mind. "Um, what did you folks have in mind?"

My mother handed me a cup of coffee and leaned back against the counter. "Your aunt Ina will be here any minute. I told her not to stop and get food, but you know how she and Louis are."

Wonderful. We'll have an entire smorgasbord before the night is out. Good thing Marshall's not home waiting for me.

I took a sip and added cream. "Um, when you said *plan*, what exactly were you ladies thinking?"

"Maybe it's the adrenaline in our systems," Myrna said, "but we actually came up with a few scenarios. Shall I tell her, Harriet?"

My mother bit into a brownie and motioned for Myrna to continue.

"We've dubbed the first plan the Entrapment."

I all but fell over on the spot. "Please. Continue." *And don't let this be something we'll all regret.*

"It's really quite ingenious," Myrna went on. "Your mother and I have that radio show with Paul this Friday morning. We'll say that someone dropped off a mystery book at the radio station with a note inside pointing to Billie's assailant and that we intend to drop the book and the note off at the posse office immediately following the show. If Billie's attacker is listening, he or she will most likely make an appearance and voilà!"

My jaw dropped. "Voilà? Then what do you have planned? A citizen's arrest? Or does Paul intend to snare them with one of his fish hooks on a line?"

"That's not funny, Phee," my mother said. Then she turned to Myrna. "Paul! We haven't gone over this with Paul. What if he doesn't agree?"

Then he gets ten points for using his head.

Myrna crinkled her nose and moaned. "Maybe we should go on to our next plan."

I nodded. "Good idea. Let's hear it."

Lucinda, who had just finished crunching on a marble Mandelbrot, leaned into the table and looked directly at me. "We call the next plan, the Reenactment."

I literally froze. If it was anything at all like the name implied, we were all in trouble. Thankfully, my aunt and uncle burst on the scene, laden with boxes from Jimmy John's sub shop, before Lucinda could speak.

"We've got turkey, roast beef, ham, Italian, and veggie," Uncle Louis announced. Stress makes everyone hungry so we figured Harriet's frozen freezer treats might need some reinforcements."

"Dibs on the roast beef," Herb shouted. "Oh, and thanks."

"Can we chip in?" I asked.

My uncle shook his head. "Got it covered. Maybe next time."

Heavens, no. Please don't tell me there'll be a next time.

My aunt and uncle arranged the subs and paper plates on the counter while my mother scurried around for more napkins. Streetman must have smelled the welcome addition to dry cookie crumbs because he stuck his head out from under the kitchen table and made a whining noise.

"I'll have to give my little man a piece of turkey or maybe some beef," my mother said. "Otherwise he'll get distraught."

When isn't the dog distraught?

As my mother reached for a half-turkey sub, my aunt grabbed her by the wrist. "Harriet, you won't believe what I heard at Jimmy John's. Louis and I were talking about Billie, and come to find out the guy who worked on our order knew her. Well, not personally, but his aunt did. Billie scammed her out of some jewelry a few months ago."

I wasn't sure I heard her correctly over the chatter in the room, so I asked, "How do you scam someone out of their jewelry? Did she sell it to get money for a bogus investment or something?"

My aunt shook her head. "According to the nice young man at the sub shop, Billie told his aunt she was friends with a retired jeweler who could clean her heirloom pieces for a fraction of the cost at a jewelry store."

"And the aunt fell for it?"

"Apparently Billie was quite convincing."

"Aunt Ina, were you able to find out who she was?"

"No, other customers came in so we had to stop talking. Anyway, he did mention she lives in Sun City West. That should narrow it down a bit."

Yep. Like identifying one of the seven continents.

CHAPTER 18

O nce everyone finished stuffing themselves with subs and pastries, Lucinda returned to the topic of the Reenactment. She gave her tussled hair a quick pat down and clasped her hands together. "Law enforcement agencies do this all the time. We've seen it on TV."

I gulped. "Seen what?"

"They reenact the crime. You know, they return to the scene of the crime and pace around reenacting it."

At that point my head spun but I kept still and let her continue.

"We figured if we could somehow get into the library tower we could role-play the situation. It might help Louise recall something."

"I've recalled enough," Louise moaned. "I told that deputy I didn't see anything. I only smelled stale smoke with aftershave or something like that. And I'm not going back in there."

"Good!" I announced. "Cross the Reenactment off your list and move on. Besides, the area is cordoned off. What else do you have?" *I'm almost afraid to ask.*

My mother, who had now stood to put some paper plates in the garbage, walked behind me and placed her hand on my shoulder. "We haven't come up with a name for our final idea. We thought maybe we'd call it the Unveiling, but then people might think it was a Jewish memorial service that's held a year after someone's death." Then she turned to my aunt. "Speaking of which, Muriel Tuttlebaum's unveiling is this July. Don't let me forget."

I knew better than to ask who Muriel Tuttlebaum was, for fear of a long-winded response, so I let it go. Instead, I cut to the chase. "What's the Unveiling, or whatever you plan to call it?"

My mother edged back to the table and took a seat. Only Herb and Uncle Louis remained standing. Then she straightened her back and starred directly at me. "As far as we know, the deputies have not been inside her house. And trust me, we know. So, with a little finagling, we figured you could get inside, snoop around and see what that deli-witch was up to. You know, unveil any secrets she might have kept hidden."

"Did you say finagling? Don't you mean breaking and entering? Good grief! That's the most preposterous thing you've come up with. Compared to that, the other two plans look like masterpieces."

"I'm not saying smash a window or pick a lock. There are other ways. Billie lived in a rented apartment in that complex near the public golf course. You could speak to the complex manager and get inside under some premise or another. And right now, that apartment is off the radar as far as the deputies are concerned. It's not a crime scene. You simply have to be convincing with whatever excuse you come up with."

"Whatever excuse *I* come up with? This isn't my idea."

Then Shirley spoke. "It may not be your idea, but heavens, Phee, you've got such a good eye for picking out details and putting them together. If that miserable woman was involved in anything heinous, and I'm sure she was, you'll be able to find out with no trouble at all."

Coming from Shirley Johnson's mouth, the idea almost seemed rational.

"You all realize I'm not a detective," I said. "Just because I work for one and am engaged to another one doesn't mean I'm—Oh, what the heck. I'll give it some thought."

My mother cleared her throat. "Well, don't think too long. Louise isn't getting any younger and she can't go on like this."

"Louise can't go on?" Herb practically bellowed. "What about me? I'm supposed to order those damn balloons and pick up the gel markers for them. The company needs at least a week's time."

"Fine." I glanced at my mother. "I'll give it some *serious* thought and talk to you tomorrow. Since everyone's okay, I need to get going. I've got to be at work tomorrow and I'd like to get a good night's sleep." I stood and walked over to where my uncle was standing. "Thanks, Uncle Louis," I said. "The subs were delicious. You, too, Aunt Ina. That was nice of both of you."

"You want to take one home in case you get hungry later?" my mom asked.

Before I could answer, she grabbed an Italian sub and raced to the cabinet where she kept the tinfoil. "Hold on. I'm wrapping this up for you."

By the time I got out of there, I felt as if I'd been on one of those whirligig rides at an amusement park. But that was nothing compared to "the Unveiling."

Rather than go full steam ahead right away, I thought I'd start with the easiest part of the puzzle—getting in touch with the guy from Jimmy John's who made the subs. At least his aunt was a genuine suspect. And one that the sheriff's office didn't know anything about. Just like Eddie Krome, before I played *Let's Make a Deal* with Deputy Bowman.

If it wasn't for the fact that I was so exhausted, I would have driven over there as soon as I left my mother's house. Those sub shops stay open until eleven or twelve and I would have had plenty of time. *Would have had* being the key words. Unfortunately, I postponed having that conversation with the guy figuring I'd be able to chat with him the next day. And I figured wrong.

When I called Jimmy John's from work the next morning and asked if someone could tell me who the guy was who worked the shift last night and when he'd be back, I found out that Richie had the week off to prep for his college finals. And when I asked if there was a number where he could be reached, the answer was a clear and unequivocal no. However, I did get a last name—Salisbury, like the steak.

Of course that didn't mean anything considering his aunt most likely had a different last name. Still, I had Augusta dredge up the Sun City West phone directory for me, but that didn't pan out either.

"I can't very well try Facebook for his aunt," I moaned. "Not without a last name. Ugh. So much for wasted break time."

"It wasn't wasted," Augusta replied. "You ate that old half of a jelly donut and had a cup of coffee."

"Don't remind me. Without Nate and Marshall here, we've gotten pretty slack at bringing in goodies."

"Speaking of Mr. Williams and Mr. Gregory, have you heard anything?"

"Marshall called late last night. Concerned they'd lose cell service over the next few days but told me not to worry. Also gave me a contact number for the sheriff's office in Cochise County if I don't hear from them in a few days. They've got a promising lead and can't afford to lose it. Needless to say, I'll be losing sleep, but that's beside the point. I'm glad I've got my own little investigation to keep my mind off of the one Nate and Marshall are on."

"And I've got a stack of work Mr. Williams left me to keep my mind where it should be—right here in this office."

I laughed. "Yeah, I've got plenty of my own, too. Still, if I don't find out something really soon about Billie's demise, I'm afraid my mother and her looney friends will pull off a stunt that will make *Monty Python* look tame." I then went on to articulate the Entrapment, the Reenactment, and the Unveiling.

Augusta's eyes got wider and wider. "It gets worse by the minute, doesn't it? Tell me, which of the three disasters do you plan to pull off?"

"I suppose the Unveiling is the least heinous of the three. That is, if I can find a way to get into Billie's apartment and snoop around."

"Good luck with that."

"I thought I'd work through lunch and check out her apartment complex after work. For all I know, maybe she kept a key under the mat."

"And to think a year or so ago you wouldn't have even rooted through someone's mail. This detective business is getting under your skin."

"No. My mother and the book club ladies are."

True to my word, I worked through lunch and only took a seven-minute afternoon break before heading over to Billie's apartment in Sun City West.

The pace in the community was certainly quieter at four thirty than it tended to be in the mornings. Still, there were plenty of bicyclists on the streets as well as dog walkers.

I found Billie's apartment complex with no trouble. It was situated off of Camino del Sol near the public golf course and consisted of one large two-story building with a few smaller casitas adjacent to the property. One of them had a sign in front that read *Manager's Office. Open Daily from 9–5.*

The clock in my car said four forty-three and I made a mad dash for the building the minute I pulled into a parking space and got out of the car.

An overhang bell announced my arrival the second I opened the door. The middle-aged brunette seated at a desk let her readers drop off her nose and dangle on the chain around her neck. She looked away from her computer screen and at me.

"Hi! I hope I'm not too late," I said. "I know you close at five but I just got off from work. I, um, wanted to ask about the apartment that Billie Churl rented. You see, I'm—"

"The fifth person who's looked at it today. No problem. It's the one-bedroom, one-bath casita two doors down. Number eleven. The door's open. You can take your time. I've got a few more things to do before I close up for the day. Just let me know when you're done. Oh, and don't touch any furniture or open any drawers. Just look around at the layout. It's a furnished rental but the prior tenant's belongings are still here. Ms. Churl did not leave us any contact information so we'll have to put her things in storage until a claim is made. And don't get me started on that new Hyundai of hers. It's parked by her casita and will most likely wind up in probate with the state."

"She didn't drive it to the library on the day of her . . . um—"

"Nope. She always walked to the library to warm up for her stair climbing."

"Wow. The walk alone would do me in. Uh, one quick question before I look at her apartment—Have the sheriff's deputies been by to check it out?"

The woman shook her head. "I would have thought so, but no, they haven't. Then again, it wasn't the scene of a crime and Billie was the victim of an altercation at the library, from what I understand."

"Good to know. I'm Phee, by the way."

"Tula McWalters. Property owner. Not to sound nosey, but you look too young to be renting in a senior community."

Thank God. "It's for my mother. I wanted to see it first before bringing her here."

"No problem." She handed me a flyer detailing the cost and the amenities. "Price includes cable TV as well."

I smiled. "Thanks. I'll go take a look."

The relief I felt, having been given carte blanche to walk through Billie's apartment, was indescribable considering I had spent the entire drive over here contemplating what sort of white lie I could come up with to get me inside the place. As it turned out, good old dumb luck prevailed.

However, I was told in no uncertain terms that I was not to touch anything. That meant I'd have to be really careful because, like it or not, I *had* this one chance only to see what Billie Churl was up to.

Thanks to my experience living with a real detective, I never went anywhere without a pair of food service gloves in my bag. Yep, food service gloves. They didn't take up much space and a full pack of ten cost ninety-nine cents at the dollar store. My mother would be proud of my frugality.

As I opened and closed the door to Billie's casita, I looked both ways to make sure I wasn't being watched. Then I flipped on the light switch by the door and took in the rental. At first glance it reminded me of one of those residence inns from Marriott or Hilton with a nondescript couch, two armchairs, a coffee table and a flat-screen TV on a credenza. A smaller TV was unplugged and on the floor by the credenza.

That's when I remembered Billie was seen purchasing a large-screen TV. That would explain the small thirty-two-inch one on the floor. Either she planned on selling it and hadn't gotten around to it or it was meant to be moved to her bedroom. Either way, it didn't matter. I had more important things to look for and I didn't have much time.

CHAPTER 19

Given the sparse furnishings in the living room, I moved to the bedroom. Not much better. A twin bed, nightstand, dresser, and small desk that housed an Acer computer with a small twenty-seven-inch screen. Evidently Billie hadn't had time to upgrade her computer hardware. Surrounding the computer were piles of papers and a few books.

I slipped on the food service gloves and moved the papers around. Mostly credit card bills. I wasn't sure if that information could help me but I had nothing to lose. I took out my phone and snapped photos of the bills. No time to boot up the computer. Besides, she probably had a password that was bound to be better than *Password, 123*, or, like my mother and her friends, her name.

The desk only had one drawer and it was unlocked. I pulled it open, but other than paper clips, assorted pens and pencils and some loose notepaper, nothing caught my eye. Then I noticed a small bulge under the papers and took a closer look. It was a flash drive with a cute depiction of Snoopy on it. Ten seconds later it was in my bag.

Heaven help me. I've resorted to thievery. What's next?

The TV sleuths like Aurora Teagarden and Amy What's-her-name from *Mystery 101* would have no qualms about pilfering clues that might bring them closer to identifying a killer, but I wasn't a TV sleuth and that little move would undoubtedly give me nightmares. Still, I kept the flash drive right where I stashed it and opened the closet door.

Not much in terms of a wardrobe. A few windbreakers, a heavy jacket, tops, sweaters, pants, jeans, and a cardboard box marked *Shoes and Boots*. I didn't notice a single dressy outfit, but given what I had been told about Billie, I doubted she went out much. *If* at all. Then, I lifted the top of the cardboard box since titles didn't mean a whole lot in our family as far as storing and identifying foods and objects.

In an effort to keep my cousin Kirk away from consuming what she had placed in the fridge, my aunt Ina would label the food storage containers with *Baked Liver and Onions*, *Boiled Halibut*, *Borsht*, and *Mashed Spinach and Potatoes*, when they really contained baked goods or macaroni and cheese. By all accounts Billie lived alone and didn't have to hide anything from anyone, but I still peered inside the box. Nothing but mounds of boots and shoes tossed every which way. I didn't bother to take a second look.

On to the bathroom. Not that I expected it to hold any trade secrets but, to be on the safe side, I opened the medicine cabinet. Other than aspirin,

Tums, and assorted tubes of sunblock, nothing shouted "Drug stash." I returned to the bedroom and gave it a quick perusal.

I knew I couldn't dillydally much longer, so I kept my fingers crossed that the flash drive would yield something and walked out of there. Last stop was the kitchen, and I didn't expect much.

It was a galley kitchen with a small bistro table and two chairs at the far end. Two opened books with pencils in the middle of their spines and a few napkins took up most of the space. A third book was facedown and off to the side. I was about to take a closer look when something hit me—people who hide important items sometimes stick them in their freezers. The exception being my mother. There was no room under those layers of frozen dinners, cookies that had past their expiration dates, boxes of matzo that had crossed the Red Sea with Moses, and ice cream that had crystalized.

Maybe Billie's freezer held the Treasure of the Sierra Madre and I'd be able to find out who really had it in for her. Unfortunately, unless Banquet found a way to reseal their frozen dinners so as to hide valuables, the freezer was a total bust. I returned to the bistro table and flipped over the books so I could read their covers. No surprises given Billie's penchant for fitness and extreme sports. One was titled *Arizona Trails for Climbers*, and the other *Hidden Arizona Trails for Hikers, Bikers, and Equestrians*," both by the same author, M. J. Evans. I figured Billie might have been interested in tackling one of those trails because the napkin sitting closest to the books had a series of squiggly lines on it with a few arrows and some abbreviations. It made no sense to me but I wasn't into hiking on uncharted trails or, God forbid, climbing on dangerous terrain.

I turned the closed book over and read the title: *Witchcraft—A Complete Guide to Casting Spells*. Yeesh! What on earth was that woman up to?

I closed the front door behind me and started for the office when I had this strange itch to go back and take another look at the cardboard box with all those boots. It was a silly thought but one that would have plagued me if I didn't bother to check it out.

This time I moved quickly for fear Tula would be wondering what was taking me so long. I dragged the box out of the closet and into the light. Then, with a fresh pair of food service gloves on, I picked up an ankle boot and peered inside. Nothing. I was being ridiculous. However, that didn't stop me from pulling out another boot. This time a hiking boot. Unlike the first one, I couldn't slip my hand into it because it had been stuffed with something.

I pulled the tongue of the boot back and gasped. A roll of dollar bills with a rubber band around it was the reason my hand didn't fit inside the boot. Unsure of the denomination of the bills, I slipped off the rubber band and took a closer look—twenties and fifties. I didn't bother to count how many. Instead, I put the roll back as it was and reached for the mate to that boot—empty. But underneath it was some sort of cowboy boot, and like the one with the money stash, this one had not only one but two rolls of bills crammed inside. This time fifties and hundreds.

No wonder she traded that Oldsmobile for a new Sonata.

It took me a few seconds to catch my breath and contemplate my next move. There was no way I could tell Tula that I had not only violated her order to keep my hands to myself in Billie's apartment, but I had gone one step further and rummaged through her stuff.

I couldn't tell Bowman or Ranston either, but I could plant a seed in one of their obstinate heads. Wasting no time, I put the money back where I found it and returned the cardboard box to the closet. With any luck, maybe that Snoopy flash drive would tell me where the money came from. I knew I had overstayed my welcome and hightailed it over to the office.

"Think the apartment will meet your mother's needs?" Tula asked when I stepped inside.

"It's a nice place. I'll talk it over with her."

"Don't wait too long. We've got a lot of lookers."

"I won't. Thanks for letting me have a peek. Have a nice evening."

All I could think about on the way home was that stash of money. True, lots of people don't trust banks, but the cliché of hiding one's savings under the mattress didn't seem to apply to Billie. If she had that much money saved up, why would she need to work at the deli? Unless it wasn't saved up. It was recent. Very recent. That would explain her high-ticket purchases. But I had no idea if she used any of it to pay off the people she allegedly owed.

Everything about that woman was an enigma. That's why I banked on that little Snoopy flash drive with who-knows-what on it in order to find out what was going on. New and equally compelling thoughts raced through my mind as I turned off Bell Road and headed north for Vistancia. Maybe Billie was blackmailing someone and things got out of hand. Then again, maybe Billie witnessed something and someone had to silence her for good . . . By the time I got in my front door, I had concocted more true crime scenarios than most well-known authors. Too bad that's all they were—concoctions.

The flash drive needed to be scanned for viruses before I dared put it in my computer, but my stomach grumbled to the extent that it was audible even over the radio on the way home. I opted to eat first and then tackle the flash drive.

Dining for one was a royal pain. I didn't have the incentive to prepare anything and nothing sounded appealing. I pulled together a quick salad and topped it off with some hard-boiled eggs I'd made a few days ago. Thankfully we still had some chocolate ice cream in the freezer for dessert.

The good news was that Marshall had downloaded a Microsoft Security Essentials program a while back and I was pretty familiar with it. Not only that, but I had taken the time to handwrite the steps on the back of an old address book I kept in my desk. By the time the chocolate ice cream had reached room temperature, Billie's thumb drive was in my computer getting scanned.

I flipped on the TV to catch the final minutes of the seven o'clock news, but like clockwork, the phone rang and it didn't take a seer to know it was my mother.

"I haven't heard from you all day, Phee. Did you figure out how to get inside Billie's apartment? The situation with Louise and her parrot is not good. Apparently the bird is not comfortable sleeping anywhere but in his own house. At three a.m., poor Shirley had to drive Louise home and spend the rest of the night over there."

"Gosh, that's—"

"You said it. It's a nightmare. The ladies and I came up with a rotation for who is going to spend the night at Louise's house. I have the day after tomorrow so I need to ask a favor."

Oh, no. It's a sleepover with Streetman. My God, I'll take the bird. Just drop off the bird. I can put a pillowcase over the cage. I heard that works to keep birds quiet.

"The dog can stay with me but I'm not sleeping at your house. I like my own bed. I can pick him up after work, then get up at some unbearable hour the next day, take him to the dog park and drop him off at your house."

"Do you hear that?" my mother announced. "You're going to have a sleepover with your sister."

I rolled my eyes and kept my mouth clamped shut.

"I'll have all of his foods, treats, and special toys in a tote bag for him. Oh, and I'll throw in the Thundershirt in case he gets stressed."

The only one going to be stressed is me and no shirt in the world will remedy it.

"Good."

"Now that that's settled, what have you decided about Billie's apartment?"

"Actually, I was able to get in this afternoon. The manager thought I was looking at it for a perspective renter—you."

"Me? You didn't give the manager my name, did you?"

"Of course not. Anyway, there's not much to tell. Not yet anyway."

"What's that supposed to mean?"

"Look, do not, under any circumstances, tell anyone about this. I mean it."

"Tell what? What did you discover?"

"Before you start shrieking, I repeat—*Do not tell anyone about this.* Billie had money stashed inside a box of old boots. And by money, I mean rolls of twenties, fifties, and hundreds."

"That's it! The woman was dealing drugs. You need to call the DEA."

"I'm not calling anyone. I wasn't supposed to go through her stuff. And the DEA? Seriously? The only thing I'm going to do is have a conversation with those deputies and sort of suggest they search Billie's apartment before it gets rented out and someone winds up with one hell of a move-in gift. But I may be one step ahead of them."

"What do you mean?"

"She had a flash drive in her desk and I took it. It's being scanned now for viruses. And before you say anything about how I could walk off with the flash drive and not the money, it's two different things." *I think.*

"A flash drive? Oh, my gosh. Like the one Streetman found. You know, if it wasn't for him that situation behind my house would still be under investigation."

"Uh-huh."

"Call me the minute you find out what that witch was up to. I don't go to bed until eleven."

"I may be asleep sooner. I'll touch base with you tomorrow."

"Don't forget, my little man will be staying with you the day after tomorrow."

"I won't forget." *He's like the gift that keeps giving . . .*

CHAPTER 20

T he more I stared at the computer, the slower the scanning process seemed to go. To get my mind off of it, I switched on the TV, but that only made things worse. The news had come on and with it, another heartbreaking human-interest story coming out of Safford, Arizona, where three more trail horses had been stolen. I turned to *Family Feud* in the hope Steve Harvey would give me something to laugh about.

Finally, the scan ended and I got the "all clear" to pop in the disk and see what Billie had copied. I held my breath hoping it wasn't in code. Rolo Barnes had enough on his plate. It turned out to be a Word file with Document 1 as the title. So much for originality. Let Microsoft do the work.

An entire flash drive and only one file. Maybe Billie was just getting started. I stared at a list of dates, first and last initials next to them, the words *delivered* or *in process* next to the initials, and a notation that read either "Paid" or "Pending." As simplistic as it was, it might as well have been in code. There were only four notations on the page, three that read "delivered" and one that said "in process," with a total of three that had been paid. But what? What was delivered?

Then I remembered the jewelry theft involving Richie Salisbury's aunt. The one whom Billie conned out of her heirlooms. I was positive it wasn't Billie's first con. And maybe that list of initials were people who fenced jewelry for her or kept it for themselves.

Much as I dreaded the thought, I really *did* need to speak with Bowman and Ranston. Maybe they had open cases of jewelry thefts either by scams or outright breaking and entering. I wouldn't have to start with the flash drive I had obtained under questionable circumstances. I could jump headfirst into the jewelry con. And my thirdhand accounting of the situation. Ugh. Not the best option but it was all I had.

So as not to worry Marshall, or cause undue stress between him and the deputies, I didn't say much about it when I spoke with him at a little before ten.

"Are you in Safford?" I asked.

"Whoa. You're either a mind reader or you've hidden a GPS with my toiletries. We're in Thatcher. A hop, skip, and jump across the highway from Safford. How'd you know?"

"A good guess. They had a segment on the news earlier about another horse theft, or thefts, in this case, from a family in Safford."

"Yeah, we're on it. Garnering a few more clues but nothing substantial. It's one hell of a situation, I'll give you that much. We've exhausted most of Rolo's leads, which brings us to the conclusion the horses aren't being used for entertainment venues. He had another thought but it's a longshot. Said he was going to pursue it. Anyway, we've got an interview lined up tomorrow with a possible witness."

"Any help from the Department of Agriculture?"

"No, but the Graham County Sheriff's Office has been helpful. Same as Cochise. I'll text you their contact information before I turn in for the night. Listen, I don't want you to be too worried if you don't hear from me. Like I explained yesterday, we're in areas with sketchy cell service."

"I know. Augusta muttered something about that along with a reference to Hansel and Gretel leaving breadcrumbs."

Marshall laughed. "Any good news with your unofficial case?"

I bit my lower lip and refrained from telling him about my find in Billie's apartment. If he thought for one minute that my discovery of those rolled-up dollar bills put me in any sort of danger, he'd be unable to focus on his own investigation. Little did I know that it was the flash drive I really needed to be concerned about.

"Hardly. Louise is terrified she'll be the next victim so the women are taking turns sleeping over at her place. That means Streetman will be my houseguest the day after tomorrow. Needless to say, I have more than one pressing reason to figure out who Billie tangled with in that tower."

"Yeesh. Just keep him off my side of the bed."

It was tough saying good night not knowing if a call would come in the next night. When we ended the call, I felt miserable. Not simply because I missed Marshall, but because I wasn't as up-front and honest with him as I wanted to be. I rationalized it was for his own well-being but that didn't make me feel much better.

I printed out a copy of the file on Billie's flash drive and, using a tissue to avoid fingerprints, put the flash drive in my bag before turning in for the night. Maybe Augusta would have better luck figuring out what it meant. If not, then I'd have to take my chances with Bowman and Ranston.

Thanks to a new Tina Kashian Kebab Kitchen Mystery book on my nightstand, I managed to read until my eyelids got heavy and I drifted off to sleep. I awoke refreshed and ready to tackle whatever puzzle Billie had written on that file. With the Keurig warming up and two slices of bread in the toaster, I turned on the news. Big mistake. I all but burnt the toast and forgot about my K-cup.

The news anchors reported a woman being held at gunpoint during a break-in at a condo apartment complex in Sun City West. The crime took place sometime after eleven p.m. when the woman, who happened to be the complex manager, was in the process of locking up the laundry facility for the night. According to the news anchors, the assailants demanded the keys to a tenant's apartment, and while one of them held the woman captive in the laundry area, the other two entered the apartment. It's not known what, if anything, was stolen, but the apartment was left in shambles according to the manager. When asked if she could identify the perpetrators, she explained they were all wearing dark ski masks, but given their voices, she was positive they were male.

As soon I heard the story, I could feel my hands shake. Unfortunately, the TV station didn't give the name of the woman or the address, but that didn't stop me from grabbing my iPhone and turning to Facebook. Three guesses told me it was Billie's place and I was right.

My conclusion was substantiated by the Sun City West News Buzz and the Sun City West Ladies Chat-About. Members of both of those Facebook groups lived in the same complex and reported posse vehicles as well as MCSO deputy vehicles on the premises between midnight and two a.m.

Like it or not, I had no recourse. I had to call Bowman and Ranston. But that didn't mean I had to spill my guts out about everything. I waited until I got into the office so I could tell Augusta what I did and show her the copy of Billie's file on the off chance she'd have a better take on it than I did.

She looked up from her desk and patted down her bouffant hairdo. "Humph. You keep getting deeper and deeper into the manure," she said. "Lucky those thieves didn't decide to break into that apartment while you were—"

"I know. Stealing a flash drive and rooting through personal property. I'm not any better, Augusta."

"Your motives are better. That much I can assure you. Show me what you printed out."

I handed her the sheet with the dates and initials. Then I stood over her desk and tapped my foot on the floor. "It's only four notations. Four sets of initials. Those must be the buyers. That's pretty obvious. And the dates are self-explanatory. Along with the status of the delivery."

"Did you want me to look at this or did you want to explain it to me?"

"Sorry. I'm antsy, that's all."

Augusta adjusted her glasses and crinkled her nose. "Pretty recent transactions. All in the last month or so. It could be anything. I don't remember reading about any high-profile thefts from businesses or individuals, but that doesn't mean anything. And if it was drugs she was dealing, like those opioids that are all over the news, there'd be no way to tell. And those initials could be anyone. If you ask me, there's got to be more to what's on this thumb drive. Most likely on her computer. And chances are, she never bothered copying that information onto a drive."

"Chances are, whoever broke into her place took that computer. Along with a decent amount of money. Drat! I should've fessed up and called those deputies the minute I made that discovery."

"No sense beating yourself up. Besides, you don't know that those crooks took the money. Only you would think to look inside of box of old, dirty boots."

I shrugged. "Only one way to find out."

"You want to call them from here or in your office?"

"My office. In case someone walks in."

"Tell me how it goes. Or if I need to post bail."

"Only if we have a bondsman on retainer." I gave Augusta a smile and turned the knob to my office door. "Pray to the gods whichever one of those two I get on the phone will be in a decent mood."

I might as well have wished for a dozen dancing leprechauns because Deputy Bowman's mood was anything but decent.

"It's only been what? Three or four days, Miss Kimball? And no, we have *not* received the lab report detailing what animal bites were found on the deceased in question."

"Um, that's not why I called. I imagine you and Deputy Ranston are looking into Tula McWalters's incident last night."

"The victim's name was not released to the public. How is it you know?"

"Her name may not have been released to the public by your office, but trust me, the Sun City West gossip crews are all over it. Look, I have information that may be of some help. And for the record, I obtained it legally." *Maybe not honestly, but legally.*

"Go on."

"I met Ms. McWalters, the complex manager, yesterday when I asked to see Billie Churl's apartment. As a possible rental for someone. Nothing wrong with that. It wasn't a crime scene and your office hadn't cordoned it off. In fact, I was one of many prospective renters according to her."

"Please get to the point."

"I may have taken some liberties to peek into her closet and peruse the box of boots she had stored. Naturally I put on plastic gloves. One can never be too careful with germs and all. Anyway, she had rolls of dollar bills in the boots. Twenties. Fifties. Hundreds. I made sure the rolls of bills were just as I found them when I left the place."

"Did you inform Ms. McWalters of your find?"

"No. She directed me to refrain from touching anything of a personal nature."

"And yet you just *had* to sift through a box of old boots."

"I *had* to get closer to finding out who was responsible for assaulting Billie in the first place. Face it, no one keeps that kind of money hidden like that. My take is that whoever held up Tula McWalters so that they could get into Billie's apartment after work hours was looking for the money. Billie had to be involved in something and that's what got her killed."

"When exactly were you going to notify my office about your discovery?"

"I just notified you."

"Yes. *After* every news station from here to Oklahoma covered the break-in."

"I can't help it if I've been preoccupied."

"Miss Kimball, these kinds of amateur investigations can get *you* killed. Now, so that we don't waste more valuable time, is there anything else you need to tell me?"

"I'd like to ask you something. Was Billie's computer still on her desk when your forensic crew went inside the apartment?"

"The initial report from the responding deputies gave no indication of a computer and the forensic team is on its way over as we speak. Deputy Ranston is already there."

"Okay then. Sounds like everything is under control. I've got to get back to work. Have a nice day."

I hung up before Deputy Bowman could growl at me again. Then I grabbed my bag and shot out of my office as if it was on fire.

"Augusta! I'm on my way over to Billie's apartment. I've got to get inside and return the flash drive before anyone knows it's missing."

Augusta winced. "How would anyone know it's missing if they don't know it's there to begin with?"

"Because I have to be the one to discover it *while* I'm there. You and I can't figure out what Billie's file was all about. Maybe the county deputies will have better luck. Maybe those initials will mean something to them. Like drug lords or shady characters who fence stolen goods. I can't stand here and talk. I've got to get over there and figure out a way to bamboozle Deputy Ranston into letting me inside. Wish me luck."

"You'll need more than luck, Phee, but I have faith in you."

"Good. By the way, if you call out for lunch, get me a sandwich, too. I'm not particular."

"It'll be ham and Swiss. Can't go wrong with that."

No, but I can go wrong with everything else.

CHAPTER 21

I raced to my car and drove to Sun City West as if I was fleeing a tornado when, in reality, I was heading straight toward one.

Deputy Ranston had his arms crossed as he paced back and forth in front of Billie's apartment shouting to the news crews to "leave and find something else to report." I parked as close to the area as I could and walked directly to him.

"Your partner and I just finished speaking," I said. "Long story but I'm here to show you and the forensic crew something I discovered yesterday."

"You were in this apartment yesterday? This *crime scene*?"

"Yes. It wasn't a crime scene at the time. I already explained that to Deputy Bowman."

"Good. Then explain it to me."

I took a breath and reiterated everything I'd said earlier. "So you see," I continued, "I need to point out exactly where that box is located and where I discovered the stash of dollar bills. If nothing else, it will save your office valuable time."

"Or, you could tell me and then go on your way."

"Why waste time when I can expedite things? This will only take a second."

Without waiting for Deputy Ranston to stop me, I ducked under the crime scene tape and made a beeline for the apartment.

"Miss Kimball! Miss Kimball! Hold on! You can't—"

The words *enter a crime scene* were muffled as I stepped inside and scanned the living room. The desktop's computer tower was missing but the keyboard and monitor were still there. Along with papers strewn everywhere. I was right. Whoever broke in was looking for something.

The forensic team wasn't in the living room but I had no way of knowing if they'd already been through Billie's desk or not. Rather than take a chance, I tried the direct approach as I peered into the bedroom from the doorway.

Two lab technicians appeared to be dusting for prints and both of them looked up when I cleared my throat. "Um, I'm Phee Kimball with Williams Investigations, but I'm not here on an official visit. If you haven't done so already, you need to go through the cardboard box in the closet to your left. There's money inside the boots. I know because I was here yesterday. *Before* it was a crime scene."

101

"Miss Kimball!" Deputy Ranston shouted from the doorway. "I need to have a word with you immediately!"

"Excuse me," I said to the technicians. "I'll only be a minute."

It was impossible for me to stash that flash drive anywhere without being seen so I pulled an Aunt Ina.

"Ew! A mouse! Did you see it? It went running by here. A big mouse. Maybe even a small rat!"

As Deputy Ranston turned in the direction where I pointed, I fell back in the armchair near the door and shoved the flash drive between the cushion of the seat and the arm of the chair. Then I realized my prints would be all over it. Too late. I had to deliver a performance worthy of an Oscar.

"Did you see it? The mouse-rat? Oh, my gosh, I shoved my hand down when I got in the chair. There's something stuck between the cushion and the arm."

"Don't touch anything!" Deputy Ranston shouted, even though he was standing inches from me. "It could be a weapon. Let the forensic crew check it out."

I immediately got out of the chair and stepped back as one of the lab techs gingerly removed the cushion. "It's a thumb drive," he said. "We'll tag it and bag it."

The deputy moved closer to the chair and all but knocked the lab tech aside. "Tag it, bag it, and make sure it gets to our office once it's scanned for viruses. It better not land in some evidence locker. It may turn out to be the only thing that's useful." Then he looked at me. "If the mouse crisis is over, maybe you can show the technicians the cardboard box."

"Certainly. No problem."

I waited for a few seconds while the tech secured the flash drive. Then I motioned him over to the closet and stood while he opened the door.

"That's it," I said. "The large box underneath those jeans on the clothing rod."

The tech pulled the box out from under the denim jeans and into the light. Unlike my food service gloves, his were heavy duty and came mid-length up his arm. "Bring the iPad over, Leland," he said to the other tech. "We need to note the exact location."

I rolled my eyes because I knew what was coming. It would be a detailed accounting of each and every boot, anklet, and shoe found in the box, complete with dissertations about any contents found within the boots. No wonder Marshall enjoyed his job as a detective for a private firm as opposed to working for a city, state, or federal agency, where more time is spent on protocol and process rather than securing results in a timely fashion.

"I take it you have reason to believe this break-in had something to do with Billie's death," I said to Deputy Ranston. "Usually the contents of a home that's been broken into aren't removed and if anything is reported stolen, the homeowners are directed to contact their insurance company."

"As you are aware, Miss Kimball, we are not at liberty to discuss our investigations."

And here I thought Bowman was the toughie.

"I'm not trying to be pushy, but as *you* know, I do have an in with the gossip line in this community. And like it or not, that's how a few recent murders were solved."

"What are you saying?"

"I will be more than willing to share whatever information wafts my way if you can reciprocate."

"Is this about the animal bites on the deceased? I thought my partner explained that the results aren't in."

"Not only the animal bites, but what you may find on that flash drive. If it has anything to do with accounting or bookkeeping"—*don't I wish*—"I'd be your best bet. That not-so-little shove Louise Munson got on her way out of the bingo hall could result in a full-blown panic about a killer loose if Billie's assailant isn't caught."

"Please don't tell me you're conducting your own investigation. That would be most ill-conceived."

"Would you at least tell me how much money Billie had stashed away in those boots? I'm pretty certain the forensic crew will need to count it and record it under your scrutiny before it's bagged and tagged and sent to evidence. And, once there, it will be recounted and verified. I'm right, aren't I?"

Deputy Ranston rubbed the sides of his temples and groaned. "Call my office later."

"That works for me. I've got to get back to work anyhow. And, by the way, you're welcome."

"Huh?"

"If it wasn't for me, the tech crew wouldn't have ventured into the closet. They would have dusted for prints in the visible areas. Oh, and if it wasn't for that mouse"—*imaginary or not*—"which you may want to report to the manager, they wouldn't have a flash drive in their possession. A good thing, considering the crooks made off with Billie's computer. It was on her desk when I saw the apartment yesterday."

Deputy Ranston opened his mouth but no words came out.

"Have a good morning," I said, wasting no time to get out of there. I could feel my heart palpitating against my chest as I unlocked my car door and got inside. Never in my life had I been so brassy. Not even when I was face-to-face with stone-cold killers. This new, undiscovered part of my personality scared me more than anything. It was one thing to be assertive and quite another to be aggressive. I made a note to rein it in the next time. *If there was a next time.*

"I'll make your day, Phee," Augusta announced the second I stepped into the office. "Your aunt Ina called. Couldn't get through on your voicemail. Honestly, taking a message from her is worse than taking one from your mother. I think I got the gist of it—'Laurel remembered something about the obstacles that stood in Billie's way.' Who's Laurel?"

"One of my aunt's Wiccan friends."

"Boy, this day just keeps getting better and better. Anyway, from what your aunt said, Laurel clearly remembered Billie asking about hypnotic spells. Laurel was so disturbed about that conversation it took her days to get over it. Not to mention the numerous purification chants she used."

"Was that all?"

"No. This Laurel person was afraid Billie wasn't acting on her own. Something about not being psychic but being in touch with the mother earth and the forces that govern her. Frankly, I lost your aunt at some point."

"Hey, you hung on longer than most people. Did my aunt want me to call her back?"

"Oh, the next part I understood—she and your uncle are going to Chompies for corned beef and chopped liver. Said to call her tonight. Okay. Enough about your aunt. What happened at Billie's apartment? Were you able to hide out and return the flash drive?"

"Yeah, with a good bit of acting on my part."

I gave her the abridged version of events, including my newfound bravado.

"I'd tone it down if I were you," she said. "Those deputies are ornery enough without you poking a stick at them."

"Believe me, I know. The last thing I want to do is mess this up. Nate and Marshall may be out of town, but I'm certain they'll be working more cases with Bowman and Ranston in the future. I don't need to put a wrench in that."

"Speaking of Mr. Williams and Mr. Gregory, still no word today. Lousy cell service once you leave the city limits. And by city, I mean Phoenix."

"Marshall said to expect that. Still, it doesn't make me feel any better."

"They're grown men with guns. And more importantly, with common sense. They'll be fine. By the way, almost forgot. Your sandwich is in the fridge in the break room."

"Thanks, Augusta. I'll eat and work at my desk. I've got tons of stuff to catch up on. In fact, I'm planning on staying late so I don't get behind."

"You're a trooper, Phee."

"Nah. More like someone who had the words *work ethic* drilled into their head from an early age."

I could hear Augusta chuckle as I opened the door to my office and tossed my bag on the spare chair.

CHAPTER 22

L yndy met me at the Angry Crab Shack in Peoria at a little past eight. We'd made plans for a Friday night fish fry a while back, long before I needed the time to decompress.

"Let me get this straight," she said. "You actually lied to get into that woman's house?"

"Not my proudest moment, but honestly, with my mother's friends going bonkers and the mere thought of hosting Streetman for sleepovers while they take turns placating Louise Munson, I've been driven to a new point of insanity."

"I guess." She pulled open the plastic bag of steaming shrimp in Trifecta hot sauce and reached in. "My aunt is convinced there's a mad killer out there, but frankly, I'm with you. I think whoever went after Billie was well-acquainted with her. And most probably saw poor Louise at one point or another in that library tower."

"Either way, Louise may be a target. Funny, but all she remembers is what she smelled. Heavy, cloying smoke. And unless Newport cigarettes changed their formula, that pack I gave to the deputy that Bowman sent over wouldn't fully explain what Louise remembered. Oh, well. Maybe I'll have an epiphany between now and tomorrow. In the meantime, I'll settle for the lobster crostini."

I went in to work the next morning even though I had that Saturday off. For some reason, I felt disorganized and discombobulated and really needed the time to catch up. Augusta had taken the day off to help a friend of hers fix some fencing around a new ranchette that the woman had recently purchased in the county land. According to Augusta, ranch owners were now getting really spooked about the horse thefts, and even though her friend only had a donkey and a few chickens, she wasn't about to take any chances.

Having the office to myself meant juggling phone calls and handling walk-in clientele, but as it turned out, it was a quiet morning and I finished up at a little past one. That left me plenty of time to pick up a few things at the supermarket and throw in a quick wash before I had to head over to my mother's house in order to get the dog.

Frankly, I still hadn't gotten over the last time Streetman spent the night with Marshall and me. My mother had joined the book club ladies for a casino night and didn't want to leave the dog alone for more than a few hours. Needless to say, we were coerced into taking him.

The dog whined, scratched at the door, even though he'd been outside numerous times, and pawed at our legs while we tried to watch TV. The only way we were able to placate him was to offer him treats. A real no-no as far as most trainers were concerned, but they weren't the ones who had to put up with that little chiweenie.

Now, I had to face Streetman alone, since Marshall was heaven-knows-where, on a case that worried me no end. I got to my mom's at a little past six, sparing me from having her "take something out of the freezer." I assured her the dog would be fine and loaded up his belongings in the backseat of the car. Most kids heading out for summer camp packed lighter than the dog.

"Don't forget his Thundershirt," my mother said, handing me the folded doggie coat. "Oh, and his dining plate. He won't eat unless it's on his special plate."

"Does his water have to be in a special bowl, too?"

"Don't be snarky, but be sure to give him the purified water from your refrigerator, same as last time. He also likes purified spring water. He won't have to go out again for a few hours and he's already eaten his dinner. Inside his sleepover bag is a plastic food container with special treats."

I did a mental eye roll and smiled.

Once we loaded the car and my mother smothered the dog with hugs and kisses, she put him on the passenger seat and told him to be a good boy.

"I really hate sending him off but who knows what Louise's bird might do to him."

Who knows what Louise's bird might do to any of us.

"He'll be fine. I'll talk to you later."

My mother blew me and Streetman a kiss as I backed out of the driveway and headed down the block.

"No theatrics this time," I said to the dog. "I've got enough to deal with."

As if on cue, the dog yawned, shut his eyes and slept until I pulled into my garage. Once I let him out, he bolted for the couch, made himself comfortable and proceeded to clean his feet. I shrugged. This was a far cry better than prior experiences with him.

I brought in his belongings and put them on the counter in the utility room. Then I made myself a tuna sandwich, grabbed a small handful of dog treats and sat down to catch the evening news. Thankfully the large-screen TV was visible from my spot at the kitchen table.

Nothing earth-shattering as far as local news. Only the usual assortment of car accidents and thefts. I ate my sandwich without incident, pausing every few minutes to hand the dog a tiny Charlee Bear liver snap. I figured maybe the sleepover wouldn't turn out so bad after all. In retrospect, I should have known better. However, in all fairness, it wasn't Streetman's fault.

After a brief walk outside around nine, we turned in for the night. No sooner did I pull down the covers and settle back to read than the dog got up from his bed and jumped into mine. At least he curled up at my feet and not on top of Marshall's pillow. A last glance at my alarm clock told me it was ten thirty-five. I shut off the bedside light and for the first four hours or so I enjoyed a blissful sleep. Then the chaos began.

Streetman let out a bark that would rival a banshee. Then, he raced out of the room while I stumbled around trying to figure out what was going on. I flipped on the hallway light and watched as he charged into the living room. Then, I remembered. Our Roomba was programmed to begin its floor cleaning routine at precisely two forty-five.

Before I could yell "Stop!" the dog lunged at the machine and snapped at it. Each snap and movement more frantic than the one before. The only way to stop Streetman was to get in front of him and hit the Clean button on the vacuum. Unfortunately, the dog and the Roomba were faster than I was.

According to the manual, the Roomba had a bump sensor and an automatic shutoff mechanism but neither of them had been activated. I tried another tactic—bribing the dog with food. While Streetman continued his assault on our three-hundred-ninety-nine-dollar purchase, I rummaged through the fridge until I found a package of cheddar cheese.

"Streetman, look! Cheese! Yum-yum cheese!"

Normally, the dog would have ceased all activity in order to devour cheddar cheese but not tonight. Instead, he growled at the Roomba and continued to snap at it. My other option was to see if pulling the charging station away from the electrical outlet would make any difference, but I didn't get the chance.

In an instant, Streetman jumped on top of the machine and tackled it like an offensive line in the NFL. Unfortunately, he and the Roomba crashed into an end table, knocking over a lamp and breaking it. The least of my worries. The Roomba kept going and so did the dog. At that rate I was certain the house would look like The Cat in the Hat came to visit, sans the bathwater.

I had to make up my mind quickly—remove the dog or remove the Roomba. Either way I'd be at the receiving end of a furry snapping turtle. I figured if I could grab Streetman from behind, I could use my foot to step on the Roomba's Clean button, thus turning it off. What I didn't count on was losing my balance at the last second. I skidded into the couch and landed on one knee. The noise must have distracted the dog for a split second because he forgot the Roomba and turned to see what I was doing.

Without wasting a second, I tossed a slice of cheddar cheese on the floor and staggered to the Roomba. In a flash, I turned the thing off and caught my breath. Small yet visible teeth marks were all over the machine.

So much for ever needing the company to make good on the warranty.

Streetman gobbled up the cheese and returned to the scene of the crime. He gave the Roomba a quick sniff and walked to the front door and scratched on it.

"Great," I mumbled. "Now you want to go outside."

I threw a jacket over my PJs, put him on a leash, and went out the front door. Like most residential neighborhoods in the West Valley, our street lighting was dim, but thankfully our coach lights above the garage and at the entrance to the house made up for it.

The little chiweenie wasted no time watering the boxwood beauties by the side of the house before prancing back to the front door as chipper as ever. I, on the other hand, had participated in a bizarre nighttime marathon. Worse yet, I still had a good three hours or so before I could take Streetman to the dog park and back to my mom's.

"Be a good boy," I said, "and let's get some sleep."

I locked the door behind me and turned off the living room lights. Streetman curled up at the foot of the bed and licked his paws. That's when I noticed it wasn't his paws that he was licking, but rather, something else he had found.

My God! Will this nightmare ever end?

Whatever the dog had, it was now between his teeth. I prayed it wasn't one of those cute geckos that are always under our bushes, or worse yet, a scorpion, but when he opened his mouth to readjust his prize, the tension in my neck subsided. It was one of his doggie toys that he must have retrieved from the bag I brought into the house.

Finally! We can get some sleep.

I flipped off the lights, snuggled under the light cover, and let my body sink into the mattress. For a brief second, I thought I heard a buzzing sound, but it dissipated. Then, it returned. This time louder than before, and I knew immediately what it was—a helicopter making its way to or from an accident somewhere in the area.

The buzzing intensified. Not one helicopter but at least two. Wherever the accident was, it had to be a pretty bad one. Vistancia was equidistant from the 101 and the 303, both major highways. No wonder the helicopter noise sounded so close.

The dog perked his ears up but then returned to his toy. I fell asleep amid chewing sounds and the muffled buzz of the helicopters. When I awoke the next morning and tapped my iPhone to glance at the news app, I expected to read about an accident. Instead, the headline read like the tagline for a suspense novel—*Fugitive escapes custody and eludes authorities.*

Terrific. It's not bad enough my mother and her friends are convinced there's a mad killer out there, now we can add a fugitive to the mix.

The news story was brief and unsettling. A well-known drug trafficker managed to cross the border from Mexico, where he was apprehended in Naco, Arizona, just south of Bisbee. However, he was able to escape from custody and has been on the loose for a few days, having been spotted in Tucson, Marana, and the West Valley of Phoenix. At least it wasn't something Nate and Marshall had to deal with. They had enough problems with the escalating horse thefts. A dangerous drug trafficker was the last thing they needed.

CHAPTER 23

Once I was up and dressed, I fed the dog, took him out to relieve himself, and loaded him in the car along with his passel of belongings before making a stop at the Sun City West Dog Park. On the way over, I grabbed a Grande mocha latte from Starbucks and a croissant, which Streetman insisted on sharing with me.

It was a little past seven and the park was a flurry of activity when I arrived. At least six or seven people were under the awning in what appeared to be a football huddle. Cindy Dolton was in her usual spot by the fence and Bundles was a few feet away. She motioned me over as soon as she saw me. "Did you hear about the police chase last night? They were in every neighborhood in Surprise along with the sheriff's deputies right here."

"I heard the helicopters and read a news app this morning. Did they catch the guy?"

"A few minutes ago. In Buckeye. That's what all the hubbub is about. Guess it's the most excitement we've had in a while. Well, *that* and Billie Churl's unsolved death. Boy, talk about creepy. I heard someone held up her landlord and ransacked the apartment."

"Uh, yeah. Guess news travels fast."

Cindy stepped closer to me. "You know about it?"

Before I could answer, she continued. "That figures. Those deputies probably keep your office in the loop with everything. If you ask me, whoever broke into her place was probably looking for something Billie took from them. Like I mentioned before, she swindled and conned people out of all sorts of things. Of course, that doesn't explain how she managed to buy a new car, or a TV, for that matter."

For a second, I thought about Richie Salisbury's aunt as a possible suspect, but according to Tula, the manager, the thugs who held her at gunpoint and rifled through Billie's apartment were just that—male thugs, not a senior citizen.

"I think once the deputies learn more about Billie they'll be able to—Oh, no! Streetman is on top of that basset hound. Not again!"

I left Cindy in mid-sentence and charged toward the dog. "Streetman! Get off of her!" With a quick shove, I removed the dog from his latest romantic interest and clasped the leash on him. "You can do your business tethered to the leash," I said. With that, I proceeded to walk him around the perimeter of the park until all business had been taken care of.

"Sorry about that," I told Cindy when I returned to the fence.

She smiled. "I think most people around here are used to your mother's dog."

"Good. Because I'm not." I then proceeded to tell her about the sleep-over and the encounter with the Roomba.

"Wow. Looks like I won't be buying one of them any time soon. Bundles may be low-keyed, but animals can turn on an instant if something spooks them."

Suddenly I remembered the animal bites on Billie's hands. What on earth could she have spooked? A raccoon? A possum? And if so, what was she doing?

"You look lost in space, Phee. Was it something I said?"

"Uh, no. I guess I'm going to need a second cup of coffee if I expect to function today."

"At least it's Sunday. Enjoy the day off."

Under ordinary circumstances, I would have done so, but the nagging threads in my so-called investigation meant I wouldn't be putting my feet up on the couch and reaching for a good book any time soon.

Cindy promised me she'd call the office if she heard anything more about Billie and swore she'd keep her ears open if she heard any good gossip. It was the best I could hope for. Then I headed directly to my mother's house.

As soon as I got to the door, my mother opened it and bent down, wrapping her arms around Streetman as if he had just returned from combat duty overseas. "My precious little man, did you sleep well without Mommy?"

It was all I could do to control the gag reflex in my throat. "He slept fine, but whatever you do, don't buy a Roomba."

She ushered me inside and closed the door. "A Roomba? I would never buy one of those. Poor Gloria Wong did and her Great Dane had an accident one night. The Roomba didn't know any better and spread that accident all around her house. The poor woman had to buy new carpeting for her living and dining rooms."

Yuck. I suppose a few bite marks aren't so bad after all.

I put Streetman's belongings on the floor near the front closet and watched as my mother continued to plaster the dog with kisses.

"How's Louise doing?" I asked.

"If it wasn't for all that helicopter noise, she'd be doing fine. Same with me. At least the Buckeye Police Department caught the man responsible for ruining our night's sleep."

Gee, maybe you can have him charged for that . . .

"Yeah. I heard the noise, too, but it didn't seem to bother Streetman.

The news said the man was a drug trafficker who managed to cross the border."

"All these criminals manage to cross the border! Why can't the good people cross the border?"

"Uh, I think that's what our government is trying to work on."

"They should stop *trying* and start *working*."

I wasn't about to get into a long-winded discussion about border security, especially since my conversation with Cindy reminded me of something I'd planned to do but didn't have time for on the weekdays. She mentioned Billie's new Hyundai, one of my dangling threads. I needed to find out how *exactly* Billie paid for the car, even if it meant stretching the truth as far as my employment at Williams Investigations.

At least I was observant when I saw the sparkling new Hyundai parked in front of Billie's condo apartment. The license plate holder boasted Peoria Hyundai, only a few miles from my house, and the perfect place to visit on a Sunday.

"I've got to run, Mom. I've got lots of errands to do and some paperwork as well."

"If that tower assailant isn't caught soon, I'll be sleeping at Louise's again next week. I'm not sure which day."

I looked at the dog, who had now retreated to his usual spot under the coffee table. "Good to know."

My mom gave me a quick hug as I reached for the door. "Be thankful Streetman isn't a Great Dane."

Uh-huh. We're truly blessed.

Once I got in the car, I drove to McDonald's for a quick breakfast before taking off to visit Peoria Hyundai on West Bell Road. And while outright lying wasn't my strong suit, exaggerating the truth had become almost comfortable for me.

I was met in the parking lot by a tall, clean-shaven forty-something man with dark hair.

"Hi! I'm Lance. Is there something I can interest you in?"

I took out my business card and handed it to him. "Actually, it's information I'd like. I'm Phee Kimball with Williams Investigations in Glendale and I'm assisting with some background work while our detectives are out of town on another case."

He read the card and tilted his head. "I'm not sure I can help but I'll give it a try. Maybe you'd like to do the same with one of our models later on."

I shrugged. "I'll keep that in mind when I decide to purchase a new car. Right now I'm looking into a purchase that Willameena Addison Churl made a few months ago. It was for a 2022 Hyundai Sonata and she may have used her nickname, Billie."

"Wonderful vehicle. Excellent gas mileage and superb safety features."

"Uh-huh. Unfortunately, Ms. Churl died as a result of an injury sustained by a fall. A fall that may have been the result of a suspicious act."

The salesman furrowed his brow. "I'm not sure I understand what this has to do with her car."

"It may have something to do with how she paid for her car. I mean, if it wasn't through a loan. Can you check the records to find out?"

"I really shouldn't be doing this but you said she died suspiciously?"

"Uh-huh. That's why we're investigating the matter."

He took a breath and looked around. "Give me a few minutes. You said this was a couple of months ago?"

"Yes."

"Okay. Follow me."

Once inside the dealership's building, I paused to take in the shiny new models as Lance walked directly to his desk. My hesitation didn't escape him.

"Outstanding vehicles," he said. "Feel free to scope them out. I'll look for you when I'm done."

I walked about the room and finally made myself comfortable in a cushy chair that faced a large-screen TV. I imagined during the week, when cars were being serviced, I wouldn't have been the only occupant in that welcoming seating area.

If Billie paid cash for her vehicle, it would further substantiate what I had already presumed—she was in deep with some nefarious operation. But what? I had no idea. And did she pay with rolled-up fifties and hundreds? It was the stuff movies were made of.

I bit my lower lip and scrolled through emails and Facebook while I waited for Lance. It was only a few minutes but it seemed longer.

"Okay, Miss Kimball. I've got the information you asked about. The purchase was a cash deal with a trade-in."

"A 1996 Oldsmobile?"

"Yep. A 1996 Oldsmobile 88 with a hundred and forty-two thousand miles on it. Valued at less than a grand given its condition, but we credited Miss Churl the thousand dollars on her new purchase."

The epiphany I'd been waiting for hit me like a ton of bricks. "Is that car still here? The Oldsmobile?"

"Don't tell me you're interested in it?"

"Um, I'm interested in taking a look but I suppose it's long gone."

"As a matter of fact, no. It's still on our lot. In back. No interest here so it's headed for auction down south once we give it a good cleanup. It hasn't exactly been a priority."

"Listen, if it wouldn't take up too much of your time, I'd really like to see it."

Lance shrugged. "No problem. Give me a sec to get the key and take all the time you need."

I couldn't believe my luck. And all because Cindy mentioned Billie's car—something I had put on the back burner until our chat. That Oldsmobile had to double as Billie's mobile office while she was on the go doing whatever grifting she was up to. That meant she might have stashed some notes or information in the console or glove compartment. I could feel my pulse quicken as Lance walked me to the rear lot.

It was a long shot and I prayed it wouldn't turn out to be another dead end.

CHAPTER 24

Notes in the console? What was I thinking? The moment I unlocked the door to the Olds and peered inside, I realized that I had taken a trip back in history. A twenty-five-year trip more or less. There was no console, only a front seat that looked more like the grand couch in my aunt Ina's living room than seating for a passenger vehicle.

The only spot for storage was the glove compartment, and thankfully it was unlocked. Unfortunately, it was also empty, with the exception of the owner's manual, a few pens, and a fairly recent map of Phoenix. I was surprised at how thin the owner's manual was compared to the tomes that come with today's new cars. And I was equally surprised that the small chrome ashtrays showed no sign of use. Maybe those smokers Billie knew from the supermarket break area weren't close enough acquaintances to have been in her car. Or maybe they became acquaintances after she purchased the new car.

The side doors didn't have any storage and neither did the backs of the front seats. I used the key to unlock the trunk but came up empty there as well. Whatever Billie had in there most likely got transferred to her new Hyundai, unlike the small plastic bag of litter that hung from the passenger door handle—two candy wrappers and some wadded-up papers.

In all probability the wadded-up papers were probably more candy wrappers but I was desperate to find any kind of clue that would get me closer to solving the deli-witch's death. The last thing I felt like doing was to stick my hand in the bag, but since I still had one food service glove left in my own bag, I took the chance.

Like a seasoned pro, I extricated the papers and wadded them up further so they'd fit in the small black doggie-on-the-go bag I still had on me.

"Any luck finding what you were looking for?" Lance asked when I returned the key to him.

"Not really."

"Hey, if something turns up, I'll call the number on your card. Meanwhile, I'd appreciate it if you'd hand out my card to any of your friends who are looking to purchase a car."

"Absolutely. And I'll be sure to keep one for myself if I'm ever in the market."

With the treasure trove of wadded-up papers in my bag, I drove home to see if my jaunt to the Hyundai dealership was worth the drive. As soon as I got in the door, I spread a few paper towels on the kitchen table and dumped the wadded-up papers on them. I hadn't felt this excited since Halloween when I was a kid. The only thing missing was my mother shouting, "Don't eat anything until I look it over."

The first paper I unfolded was dated a week or so before Billie was found dead. It was a partial cash receipt from Dale's Country Store in Surprise for a fourteen ninety-nine nylon Dura-Tech something-or-other. Something-or-other because that part of the receipt was missing. I figured it had to be clothing or gear for one of her extreme sports.

Next was a trail map of the Hassayampa Bird Preserve off of Route 60 in Wickenburg. I tossed it aside and reached for another receipt. This time from A & G Rentals on Deer Valley Road near the small single-engine airport and not for chump change. The receipt was for eight hundred dollars, also cash. I checked the date. Same time frame as the Dura-Tech purchase.

I knew climbing equipment was expensive, but eight hundred dollars? It had to be something else.

There was only one other piece of paper left and it was a note on lined paper that read, "Just stick to your end of things. We've got the lower corridor covered." Large swirly initials followed the word *covered* but it was impossible to figure out what the letters were, or if it was a name and not initials.

By "lower corridor" I wondered if they meant the Sun City West Library since it had a short corridor going from the reading area to the computer room. But then again, why say "lower corridor" if there was only one.

I was positive Nate or Marshall would have been able to piece Billie's notes together and figure out what they meant, but I was at a total loss. I took a second gander at the flash drive information with the misguided notion that it would somehow cement all the information in those wadded-up notes into something meaningful. It didn't. So when Herb Garrett phoned a few minutes later to tell me he found out who Billie owed money to, I was more than ecstatic.

"I'm a man of my word," he said. "I told you I'd find out whose pockets that witch was picking and I did. Well, not me, exactly, more like Wayne and Kenny, but still, I was able to get it out of them."

"Who? Who did she owe money to? Was it a lot? A little? What?"

"Don't know the exact amount. Only know that she owed some guy who hangs out at Curley's a boatload of money."

"That's it? Some guy from Curley's Bar? It could be anyone."

"Not anyone. The guy's on one of the water volleyball teams so he's a resident here. And, he's really recognizable."

"How so?"

"The man's got a heavy-duty tattoo of a Gila monster on his arm. You don't see those every day."

No, you certainly don't.

"Do Wayne and Kenny know anything more about this guy?"

"Yeah. He quit smoking not too long ago, and according to Wayne, he's been in a bad mood ever since. Glad I'm not on *his* volleyball team. Hey, you don't think he's the one who sent that deli-witch flying, do you? I heard people can get really volatile when they stop smoking."

"Um, uh, I'm not sure but it's the best clue I've had since I started to look into Billie's death. Thanks, Herb. I really appreciate it."

"If you decide to meet up with the tattooed ex-smoker, do it in a public place or your mother will have my head on a plate."

"Don't worry. I'll be fine. And thank Wayne and Kenny for me, too."

I grabbed my iPhone and pulled up the Sun City West Boomers club water volleyball schedule for the coming week. Like it or not, the guy with the Gila monster tattoo was turning out to be my best lead. If I didn't wind up underwater.

That night I got a quick call from Marshall. From someone's landline somewhere south of Safford. He and Nate were still pursuing leads and optimistic about their progress. I told him the same thing about my amateur sleuthing but left out the pertinent details. Hearing his voice enabled me to sleep through most of the night, so when morning came I wasn't a total zombie.

• • •

"I'm playing water volleyball tomorrow night," I told Augusta when I got to work the next day. "I called the woman from the Boomers club, Julia Ornstern, and the B team can fit me in."

"And I'm playing canasta. No need for a bathing suit or towels. Only a deck of cards. Did you get any information from Mr. Gregory last night?"

"Huh? How did you know he called?"

"Because Mr. Williams left a message on the machine. Said Mr. Gregory called you."

"He did. From a landline. Marshall didn't say much about their investigation but he sounded chipper."

"Naturally he sounded chipper. Like Hopalong Cassidy on the trail. Well, I hope those two hop along pretty quick and get back here. We've got clients who are chomping at the bit to find out if their spouses are cheating on them, stealing from them, or planning to walk out on them."

"I'm chomping at the bit, too. I could really use their help tracking

118

down Billie's assailant. One more sleepover with Streetman and I'd gladly trade places with Marshall."

"The little bugger bark all night?"

"Worse."

I gave Augusta the rundown, and as much as she tried to keep a straight face, she couldn't. "You'd have been better off taking Louise Munson's bird for the night."

"Perish the thought. Um, aren't you the least bit curious about why I'm going to play water volleyball?"

"Nope. I already figured it out. It has to do with the Gila monster tattoo guy you told me about. You think he's one of those smokers Billie knew from the supermarket."

"Augusta, I think you and I both missed the boat. We should be detectives."

"Thanks but no thanks. I like a comfortable chair, a climate-controlled room, and a good distance from the crazies out there."

"I was only kidding. This stuff scares the daylights out of me if you must know the truth, but I seriously hate to think someone is after Louise. Not to mention that ridiculous Bye Bye Birdie event and my mother's dream of being a guest on *Sonoran Living*."

"Hate to ask this, but do you have a plan if the Gila monster tattoo guy shows up for water volleyball? If he did have anything to do with Billie's fall in the tower, I guarantee he's not about to admit it to you."

"I know. That's why I intend to coax it out of him a different way."

"Humruph. If anyone else said that I'd think they were about to use their feminine wiles on him."

"Ew. Not on your life."

"Then what?"

"I'm going to tell him that I know Billie owed him money and I know they worked together."

"But you *don't* know that they were in cahoots together."

"It's an educated guess."

Augusta groaned and I kept talking. "I'll tell him I can step in for Billie. I'll let him believe I was familiar with her operation and that I can seamlessly pick up where she left off."

"That's the worst plan ever! Worse than the looney stuff those book club ladies come up with. You have no idea what that witch was up to."

"Nooo . . . but it's one way to find out."

"One way, all right. One way to be the next person at the foot of the stairs."

"Without Rolo Barnes to figure out whose initials those could be on that flash drive and me coming up empty regarding the wadded paper notes and receipts, I don't have a whole lot of choices."

Augusta didn't say a word. Instead, she lifted her right pant leg and pointed to a small pistol.

"I'm not good with guns," I said. "I'd probably shoot myself in the toe. Besides, I don't have a permit to carry like you do." *Or lots of experience with rifles from living in the Wisconsin boonies.*

"Then go to Cabela's Sporting Goods and buy yourself a nice can of bear spray."

"You don't have to worry. All I intend to do is eke some information out of the guy. Then I'll come up with some excuse later as to why I can't do whatever it is that Billie did."

"And here I thought Mr. Williams and Mr. Gregory were the ones who took chances."

Yeah. Me, too.

CHAPTER 25

I arrived at six thirty on the dot at the RH Johnson pool the following night. The temperature was in the mid-seventies according to the large thermometer on the wall by the entrance, but I knew they kept the water at a comfortable eighty-seven. A quick scan of my guest pass and I was in. The large net was already set up across the lane section of the pool and a few swimmers milled about.

"Hi, everyone!" I called out as I approached the group. "Julia said I could join you tonight."

The man I recognized as Harold walked toward me and pointed to the net. "Welcome. Glad you could join us. Phee, right?"

"Uh-huh."

"Stash your towel and bag on one of the chairs and jump in the water. We were just about to get started with a quick warm-up. You've played before, I presume."

"Uh, volleyball. On dry land."

"It's the same thing. Only wetter. We play an eleven-point game with a two-point lead to end the game. We rotate clockwise after the other team returns the serve."

I nodded. "No problem."

"I guess I don't have to tell you no pushing, shoving, carrying the ball, deliberately splashing water on other players, or kicking them under the water."

"Kicking them?"

"Yeah. Billie was known for that if they got too close to her."

"It's a wonder she was allowed to play at all."

"Let's put it this way, no one wanted to mess with her. Even Julia. And she's the queen of spiking. I think they called her 'Spiker' or 'Slammer' back in college. Oh, look! Here comes Denton. He must have gotten back early from that business trip of his. I swear, for a retiree he's busier than most full-time workers."

I turned to my left and locked eyes with the middle-aged man with the light stubble on his face. He pulled a gray sweatshirt over his head and in the process revealed the Gila monster tattoo on his right forearm.

Hallelujah! With any luck, I won't have to play water volleyball again.

"You're on the far side of the net, Denton," Harold said. "We're breaking in a new player on this side. Phee something."

"Kimball," I muttered. "Phee Kimball. I'm thinking about joining the Boomers club."

Denton took a few steps toward me and winked. "Watch out for my fast serves." Then he retreated to his side of the net and joined the other players who were already in the water.

"This is warm-up, everyone, so go easy," Harold shouted.

Next thing I knew, the volleyball was lofted in the air by a red-haired woman in a floral tankini. It sailed smoothly back and forth across the net before I got a chance to give it a shove. So far so good. The pace was slow and easy and I began to relax. My only concern was how I was going to approach Denton with my concocted plan.

I was a terrible liar and I would have made an awful poker player. However, I had become more brazen recently, especially in my conversations with Bowman and Ranston. I supposed that was because I was familiar with them and had some idea about how far I could push them. Denton, however, was an enigma. And a possible murderer. I had to broach the subject of taking over for Billie with the right blend of assertiveness and diplomacy. Not to mention I had to gain the guy's trust. All while dripping wet after a rigorous water volleyball game. Too bad I couldn't get someone to cast a spell and get it over with.

After a five-minute warm-up, Harold announced the start of the game. Suddenly the pace changed and I was all but out of breath as I responded to bangs, bounces, and thumps. Surprisingly, I was able to execute a decent serve but didn't score any points.

The first game ended with Denton's team winning. Then, we switched sides for the second and final game of the evening. Like the first one, I responded to the ball with lots of assists but nothing spectacular. Still, I prided myself in being able to keep up with everyone. If the team expected an ace player, they were out of luck. Nevertheless, I persevered until we lost again to Denton's team.

"Want a third chance to redeem yourselves?" someone from his side of the net yelled.

A chorus of "I can't stay I have to let the dog out," "I've got to get home in time for *NCIS: Hawaii*," and "I haven't eaten dinner yet" followed.

I got out of the water, grabbed my towel, and hustled over to where Denton stood. He ran a small washcloth over his hair and had just reached for a larger towel when I got there.

"You played a good game," I said. "Is this your only sport?"

"Pretty much. I'm not a golfer or a bowler, and up until recently I've been a smoker, so that lets out the more energetic games. Of course, that may change. What about you? You seemed pretty confident."

I shook some of the water from my hair. "I like water sports. It's a good way to unwind."

"Think you'll join the Boomers club?"

"Maybe. I like keeping my options open." At that point I looked around to make sure no one was near us. "Don't ask me how I know this because I'm not at liberty to say. I'm aware that Billie owed you money and that probably ticked you off considering she bought herself a new car and a new TV. I also know you and Billie had a sideline going. A profitable one."

Please let me be right on this one.

Denton didn't say a word and I hoped his silence wouldn't unnerve me.

"Face it," I continued, "no one goes from owning a relic of a car to acquiring a new SUV."

"What are you getting at?"

"I wouldn't mind stepping in where she left off."

Now it was Denton who looked around. A few people were still gathering their bags and towels but they were out of earshot.

"If you're with law enforcement, I can save you the trouble. She wasn't dealing drugs or anything of the sort."

"I'll save *you* the trouble. I'm not with law enforcement but I've got the kind of skill set you might need. And I always pay my debts."

"Always pay my debts?" "The kind of skill set you might need?" Have I lost my mind completely? What skill set? What am I getting into? Next time I'll listen to Augusta.

"Now's not the time or place. How about we meet tomorrow night at the Starbucks on Reems and Grand? Normally I'd suggest Curley's or a similar venue, but with all the smokers, it would be way too tempting for me to backslide."

"Starbucks is fine. What time?"

"Let's make it eight. The place is pretty empty by then and we can sit outdoors."

"Fine. Eight at Starbucks."

I retrieved my tote bag and walked straight to the locker room before I had a chance to change my mind. This was, by far, the stupidest, most dangerous situation I walked into. And not *walked,* I orchestrated it. In retrospect, the Entrapment and the Reenactment sounded like brilliant ideas.

The more I thought about it on the way home, the more concerned I got. It was like Shoeless Joe making a deal with the devil in *Damn Yankees.* True, I had time to back out, but Denton was my only chance of finding out what the heck Billie had been up to that got her killed. At least Starbucks was a very public place and one that the book club ladies only frequented once in a while. And only when they ran a special on seasonal lattes.

I didn't sleep well that night. There was no call from Marshall, although that was to be expected, and my late-night foray into the kitchen for assorted odds and ends from the fridge resulted in a bloated stomach and indigestion. But the real reason for my miserable night was the gnawing fear that I might wind up in the same predicament as Billie.

There was only one way around it and that was to convince Lyndy to play along. After all, wasn't there such a thing as safety in numbers?

"Help me understand this," she said when I called her from work the next morning. "You want me to go with you to the Starbucks in Surprise tonight so you can coax a possible killer into offering you the same job Billie had?"

"Possible assailant."

"Same thing. The woman wound up dead. And you have no idea what she was involved in. Or even if this tattooed guy was working with her."

"Uh, yeah. More or less. But I have a really strong hunch they were embroiled in something nefarious."

"Wonderful. And now we'll be embroiled too."

"Think of this as a fact-finding mission. Not a commitment."

"Aargh. What is it you want me to do?"

"Ferret out information along with me in case I get tongue-tied, or worse yet, make a serious blunder."

"Granted, I've told you how much I enjoy living vicariously through your sleuthing, but that's because I don't have to stray too far from my couch."

"Starbucks isn't that far."

"You know what I mean."

"So will you do it? I'll buy you whatever size latte you want."

"Yeah. I'll do it. I have to work late so I'll meet you there. It beats watching reruns, and who knows, maybe you'll be able to get that one clue that will put everything together."

Or make that one mistake that will change everything.

CHAPTER 26

"**K**eep your car keys in your pocket and be ready to make a mad dash from the place if you have to," Augusta said when I told her about my plan to meet Denton at Starbucks. "At least you'll have backup. Does your friend have a pistol permit?"

"Only if they start issuing them for water guns. We'll be fine, Augusta. It's a public coffee shop."

"If that lizard man wants you to sign anything, tell him you'll take it under advisement."

I smiled. "I doubt he'll ask me to sign anything. If he decides to include me in his dealings, I guarantee payment will be under the table."

"As long as they don't find you under there along with your girlfriend."

While I focused on invoices and billing, Augusta typed up a stack of notes Nate had left on her desk and worked on some marketing for the business. The phone rang intermittently throughout the day and I wondered how long she could keep reshuffling appointments.

When lunchtime rolled around, we ordered a medium veggie pizza and split it. I figured it would be my "big meal" for the day since I hadn't been that hungry in the evenings with Marshall on the road.

At five we closed the office and headed home.

"Be on your toes tonight," Augusta said as she double-checked the lock on the door. And if you don't want to take along some mace, you can always push the alarm button on your car's key fob."

"Yeesh. You're getting as bad as my mother."

"As long as you're in one piece tomorrow, I'll be fine."

With three hours to spare before I had to be at Starbucks, I did a bit of food shopping, mainly because I was antsy, and threw in a pile of laundry. Then I paced around the house rehearsing my end of the conversation I planned to have with Denton.

It was useless. I needed a screenwriter to come up with an intro that had the right amount of innuendo so that Denton would think I knew what was going on. At seven fifteen, I gave up and got in my car. Maybe I'd have a brainstorm between Vistancia and Surprise.

Lyndy's car was parked to the right at Starbucks, just past the handicapped spots. I pulled in next to it and looked around. No one was seated outside. A good sign. Unless Denton was at the counter placing an order, we had arrived before he did.

Other than Lyndy, who stood at the counter, the only customers were a senior couple and a young woman with a child in tow. "Hope you haven't paid yet," I said. "It's on me."

"Nope. Just got here. Trying to decide if I want the black and white latte or the mocha java chip."

"We've got a few minutes. It's only quarter to eight."

Both of us decided on the java chip and stepped outside to secure the only corner table away from the others. The barista said he'd bring the drinks outside for us so that meant neither of us had to stand at the counter and wait. Instead, we stared at the parking lot while I tapped my foot, pausing occasionally to sigh.

"I don't think you're cut out for this kind of stuff, Phee," Lyndy said from across the table. "The espionage, for lack of a better word. You're great at snooping around and getting info from the senior crowd, but this is something that trained professionals pull off."

"Not according to my mother, who's seen one episode of *Shakespeare and Hathaway* too many. Uh-oh. That's Denton now, coming out of his truck."

With his facial stubble, well-worn jeans and dark T-shirt, Denton almost looked ominous. The tattoo, clearly visible, didn't help. I waved him over the second I saw him.

"Hi! Hope you don't mind but this is my friend Lyn—Lynn." It was bad enough he knew my name, he didn't need to hear hers. "Lynn and I have worked together and she can be trusted."

As I glanced at Lyndy, her face looked ashen and all she could do was nod. Denton pulled out a chair and sat. At that moment, the barista arrived with our drinks.

"Enjoy your evening," he said and then took off.

Denton propped an elbow on the table and leaned in my direction. "It's a simple loading and unloading process but you have to be quick. I might have something the end of the week. South of Queen Creek. Real easy to hop on 87 and go south from there."

Loading and unloading . . . 87 south? He has to be dealing in stolen goods.

"When will you—"

I never got to finish my sentence because in that exact moment, a voice exploded from behind us. When I turned my head, I saw a heavyset woman sporting a straw hat with colorful beaded accents. My jaw dropped. It was Eunice Berlmosler, the publicity chair for the local theater group.

"Phee! I thought that was you! Goodness, imagine seeing you here. I haven't seen you since you worked the ticket booth for the Sun City West Footlighters. Wonderful play. Your mother's performance was spectacular. Tell me, does she plan on auditioning for the fall production? They start rehearsals this summer."

Denton pushed his chair back and edged forward. "I should get going."

Too late. Eunice put her hand on his shoulder and didn't remove it. "Oh, no. Please don't leave on my account. I was just telling Phee how impressed everyone was with her mother's acting skills. Have you met Harriet? Lovely woman."

The expression on Denton's face was indescribable. I was positive my plan was about to implode. And given the look on Lyndy's face, she agreed.

I opened my mouth to speak but Denton beat me to it. "Sorry, I don't get out that much for entertainment. My work keeps me pretty busy."

Suddenly, the door to Starbucks flung open and a gray-haired lady shouted, "Eunice! Are you going to be gabbing all day? I've been waiting a full ten minutes for you. The programs aren't going to print themselves."

"I'm dreadfully sorry." Eunice leaned into the table and adjusted her hat. "Maybe we can all chat another time. Nice seeing you."

"On second thought," Denton said once Eunice stepped inside the building, "this won't work. You're much too high-profile around here."

Thank you, Eunice.

"I'm not," I stammered. "Really, I'm not."

"Give me a sec. Might as well snag a coffee while I'm here." He stood and pushed his chair back when the classic ringtone went off on his phone. As he took it out of his pocket, I got a good look at the initials in the little circle. Not that it mattered. I had no idea who the caller was or if it had anything to do with his business.

Denton glanced at the screen and pocketed the phone. "They'll leave a voicemail." He started for the entrance but instead turned around. "On second thought, I'll skip that coffee."

"Will you be getting back to me?" I asked.

He shook his head. "Like I said, you're way too high-profile. Don't sweat it. Maybe I'll see you again at water volleyball." He gave Lyndy a quick look and smiled. "Maybe you, too."

Speechless, we watched him get into his Dodge Ram truck and take off.

"Maybe we should have picked another Starbucks," Lyndy said.

"Of all things. Eunice Berlmosler. I suppose we're lucky she didn't pull up a chair and pepper Denton with questions."

"She might have had better luck. I'm sorry, Phee. You were so close. Now it's back to square one, huh?"

"I'm not so sure. Did you see the way he froze when he saw who called him? I'll wager that was the real reason he left. Well, *that* and the fact he really didn't want anything to do with me after Eunice burst on scene. Anyway, I got a good look at the initials, and if I'm right, they might match one of the four sets of initials from that list I found on Billie's flash drive.

Too bad I didn't bother to memorize them. Now I'll have to wait until I get home."

"Isn't that flash drive in the possession of the sheriff's office? I thought you pretended to find it in a chair at Billie's place."

"I did. And it is. But I ran off a copy of the file."

"Good thinking. Of course, you can't very well call those two grouches over there and tell them you might have a matchup for the initials."

"Not without getting another lecture about leaving the investigation to the professionals. And even if the initials from that phone call are the same ones on the flash drive, it's coincidental at this point."

"Coincidental until it's not. So, now what do you propose to do?"

"Find out how much money Billie stashed away and have another go with Denton. When he figures out I know more about his operation than he thinks, he may want to let me in so I'll keep quiet."

"But you don't know."

I sighed. "Deputy Ranston wasn't altogether averse to telling me how much money was rolled up in those boots. He pretty much said as much when I left Billie's apartment during their search. He said, 'Call me later.' And when I do, I'll ask if the flash drive yielded any vital information as well."

"What makes you so sure he'll share that info with you?"

"Oh, he won't *share* it, but I'll bet he'll trade it. I gave his partner the lowdown on Eddie Krome and Bowman was like a kid at the circus reaching for some cotton candy. Now I can offer up Denton. Once I find out his last name. And that shouldn't be too hard. I'll call Julia from the Boomers club."

"You're starting to scare me. You're beginning to think like a detective."

"No. If I really did, I'd have Billie's death figured out by now."

CHAPTER 27

W hen I got home, there was one message waiting for me on the landline—my mother's.

"I hope you're happy, Phee. Finding Billie's attacker, who most likely is the person who tried to do Louise in, has taken so long that now it's too late to order the large multicolored balloons for the Bye Bye Birdie event. Herb's tried all three distributors in Phoenix and the only large balloons he can get are black. Black balloons! It's not a funeral. It's a send-off. Call me. And by the way, your voicemail box is full. Empty it or something."

Unlike Lyndy, who had a late lunch at work before driving to Starbucks, my last meal was the pizza I shared with Augusta and I was hungry. Enough so that I waited until I'd eaten an egg salad sandwich before returning my mother's call. I didn't feel like fending off hunger pangs while listening to her complain.

"Hi, Mom, got your message. Uh, too bad about the black balloons, but people can write their names and messages with those silver or gold pens and it'll look fine."

"It will look like a funeral. Are you sure you can't do anything to hurry Nate and Marshall along so they can get back here before it *will* be a funeral?"

"I can't. You know how these investigations go. They seem to take forever and then, voilà! The right clue and everything falls into place."

"Fine. Speaking of clues, were you able to find out anything from those water volleyball Boomers last night?"

"How did you—"

"Gloria Wong thought she saw you at the RH Johnson pool but she wasn't sure. She takes her glasses off so they won't get wet in the water. She was in the large walking circle past the volleyball area."

"Yeah. It was me. Gloria's eyesight must be better than she thinks. Look, I meant to tell you but I haven't had a free minute in the past twenty-four hours."

"Well? Did you find out anything? Who had it in for that deli-witch?"

"Who didn't? Lots of people had lots of motives."

"Harrumph. That must mean you didn't find out anything."

"I found out enough to pique my interest. And I intend to do a bit more probing if you must know."

"Myrna's played water volleyball before. I can ask her to join you if you want."

"Good grief, no! She'd be likely to zoom in on the players with a clipboard in her hand if she doesn't drown one of them first by splashing around. One look at her and they'll clam up for good. Thanks anyway, but I'm doing fine on my own."

And I'll do much better once I get Ranston and Bowman to open up.

"Let me know. The mattress in Louise's guest bedroom will give me a permanent back condition if I have to stay there again. Not to mention being away from my precious little man. I made it up to him, though. I got him the deluxe Charlee Bear treats this time."

Wonderful. And what did I get? A nightly bout of indigestion.

"I'm sure he appreciated them. If I find out anything earth-shattering, you'll be the first person I call."

"Good. And be careful. Just because this is a senior community doesn't mean we don't have our share of lunatics."

Indeed!

It was too late to phone Julia in order to get Denton's last name, and much too late to reach Bowman and Ranston without incurring their ire. Instead, I made myself comfortable, stretched out on the couch, and turned on the news.

As the commentators described yet another heroic rescue on Camelback Mountain, followed by the usual litany of car crashes in the valley, I picked up the printout from the flash drive and scanned the initials. It was the third entry on Billie's list and a perfect match with Denton's caller. Unfortunately, no one in the widening circle of people who surrounded Billie had a first or last name with either of those initials. Not the deli workers, not Tula, and not any of the Boomers whose names I did manage to glean.

As for my aunt's Wiccan friends, their names didn't match either. Whoever those clients were on Billie's list, they were an enigma as far as I was concerned. And for all I knew, they could be right next door or as far away as Saskatoon. If I was lucky, Bowman and Ranston might be in good moods tomorrow and might be inclined to open up. If not, I'd have to rely on my "people skills," and I wasn't so sure they were as polished as I would have liked.

At five minutes to ten my phone vibrated and every hair stood up on my arms. I had dozed off on the couch watching an old rerun of *Death in Paradise*. My first thought was that it was my mother calling to tell me something catastrophic had happened to Louise, but when I saw the call was from Marshall, I was elated.

"You must be going out of your mind, hon," he said. "We're fine so you can take a deep breath and relax. The cell service is worse than spotty so this call may end without notice."

"Where are you? What's going on?"

"We're in Sunizona, halfway between Willcox and Douglas. Rolo tracked down a money exchange that prompted us to—"

"To what? Hello? Marshall?"

I tried to redial his cell but the call wouldn't go through. At least I knew he and Nate were safe, but for how long? I tried not to think about it but it was impossible. There was no way I'd be able to fall asleep at this point. Instead, I went back to my murder map with its hubs of suspects. I had added small cartoonlike balloons that linked with each player so I'd have a spot to jot down my thoughts. I was still way too far off to include any possible evidence, unless the combination of that smoky cloying smell Louise remembered could count as evidence.

As I looked at the notebook, I realized something. I hadn't bothered to create a section for the few clues I'd been able to muster, namely the two receipts I found in Billie's old car along with a map of the Hassayampa Bird Preserve and that cryptic note. At least I had the good sense to put them in a manila envelope by my computer so I wouldn't be chasing all over the house for them.

Adding the clues to my murder map gave me something to do in lieu of eating junk food. I flattened out the creases in the two receipts and wrote down the information. That was the instant I could have kicked myself in the rear for being such a dunce. I had *partial* clues but that didn't mean I couldn't get the rest of the information.

Billie paid eight hundred dollars cash to A & G rentals. Since the receipt had the date, all I needed to determine was what she rented. The other partial receipt was for fourteen dollars and ninety-nine cents from Dale's Country Store. Almost not worth the bother, especially if it was for something innocuous, but I knew it would plague me if I didn't find out.

As far as the note went, it was anyone's guess. And the map? That was a no-brainer. Billie trekked all over the place as part of her active lifestyle obsession. No matter, I included all the info on my murder map and went to bed determined to call A & G and Dale's in the morning during my break.

• • •

"Marshall and Nate are alive and well," I said the moment I opened the door to the office. Augusta, who was standing by the copier, coffee in hand, looked up. "I know. Shortest phone message on record. Give me a second and I'll replay it for you. According to our answering machine, the call came in at ten fifty-three last night."

"Hmm, about the same time as Marshall's call to me."

Augusta put her coffee mug on her desk and pushed the playback button on the phone. Nate's voice was loud and clear. And brief. "Caught a hot trail from Rolo and—"

"I can fill in the blanks. They're midway between Willcox and Douglas. In a place I never heard of—Sunizona," I said.

"No wonder the cell service stinks. At least they caught a decent lead. And talking about leads, how'd it go with your lizard man? I see you're in one piece, so either he didn't show or you and your friend scared him off."

"Not me. Eunice Berlmosler. She's the publicity chair for the Sun City West Footlighters. She barged over to where we were seated and literally took over the conversation. Denton all but flew out of the place. Said I was too high-profile to deal with."

"Guy makes a good point."

"Not funny, Augusta. I was so close. Now I'm back to putting little puzzle clues together. Namely, the receipts I found in Billie's old car. I need to track them down. And I plan to have another go at Denton once I do."

"Again, public place and preferably with a concealed weapon."

When ten fifteen rolled around, I grabbed another cup of coffee and one of the mini-donuts Augusta brought in. Then I phoned A & G rentals on Deer Valley Road. I explained I worked for Williams Investigations in Glendale and that we were looking into the unexplained death of Billie (Willameena) Churl. Not exactly a full-blown lie, but certainly an exaggeration of sorts. Especially the *we* instead of an *I*. *I* was looking into her death, not Nate or Marshall. But A & G Rentals didn't need the specifics.

"I'm looking at a receipt for eight hundred dollars," I told the man at the other end of the line. "It's got the date but no specifics. I was hoping you could provide that for me."

"Got a number on that receipt? We file by numbers."

I read off the letter and number at the top of the receipt and held my breath.

"Aargh," the man groaned. "I keep telling Chuck to write down every blasted thing on those receipts, but between you, me, and the lamppost, he takes every shortcut he can get. If he wasn't my nephew, I'd send him packing. Hold on a sec, will you?"

Before I could reply, it was nothing but dead air space. Not even elevator music. I tapped my foot on the floor and thumbed the fingers of my right hand on the desk. Finally, a voice at the other end. "Yep. Got it right here. Hmm, no wonder there was an extra hundred-and-fifty-dollar charge. Usually those rentals are a straight six fifty and that includes the hookup."

"The hookup?"

"Yeah. Lots of folks don't want to monkey around hooking up a trailer to their truck. Rather have us do it."

"A trailer? She rented a trailer?"

"That's what it says—livestock trailer. The extra cost was because she returned it to our drop-off location near Laveen and not here on Deer Valley Road."

My mind whirled and it amazed me that I had the wherewithal to ask if anyone remembered what kind of truck she drove.

"Hold on. Maybe Chuck can remember."

Again, dead air space.

Finally, the now-familiar voice. "A beat-up old Chevy Silverado. Maybe a 2014 or 2015. Chuck said it looked like it had been driven on Mars. That much red dirt. Even the driver's seat. That's how he remembered. Said he was coughing up dust all day after moving the truck around back for the hookup."

"Uh, thanks. You've been a big help."

"No problem. If you need to rent any equipment, on or off road, A & G Rentals is your place."

"I'll spread the word."

The instant I got off the phone I charged over to Augusta's desk. "I might be on to something. Oh, my gosh. I might *really* be on to something. Of course, it's too soon to tell. One more call to make."

I ran back to my desk as Augusta shouted, "You've got to stop hanging around your mother's friends. They're rubbing off on you."

Dale's Country Store said they'd be glad to help but I'd have to bring the receipt to them in person so they could verify it. Five seconds later, I was back at Augusta's desk.

"I'm driving to Surprise during my lunch break and I'll stay late if need be, but I have to check out this fourteen ninety-nine receipt of Billie's. It was the same day as the other one."

Augusta looked up from her computer screen. "Knock yourself out."

The next hour and a half moved like sludge. I swear, even entering numbers on my spreadsheet took an inordinate amount of time. At last it was almost noon and I flew out the door. Bell Road traffic wasn't too bad, but it wasn't too good either. It took me a full twenty-three minutes to get to Surprise. I turned south on Litchfield Road and west on Waddell. Dale's Country Store was on my right and I pulled into their gravel parking lot at the same speed my mother and her friends do when there's a sale at Shers' Clothing.

With the receipt neatly folded in my bag, I approached the cashier. "I'm Phee Kimball, the person from Williams Investigations who called about a receipt."

The woman behind the counter looked around. "I can look into it. Doesn't appear as if we have any customers headed this way."

I took out the receipt and handed it to her. "The paper's yellow. Looks like it might be a carbon. If so, can you find the original for me so I can see what's missing?"

The woman nodded. "That's the good thing about going old school. Everything's easy to find."

She immediately opened a drawer behind the counter and pulled out a small booklet. Then she thumbed through the pages. "Got it right here. The purchase was for a nylon Dura-Tech halter. Eight hundred to one thousand pounds."

"Halter? Like on a horse?"

The woman laughed. "Unless you've got one hell of a dog. Did you want me to make you a copy?"

"Yes. Please."

I couldn't wait to get back to the office to tell Augusta what I'd learned. Instead, I phoned her, oblivious of how I sounded.

"A halter. For a horse. And the trailer. Livestock. Had to be a horse. And that explains the damn bite marks. Oh, my goodness. The map of Hassayampa. And that book by M. J. Evans. It's still on Billie's bistro table. Unless Tula cleared out the place. Oh, no. I've got to drive over there."

"Whatever you do, don't drink any more coffee. And call me when you get there."

CHAPTER 28

I pulled into Billie's condo/apartment complex for the third time since her death. The first, under false pretenses, and the second, under unbridled enthusiasm. Not to mention curiosity. Now, I had to own up.

The sign on Tula's office door said *Open* but I gave a quick knock before I let the overhanging bell announce my arrival. Tula was seated at her desk sifting through papers. It was only when I said "Hi" that she looked up, letting her readers drop from her nose.

"I'm not who you think I am," I said. "I need to get that out in the open."

Tula didn't look surprised. "I figured as much when I saw you on Friday, leaving Billie's apartment the second time. I take it you're an undercover deputy. That would make sense."

Only in my nightmares.

"Um, actually I work for an investigative agency in the valley. One that consults with the Maricopa County Sheriff's Office."

"Hmm, guess that explains it. Too bad, your mother would have liked the apartment. That is, if your mother really lives here."

I tried not to roll my eyes. "Oh, she lives here. No doubt about that. By the way, I'm Sophie Kimball but I go by Phee. I didn't introduce myself fully the last time."

"Nice to meet you, Phee. What can I do for you? The deputies must have taken what they needed because they removed the crime scene tape and it's a go as far as removing Billie's things and re-renting the place."

A sudden sense of relief washed over me. Billie's stack of books would still be on her desk.

"I think the deputies may have overlooked a vital clue on Billie's bistro table. Would you mind terribly if I went in there to look? It's one of the books she had. It may get us closer to finding out who assaulted you and who ransacked her place."

Tula gave me a nod, reached in her desk and handed me a key. "It's the master key to all of the condo apartments. Listen, if it's just a book, take it and return it when you're done. I have no idea how probate works in this county but I'm about to find out. That's why I can't simply give you the book or I would. I'm stuck getting all that stuff into storage until I'm told what to do with it. Talk about a mess."

"Maybe Billie's last will and testament will show up."

Tula shook her head. "I don't think I'll be that lucky."

I took the key, thanked her, and told her I'd be right back.

The apartment looked the same as it did the last time I'd been there. Ranston must have read the forensic crew the riot act about leaving everything the way they found it—in shambles from the break-in. It took me all of three or four seconds to march over to the bistro table and zoom in on *Hidden Arizona Trails for Hikers, Bikers, and Equestrians.* Apparently the books were the only things that weren't disturbed. The tome I needed was wide-open with a pencil down the spine, and the napkin with those squiggly lines and abbreviations hadn't budged from its spot between that book and the one about climbing.

I picked up the hidden trails book, put the napkin inside of it and glanced at the bistro table. The only other book was the one about casting spells and that was the last thing I needed to do. So as not to overstay my welcome as far as Tula was concerned, I closed the door behind me, locked up the place and returned to the office.

"Did you find what you were looking for?" Tula asked when I handed her the key.

"This is it." I waved the book in front of her and she nodded. "Like I said, I'd let you keep it but for all I know, those deputies took a video of the place and I'm responsible for its contents."

"No problem. I'll make sure to return it. I'll also let them know I have it."

"You probably can't answer this, but do you think I'm in any danger? The sheriff's office has a posse car swing by here every few hours, but what good's that going to do if I'm gagged and hogtied somewhere? Frankly, I'm not worried about daylight when everyone's out and about, but I do work evenings."

"I can't speak for the sheriff's office, but I'd be very cautious if I were you. True, the thieves made off with Billie's computer, but who knows if they want something else?" *Like reams of money.* "If I were you, I'd lock up before dusk and take my work home with me. Oh, and I'd buy myself one of those Screamers."

"Screamers?"

"Uh-huh. They're little handheld devices that let out a piercing sound if you push the button. My mother and all of her friends bought them after that body was found a year or so ago in the Stardust Theater. It goes without saying that you can always hit the siren button on your car's key fob, but that will sound like a whimper compared to the Screamer."

"I'll google it on Amazon, Best Buy, or Walmart tonight. Thanks. I appreciate it."

"No problem. And thank you, Tula, for letting me peruse Billie's book."

• • •

In all my excitement, I'd forgotten to call Augusta when I got there. Last thing I needed was a cavalcade of her gun-toting canasta crew showing up to extricate me from whatever she envisioned had happened.

I immediately dialed the office and spoke before she could utter a sound. "I'm on my way back to the office and I think I know what got Billie killed. I won't be a hundred percent sure until I scour through the hiking and biking book. But put it this way, I'm eighty percent sure. Maybe seventy."

"Glad you're not putting odds on a horse race."

"Oh, it's a horse race, all right, and the head jockey's sporting a Gila monster tattoo."

"Translate that to English when you get here. And from now on, I'm buying decaf for the office."

After spotting two Surprise Police Department cars on Bell Road, I slowed down. Good thing because there was a Peoria Sheriff's vehicle just past the entrance to the 101, and another from its Glendale counterpart three blocks from our office. With the book under my arm and my bag hanging from my shoulder, I hightailed it to the office the second I parked the car on the street. At least I didn't have far to walk, only twenty or so yards.

"I've seen storms blow in with less energy," Augusta said the moment I stepped inside the front office. "Take a breath, pull up a chair, and tell me what's going on. I'm too old for puzzle solving."

"Sorry. It's just that I'm pretty sure I stumbled onto something, and if I'm right, Nate and Marshall may be up against a whole lot more than your average horse thieves. First off, the receipt from A & G Rentals was for a livestock trailer, but the real kicker was the one from Dale's Country Store. Billie bought a halter. A halter! She probably needed an extra one. My God, Augusta, that's how she wound up with all that newfound money. She was stealing horses! That's the underhanded business she and Denton were into. And Denton's still in it. With accomplices, no doubt. Probably the men Rashida from the deli mentioned when I met her."

Augusta fluffed her bouffant-styled hair and leaned back in her chair. "Hmm, the receipts make sense but I can tell you right now, unless you've got other, more compelling evidence, you'll just be spinning a tale as far as those deputies are concerned."

"That's why I had to get into her apartment and go through this book." I handed her the hardcover tome M. J. Evans had written about hidden trails, making sure to pull out the napkin with the squiggly lines that I'd placed inside it. When Augusta reached for the book, it dropped on the floor and the well-worn cardboard cover broke apart, revealing a piece of paper that someone had carefully glued to the underside of cover.

My hand shook as I reached for it. "Hold your breath. This could be the compelling evidence." Then I took a closer look. "Drat! It's those initials again. Same as the ones on that flash drive. Only there's other stuff written, too, but I can't make it out. Can you?"

Augusta took the paper from me and nodded. "I can make it out, all right, but it's in Spanish. I recognize the word *caballero* from the sign on the men's restroom door at Master Taco. At least they had the good sense to have stick figures on those doors so we'd know which one to open."

"I know someone who can translate it—Lucinda Espinoza from my mother's book club. She's always translating those Telemundo soap operas for the ladies. Would you do me a favor and find her phone number from the directory? I'm going to skim through this book and see if Billie wrote anything on any of the pages. Like it or not, I'm going to be staying real late today to get caught up with my work."

"Harrumph. If you'd simply trade your bookkeeping and accounting for a detective's license, you'd be all set."

"No, thanks. I need some sanity in my life."

"By the way, there's a leftover bagel and cream cheese in the fridge. You can eat it while you turn the pages."

I plopped myself at my desk and began to study M. J. Evan's book in earnest. It was filled with detailed maps of the terrain as well as important pointers for using certain trails in rainy conditions. There were a few handwritten side notes that I presumed came from Billie but nothing out of the ordinary. Her comments included things like, "would be good in summer," "lots of shade," and "close to streams."

Twenty minutes later, I took Augusta's suggestion and ate the cold bagel. It sat in my stomach like a rock but I kept turning the pages in that book, certain I'd find something that would cement those other clues.

"Got the number for you!" Augusta called out. "Good thing she still has her landline. Want me to bring it in?"

"Sure."

She handed me Lucinda's phone number and glanced at my desk. "Still no luck, huh?"

"Not yet. Guess I might as well give Lucinda a call."

The first words out of Lucinda's mouth were, "Is your mother all right? Is Louise all right? I haven't spoken to anyone since yesterday."

"Everyone's fine," I said. "I called because I need you to translate something that could be important."

"Not a recipe? Don't tell me your aunt Ina found some old Aztec recipe and wants to replicate it."

"No, thank goodness. It's something I found in one of Billie's books. Her condo manager let me take the book when I told her I worked for Williams Investigations and we were looking into Billie's death."

"That's wonderful. Nate and Marshall are on the case."

"Uh, no. *I'm* on the case, but not officially. So, um, will you do it? Translate the note?"

"Sure. Can you read it to me?"

"How about if I take a photo of it and send it to your cell phone? I just need the number. You can call me back on mine. I should probably keep the office line free."

"Sure. I'll call you back with the translation."

"Great! Oh, and whatever you do, please don't tell my mother. She's convinced I'm in mortal danger."

"Honey, we all are until that stairwell lunatic gets caught. Here's my number . . ."

While I waited for Lucinda to return my call, I continued to peruse through the many hiking, biking, and equestrian trails our state had to offer. And as I continued to turn the pages, Billie's notes got more detailed and more perturbing, especially when it came to the equestrian trails.

She noted places that riders should avoid at certain times of the day as well as trails that should be taken at nightfall. Nightfall? Who the heck rides a horse at night? In the dark. Maybe with a flashlight, I suppose. But still . . .

CHAPTER 29

I kept reading, unable to take my eyes off of her side notes. Maybe M. J. Evans could have used her as a coauthor. Then, I spotted something that made the little hairs on the back of my neck tingle. It was a sketchy drawing that linked the Hassayampa Bird Preserve map to a trail that led to ranch properties outside of Wickenburg. Billie had made a side note that read, "park truck and trailer here and walk."

Not far from the trail was a paved county road that anyone could have accessed in a vehicle. I was about to confirm my suspicions with Augusta when my cell phone rang and I jumped. Lucinda!

"I've got your translation, Phee, but I have no idea what it means."

"What does it say? Maybe I do."

"I'll skip past the initials. It says, 'BC to oversee W Corridor, DD or BC for SE Tuc, two stops, DD or BC for Naco. Expect resistance on last stop. Clear shots only. Can't afford to lose a horse.' At first I thought the note referred to a train or something, but this mentions shooting and horses. Are you sure it has something to do with that assault on Billie in the library tower?"

"Oh, yeah, more than ever. Did you notice anything else?" I asked.

"Only that the first set of initials has a small checkmark next to it and the words 'Paid in full.' Nothing is written next to the other three sets of initials."

I was so focused on the note, I hadn't noticed the checkmark. "Lucinda, you're a lifesaver. Read it again slowly in English while I write it down."

"What does any of this mean? What was that deli-witch up to?"

"I'm pretty certain she was involved in those Wickenburg horse thefts and would have stolen horses from other parts of Arizona if she hadn't fallen to her death. I'm guessing SE Tuc is southeast Tucson and I know for sure horses were stolen from that area. Nate and Marshall are investigating. Listen, this can't leak out. Not until I've talked with our sheriff's office. I could be really off course."

"Mum's the word."

"Thanks, Lucinda. I appreciate it."

The second the call ended, I raced to the outer office, where Augusta had just removed some papers from the copier. My voice was high-pitched and louder than usual. "It was her. It was her all along! Billie! She's the one who stole those horses from Wickenburg. Well, she and Denton. And probably the other two men that Rashida mentioned. The smokers who hung out in the break area behind the supermarket. I don't think the thieves have reached Naco yet but Nate and Marshall are in that area. Oh, crap. This could get ugly. Billie used the words *clear shots*. That means someone's got a gun. Or guns."

"Calm down. Like I've said before, Mr. Williams and Mr. Gregory have guns, too."

"A barrage of bullets doesn't make me feel any better. I'm trying Marshall right now on his cell."

I reached in my pocket, where I'd put my phone, and dialed Marshall's number. Voicemail. I left a frantic message. Then I tried Nate's but his also went to voicemail. I bit my lower lip and dialed another number. One I'd been avoiding all week.

"Rolo? It's Phee. Phee Kimball. Have you been in contact with Nate and Marshall in the last twenty-four hours? I can't reach them and I think I stumbled onto something. I hope I'm wrong but if they're headed to Naco there's going to be trouble."

"Naco? How'd you find out about that? Never mind. And no. I haven't been able to reach them. I left a message at the Cochise Sheriff's Office but I couldn't be too specific with them. They'd want to know who I am and all that hullabaloo. Can't very well tell them I've been swimming around on the dark web."

"What *did* you tell them?"

"That I consult for Williams Investigations and that two of their detectives may be met with gunfire in Naco over some stolen horses in the next day or so. I was about to call your office when you beat me to it."

"Rolo, what's going on? What's this about? A drug cartel?"

"Nope. Worse."

I swallowed and tried to stay calm. "What?"

"Getting certain people across the border illegally. People who have more than enough money to make it well worth the risk. Forget car trunks and the usual means. The team behind this operation uses stolen trail horses to do the trick. And not just your run-of-the-mill horses. They look for horses that have been used on tough terrain and aren't afraid of crossing streams or maneuvering through brush. It's damn well-thought-out if you ask me."

"And you were able to find this out on the internet?"

"Not that easy. Not like going on eBay. It involves deciphering messages and breaking down codes. Good thing I'm fluent in more than one language. Anyway, unless Nate and Marshall get some backup, they're going to be in for a hell of a ride."

"Rolo, can you get a better time frame than 'the next day or so'?"

"I'm working on it. Tell me, how'd you figure it out?"

"Long story. I'm looking into the possible murder of a former delicatessen worker who fell to her death in the Sun City West library tower as the result of an assault."

I then went on to give Rolo the details surrounding Billie's death, including her relationship with Denton and the unidentified smokers.

"Oh, yeah," I said. "This probably doesn't mean anything, but this Denton guy has a tattoo of a Gila monster on his arm. Very unique."

There was dead silence on the line as soon as I said that, and for a minute I thought I'd lost the connection. "Rolo, you still there?"

"Uh-huh. Listen. I've got to make some more calls. I'll be in touch."

The call ended before I could utter a syllable and I stood in front of Augusta and didn't move.

"You okay, Phee? All I heard was you asking Rolo questions. I didn't hear his answers."

"Maybe that's just as well. It's awful and I'm stuck here unable to do a gosh-darn thing. According to Rolo, those horses were carefully chosen. I figure Billie did the legwork and that info is on her computer with the person who broke into her place. The thieves stole highly trained trail horses in order to smuggle people across the border. And I was right about that note I found. They expect trouble in Naco and who knows what they'll do."

Augusta held up the receiver to her phone. "I'll tell you what you should do—call Ranston and Bowman now."

I nodded and used the office line. Bowman picked up the call but the minute I told him what I'd gleaned from Rolo, he replied that, number one, it was out of his jurisdiction, and number two, it was a matter for the Arizona Department of Agriculture. I slammed the phone down and leaned across Augusta's desk.

"Do we have the phone number for that field rep? The one from the agriculture department? What was his name? Martin something. Or Winston something."

"Martin Winston-Featherly. Hold on. I've got it. I take it whichever one of those two deputies you got on the phone didn't want to deal with the matter."

"It was Bowman and you got that right. Geez, I didn't even get a chance to let him know how Billie figured in all of this. Never mind. I've got to call that field rep."

Augusta handed me a small pad that had Martin's number on it. "Want me to call him? You look as if you're about to have a stroke."

"I'm fine. Perfectly fine."

Immediately following the first ring was a recording from the Arizona Department of Agriculture. I felt as if I'd landed in the pit of hell. "You've reached the Arizona Department of Agriculture. If you know your party's extension, you can dial it at any time. For a directory, press one. For the livestock department, press two, for the—" I didn't wait. I pressed one for the directory and held my breath until they got to the *F*s. I lunged for the nearest pen I saw on Augusta's desk and wrote the number on the nearest piece of paper I could find.

"He'd better pick up this call," I said. "Or I'm likely to drive down there and forcibly remove him from the break room or wherever he's hanging out at taxpayer expense."

Martin's voice was chipper and businesslike. "Good afternoon. This is Martin Winston-Featherly, field rep."

I didn't give him a chance to go any further. "Mr. Featherly, this is Sophie Vera Kimball from Williams Investigations in Glendale and I believe you are familiar with the detectives in this agency—Nate Williams and Marshall Gregory." Again, I didn't give the guy a chance to respond. "For your information, they've followed a lead on those stolen horses and are downstate near Sunizona. Our office was able to determine that the horses were stolen by a human trafficking ring that brings wealthy clientele into this country illegally by using trail horses to evade the authorities. Their next pickup will be in Naco. In a day or so. I hope to have more details from our cyber investigator." *Or whatever the heck Rolo is . . .* "Anyway, our office has reason to believe these thieves are extremely dangerous. You've got to send help down there ASAP. Sheriff's deputies, border patrol, Homeland Security."

My God! I'm sounding like my mother, only worse.

"You said Naco? Hmm, we've got someone working on an agricultural pesticide issue down in Bisbee right now. I'll give them a holler."

"A holler? You need to give them a Smith and Wesson and send them straight to Naco."

Oh, no. Now I'm sounding like Augusta.

"We can't send officers of the law to an area without sufficient information. Time. Place. Details. Like I said, I will contact our rep in Bisbee and give him the heads-up."

I knew I was wasting my time. That's probably what Perry Gaynes and those other horse owners thought when they elicited Nate's help. "You do that," I said. "Give him the heads-up." *A heck of a lot of good that's going to do.*

I hung up and crashed on the chair next to Augusta's desk. "This is horrible. Absolutely horrible."

She crinkled her nose and motioned for me to calm down. "Didn't Mr. Williams say that the Cochise County Sheriff's Office was really cooperative? Not that I'm telling you what to do, but that would be my next call."

"I suppose you've got the number in front of you, huh?"

"Better yet, I'll dial it for you and get someone on the line. Meantime, make yourself a cup of coffee. On second thought, make some of that minty tea in the green K-cups. I haven't bought decaf coffee yet."

"Are you implying I'm overwrought?"

"You said it, not me."

CHAPTER 30

B y the time Augusta got a deputy on the line, I had calmed down sufficiently to speak in a normal voice and not one that sounded like I was auditioning for *The Taming of the Shrew*. I explained about acquiring evidence regarding a horse stealing ring for the purpose of human trafficking and told the deputy that Naco, Arizona, was going to be the next stop. But where exactly, I had no clue.

"Lots of undeveloped land out there," the deputy said. "And hilly terrain north of there in Bisbee. Plenty of horse trails, too. Not to mention abandoned barns and lean-tos that could be used to hide the horses. Listen, as soon as you get some more definitive information, call us. That's the same thing I told the two private investigators from Maricopa County. Here's my direct number. Just in case. Name's Emilio Ramos and I've been with this office for the past fifteen years. Meanwhile, I'll have our office scour the area and do some poking around as well."

"Don't you have to check with the Department of Agriculture?"

Deputy Ramos laughed. "For what? An update on crop rotation? When it comes to matters like this, they always wind up in our hands."

It was the first bit of good news I'd had since I walked into the office, but unless Rolo could come up with a meeting time and a place, it wouldn't matter.

"I suppose I should get back to the real reason I've been hired," I said to Augusta once I told her what Deputy Ramos said. "Maybe looking at spreadsheets will get my mind off of the soon-to-be situation in Naco."

"Good idea. And remember, Mr. Williams and Mr. Gregory know what they're doing."

Terrific. I only wish I did.

The afternoon plodded along and I stayed late to catch up on my own work. I knew once Rolo set his mind to something he'd be relentless, but it still wasn't much consolation. I locked up and left the office at a quarter past seven. From there, I grabbed a take-out dinner from Boston Market and drove straight home.

I was famished and didn't even bother to change into comfy clothes before chowing down. I glanced at my landline but no red light blinked. Thoughts of Nate and Marshall walking into a modern-day Gunfight at the O.K. Corral left me nervous and antsy. I did more channel flipping in the next hour than anything else. And while I was worried sick about my fiancé and my boss, I was positive my mother was fretting about that ridiculous Bye Bye Birdie snowbird send-off.

That event was approaching like a freight train but I had a downright emergency on my hands. I made sure my iPhone was set at full volume in case Rolo decided to use that number, but no calls came in. At a little past eleven, I forced myself to go to bed, but after a restless hour of changing positions from my back to my sides, I gave up and made myself a cup of tea, knowing that the only thing it would really be good for was frequent trips to the bathroom.

Rather than turn on the TV again, I unfolded an old AAA map I had of Arizona that my mother had sent to me a few years ago when she insisted I fly out here to solve a book curse. I told her I could google the map but she didn't trust anything that had to do with the internet.

I wanted to see exactly where Naco was situated, even though I had a general idea of its location. The old AAA map would suffice. New roads might have been built, but Naco wasn't going anywhere. As I sipped on the spicy Constant Comment tea, I studied the cities, towns and roads that surrounded that border city. Suddenly, the name Nicksville popped up and I remembered where I'd last heard it. Tersee, my aunt's Wiccan friend, mentioned it when she met with my aunt and me about Billie.

Nicksville was a stone's throw from Naco, and if I wasn't mistaken, a whole cadre of nature-worshiping Wiccans were about to descend on it for their annual Beltane celebration. It was late and my mind was foggy, but somewhere in that mess of illogical reasoning and insomnia, I came up with a plan. Had I given it more thought, I would have dropped it immediately, but it wasn't as if anyone else offered up another solution.

Billie's gang of horse thieves had to be apprehended and the horses needed to be returned to their rightful owners. I couldn't bear watching another TV segment with some poor kid bawling his eyes out over losing his best four-legged friend.

Confident my idea would work, I crawled back to bed and managed to get a few hours of sleep before hurrying off to work so I could call my aunt Ina when she woke at her usual "any time after nine thirty." Clearly, I still needed to hear from Rolo, but I was pretty sure he'd come through. The only thing that plagued me was the abrupt ending to our last call. It wasn't like Rolo to end calls without mentioning at least one new aspect of whatever loony diet he was on, but then again, the urgency of the situation might have been to blame.

"Any news from Mr. Williams or Mr. Gregory?" Augusta asked as soon as I opened the door to the office. "Or Rolo, for that matter?"

"Not yet, but I guarantee Rolo will phone us before the day's out. And when he does, I came up with a plan to help locate those thieving chain smokers. I just need to call my aunt Ina to set it up."

Augusta opened her mouth and then closed it without saying a word.

"That's right. My aunt Ina. She's very gifted when it comes to persuading people."

"What people?"

"Her Wiccan friends. Their coven is going to combine with two larger covens in Nicksville, not far from Naco, for the annual Beltane celebration. The timing couldn't be better. They can be on the lookout for anyone suspicious on horseback and notify Deputy Ramos. If they're discreet enough, it would allow the Cochise Sheriff's Office to swoop in and round those bad boys up."

"Or maybe they can just cast a nifty little spell."

"Honestly, Augusta."

"You want three covens of witches, who will be in the midst of celebrating who-knows-what, to be discreet if they see someone on horseback? What are they supposed to do? Stop dancing and chanting so they can run for the nearest cell phone? And what good is that going to do if there's no connection? Mr. Williams and Mr. Gregory can barely get through to us. Worse yet, what if they decide to converge on those horse thieves? Then what? Honestly, Phee, your plan has more holes in it than a moth-eaten sweater. At least wait until you hear from Rolo."

"Don't worry, I can't put anything in motion until I speak with Rolo. But that doesn't mean I shouldn't run my idea by my aunt."

"As long as that's all you do."

Like it or not, Augusta was right. In theory, my plan sounded feasible, but it was the what-ifs that worried me. Nevertheless, it was still a golden opportunity and one that I wasn't about to lose.

I waited until my break time to call my aunt Ina. Number one, I had to be reasonably assured she was awake and functioning, and number two, I held out hope Rolo would call me first. He didn't.

My aunt answered on the third ring and in the background I could hear my uncle's saxophone.

"Hold on a minute, Phee," my aunt said. "I need to close the bedroom door. Your uncle has a double engagement this weekend. Tomorrow night is the Abromowitz Bat Mitzvah and Sunday afternoon is the Cooperman bris. Both in Fountain Hills."

"Uncle Louis and the other musicians are playing for a bris?"

"Not the bris itself. That took place yesterday. The extended family is holding a party at some fancy-schmancy hotel to celebrate. Louis and his buddies will be staying in Fountain Hills all weekend. Too far to drive back and forth. Anyway, enough about your uncle, tell me, has any progress been made on that murder?"

"Sort of. Well, maybe. Um, remember when Tersee invited us to attend that Beltane celebration? It's Sunday night, isn't it? I looked up the date on a calendar of Wiccan celebrations and rituals."

"Goodness. You've had a change of heart, didn't you? That's wonderful. Here I was, contemplating how to spend the weekend with Louis gone, and now the two of us can drive to Tucson in the morning, stay at a wonderful spa that's known for its Reiki healing, and then head on down to the Wiccan celebration on Sunday. I'll need to call Tersee or Serena to let them know we're coming."

"Huh? No. Don't call and tell them. I mean, yes, I'd like you to call them but—"

"Make up your mind, Phee. You sound worse than Louis when he's not sure what he wants for dinner."

"What I'm about to tell you cannot be repeated to anyone. Understood?"

"Of course. Go on."

"Billie was involved with an unscrupulous gang of horse thieves who stole trail horses to be used to move wealthy clientele through our state once they snuck them over the border. It's the case Nate and Marshall are working on. No time to get into the details but those scoundrels will be making a crossing around the same time your Wiccan friends hold their celebration. And, in the exact same area. We need your friends to be on the lookout so they can contact the Cochise Sheriff's Office if they spot anyone suspicious on horseback. Will you please call Tersee or Serena to ask if they'll help?"

"I have a better plan."

Oh, God help me.

"You and I need to join their celebration. We can't expect those covens to do all the work for us. It isn't right. You and I can seamlessly blend in and while the coven is doing whatever it is they do, we can mosey about the area and listen for the sound of people on horseback. If we hear those thieves, we take action."

"You mean we call the sheriff's office and try to reach Nate and Marshall."

"Yes. That, too."

It was the way my aunt said *too* that unnerved me but I supposed in order for my plan to work, I'd have to take a more active role even if it meant trusting my aunt's judgment.

"Fine. I'll go. Now, will you call Tersee or Serena?"

"Yes, yes. Oh, before I hang up, you said not to say a word of this to anyone. Does that include your mother?"

"Include her? That goes without saying! She's the last person you should tell. She'd round up your book club, deck the dog out in some godforsaken witch costume, and have a lineup of Buicks descend on the area like one of the ten plagues of Egypt. Whatever you do, don't breathe a word of it to her. Although I'll have to tell her something. Hmm, I'll just say you and I are going on an overnight spa retreat. It's not exactly a lie. Part of it is true. I'll simply leave off the rest."

"Smart idea."

"Thanks, Aunt Ina. Talk to you later."

When I stepped to the outer office for another cup of coffee, Augusta looked up from her desk and gritted her teeth. "You put that plan in motion, didn't you?"

"How did you—"

"I can tell by the guilty look on your face."

"The plan's not really in motion. Not until we hear from Rolo and my aunt sets things up with her Wiccan friends. Then I can contact Deputy Ramos and see what he thinks."

"I don't know the man but I can tell you what he'll think. He'll think you're muddying the waters and he'll nix your plan."

Augusta was rarely wrong when it came to reading people, but I still held out hope she was wrong.

CHAPTER 31

At a little past three, when I figured Rolo had hit a dead end, he called. Augusta transferred the call to my office, then shouted for me to hold off. "It's Rolo. Sounded stranger than usual. Thought I'd give you the heads-up before you took the call."

"Thanks."

Rolo always sounded a bit peculiar, but given the circumstances, I was worried. "Rolo! Thank goodness. What did you find out?"

"Does your office have any burner phones?"

Yep. "Stranger than usual." Augusta was right after all. "Huh?"

"Burner phones. Prepaid untraceable phones."

"Uh, yeah. I know what they are. Nate has a few of them in a file cabinet. Why?"

"Get one and call me back on it."

The call ended but it took me a second to replace the receiver on the phone and digest what he'd said. I walked to Augusta's desk and told her about Rolo's demand.

"He must think our line is bugged. Same deal with your cell. Guy's as nutty as a fruitcake but his intuition's damn good. Hold on, I'll unlock the cabinet and get you a phone."

A minute or two later, I was back at my desk tapping in Rolo's number.

"Okay," I said. "I'm on a phone with a prepaid cell number. Now can we talk?"

"You bet. I was able to piece together enough chatter to be fairly certain that eight or nine affluent wheeler-dealers who need to get the heck out of Mexico will be escorted by a little-known trafficking operation that relies on trail horses to make the initial trek until more substantial transportation is used."

"Yeah, that's what you mentioned before. Not the numbers of people, but the process. Were you able to find out when and where?"

"That's why I called. They'll be entering the U.S. around dusk on Sunday. Above Pozo Seco off of Route 2 in Mexico. The border wall's not fully established in that part and they'll use any soft spots to enter."

"What about the horses?"

"My take is that they'll have them fanned out in the area so it will look like any old ordinary rancher checking out his or her land."

"About this trafficking operation, how dangerous are they?"

"Dangerous enough to be in that business. Those guys don't mess around. They'll be armed and who knows how they'll react if they're confronted. That's why Nate and Marshall can't just barge in on them."

"I've spoken with a deputy from the Cochise Sheriff's Office and they'll step in. At least I can give them the time frame and general location."

"The general location's huge, that sheriff's office is going to need more than a few deputies. Look, I'll keep trying to reach Nate and Marshall. Guess you'll be doing the same."

"No guessing about it. If I could send a carrier pigeon, I would. Look, Rolo, if you hear anything else, *anything at all*, call my cell or call the office. Got it?"

"I'll call the burner number. Give it to me."

I gave him the number, thanked him, and returned to the outer office.

"Rolo's got the time frame narrowed down as well as the general entry point. I need to call Deputy Ramos and let him know. The fact Rolo insisted on using the burner phone has me worried. Augusta, do me a favor and try to call Nate and Marshall, will you?"

"I've been trying since I got in this morning and all I get is their darn voicemail. I'll keep at it."

I went back to my office, left word with Deputy Ramos, and forced myself to focus on reconciling the numbers on my spreadsheets. The data was clear and so was the process. That's what I liked about bookkeeping and accounting. Nothing iffy. And if it *was* iffy, then someone was cooking the books.

About an hour into the process, I got an unexpected call from Deputy Bowman. I thought maybe he had second thoughts following my call to him yesterday.

"Miss Kimball? Since you were so forthright in providing our department with possible evidence in the Billie Churl investigation, I thought it only fair to inform you that our lab was able to secure a fingerprint on that pack of Newport cigarettes. Report came in a few hours ago. Good thing that tobacco company used cellophane on the wrapper."

My pulse quickened and I sat up in my chair. "It was Eddie Krome's, wasn't it? I knew it. He had something going on with Billie."

I couldn't tell if Bowman groaned or had simply cleared his throat. "No, the print did not belong to Eddie Krome. But it *was* in our database. Seems it was a positive match to a man by the name of Ted Gillian. Convicted felon. Bank robberies in Portland, Oregon, and Redding, California. Served a few years, and when he was done with his parole in California, he moved on. Suffice it to say, the guy's most likely in this area."

"Oh, my gosh. Do you think he was the one responsible for that assault?"

"Our office does not speculate."

"Fine, forget speculating. Is your office beefing up its patrols of the area? Especially in light of this evidence?" *And the fact that if my mother and her friends got wind of it, I'd never get a decent night's sleep.*

"Yes. The Sun City and Sun City West Posses have been duly informed, as were the Surprise, Peoria, and Glendale Police Departments. In addition, MCSO has added more patrol cars in those areas."

"Um, about this Ted Gillian. Do you know what he looks like? There must be an old mug shot or a prison photo if there's such a thing."

"It was sent to the law enforcement agencies but it was taken years ago. Caucasian, average height and weight. No facial hair."

"What about tattoos? Did he have any tattoos?"

"One on his left forearm. Tattoo of a snake."

"A snake? Are you sure it was a snake?"

"Miss Kimball, while I do not possess the expertise to identify the type of snake Mr. Gillian chose for his body art, I certainly can recognize a drawing of one when I see it."

"Uh, sorry. I was hoping it was a different tattoo."

"You're probably not the only one. It wouldn't be my choice, either, if I went in for that sort of thing. Listen, about that other matter. The stolen horses. Like I said before, it's out of our jurisdiction, and our purview, but we've got our own contacts down in Cochise County and we've been on the line with them. They know your boss and your fiancé are in the area. Since that information didn't come from our office, I can only presume it came from yours."

"Of course it did. What did you expect?"

"That's exactly what I expected and you made the right call. If that gang of horse thieves is going to break through the border this weekend, they'll be met by a substantial showing from our partners in Cochise County. Law enforcement has got this covered."

"What about the Department of Agriculture? I thought it was their job to track down and deal with horse thieves."

"Horse thieves, yes. Illegal border crossings, no. It's a complicated issue. Call our office as soon as you hear from Nate and Marshall."

"I will. And thanks for letting me know about the fingerprint match."

"I think I may have gotten some good news from Deputy Bowman but I'm not sure," I said to Augusta. She was sifting through some papers on her desk and put them down.

"What do you mean by 'may'?"

"They found a match for that pack of cigarettes I found but it doesn't belong to Eddie Krome. Boy, do I make a lousy detective. But right now I'm less concerned about who sent Billie to her death and more concerned about what Nate and Marshall may be walking into. Bowman said his office is in contact with the Cochise Sheriff's Office but I don't know what good that's going to do."

"It's four fifty already. I'll try Mr. Williams again."

I held my breath and watched as Augusta picked up the office phone and dialed. She shook her head and put the receiver down. "I can try tonight from home."

"That's all right. No sense in having both of us do that. I'll call you if I hear anything."

No sooner did she power off her computer and shut down the copier than the phone rang. Augusta grabbed the receiver in a nanosecond but didn't get a chance to finish her usual, "Good afternoon, this is Williams Investigations . . ." She uttered the first few words then mouthed the word "Nate" to me.

By now every nerve in my body was on high alert. I stood at her desk with my hands shaking as I watched the expression on her face. Thirty seconds later, the phone call ended.

"The line went dead," she said, "but you can breathe. Nate started the call with the words *crappy cell service.*"

"Where are they? Are they all right? What did he say?"

"Said they were fine and to call Rolo. Something about a ham radio operator. That's as far as he got."

I flew to my office, snatched the burner phone out of my bag, and dialed Rolo's number. Busy signal. Damn. I took a breath, counted to ten and tried again. Still busy. By now Augusta was leaning against my doorjamb. "Catch your breath, Phee, and try again."

No sooner did I pick up the phone than I heard its ringtone.

"Rolo?"

"Who else were you expecting? Did you give this number to anyone else?"

"No, only you."

"Good, because I've got news."

CHAPTER 32

G ranted, it was sketchy news, but it *was* something.

"Nate mentioned ham operators or ham radios before the line went dead," I told Rolo.

"That's a darned good break. Means he and Marshall spotted a tower or two in the area. I'm on it. Oh—and whatever you do, call me on a burner phone."

"Got it."

An instant later, Rolo ended the call and I turned to Augusta. "Rolo thinks the guys spotted ham radio towers in the area. He's checking it out. Anyway, no sense in hanging around. We've shut everything off. I'll call you if Marshall gets through to me."

"Whatever it is you and your aunt are up to, be careful this weekend and keep me posted. I'll be in the office in the morning."

Augusta and I turned off the lights and exited the building. I stood and waited while she locked up before we went our separate ways to our cars. There was one more thing I needed to do before driving to Tucson with my aunt in the morning. I had to let my mother know I was going out of town. Knowing that the call would be uncomfortable at best, I rehearsed my end of the conversation on the drive home.

Luckily everyone was glued into Bluetooth so having a conversation with myself probably didn't seem too odd to the other drivers. Once I got in the house, I raced for the landline in case there was a message. Sure enough, the red light was blinking, but the message was from my mother.

"Put a firecracker under those deputies before Louise is forced to get a prescription for antianxiety medicine. She had an incident today while she and Myrna were at the thrift store. Not the resale store, the big thrift store. The one where everyone smokes in front of it. Call me."

As if it wasn't bad enough I'd have to break the news I'd be with Aunt Ina at a spa, now I prayed Louise's "incident" didn't include another shove or worse. I went into the kitchen, poured myself a tall glass of iced tea, and composed myself before returning the call.

"Phee! You got my message. Good. Louise is beside herself. While she and Myrna were shopping in the thrift store, she smelled that same saccharine and smoke smell she detected the morning Billie's body was found. What did she call it? Oh, yes—cloying. Sounds like a word that should be used in one of those Bronte novels. Anyway, it brought back the memory of that awful morning and the poor woman had an anxiety attack right in the middle of the store. Three people offered her their Xanax and another two had lorazepam they wanted to give her."

"Oh, brother."

"You can say that again. Suffice it to say, Louise didn't take anything. She just sat and took deep breaths until she felt better. But that's not the real reason I called."

Oh, dear Lord, help me.

"I, um, er . . ."

"Myrna had the most ingenious idea. Whatever it was Louise smelled had to be the same smell from whoever was in the tower with Billie. Maybe a man's cologne. Maybe a woman's perfume. So, Myrna came up with the Inhalation. It's a new plan. Once Louise calms down, we'll return to the library where it happened, and have her sniff around at the patrons to see if she smells that scent."

I clenched my fist and tried to stay calm. "I'm not sure that's going to get you the results you want, and besides, it may get all of you thrown out for annoying the library patrons. Look, the deputies have some decent leads, let them deal with it. Um, by the way, I was going to call you tonight. Uncle Louis has a double gig out of town and Aunt Ina wants me to join her at the Soulful Serenity Spa tomorrow night. It's in Tucson."

"Tucson? My sister wants to drag you to Tucson to stay at one of her rejuvenation spas? What's it this time? Don't tell me. It's the place with the Nova Scotian seaweed wrap, isn't it? Ina was raving about it. Well, if the two of you want to soak in mud and get wrapped up in kelp, who am I to stop you?"

Hmm, she's taking this much better than I thought.

"Uh, no. Not seaweed wrap. Something about hot stone massages and warm herbal soaks."

"Massages and soaks?"

"Uh-huh."

"You know what? I think I'll join you. Those places always allow pets and Streetman deserves a break. I'm calling my sister right now."

Me and my enormous mouth. Now I'm really sunk.

"Maybe now's not the best time. What if Louise needs you?"

"Shirley and Lucinda have her for the weekend. Louise will be fine. Did you and your aunt pick a time to head out tomorrow? Never mind, I'll ask her. I imagine you're driving since no one wants to be in a vehicle with Ina behind the wheel. Pick Streetman and me up first, then we'll get your aunt. See you in the morning."

And, for the second time in the same day, someone ended the call before I could utter a word. The minute I realized the line was dead, I phoned my aunt, but her line was busy. Drat! My mother must have had her on speed dial. Now all I could do was try to figure out how I could salvage this mess.

A half hour later, my aunt called and told me we were sunk.

"Did you mention the Wiccans?" I asked.

"Are you kidding? We'll just deal with it when the time comes. Pick me up at nine thirty, okay? And make sure your mother's in the backseat with the dog."

"No problem. By the time we get to Tucson, all of us will need a nice long soak and an endless massage. The dog's fine on short trips but moans like nobody's business if it's longer than a half hour."

Just then, I heard my aunt yell, "Louis! Where did you put those noise-canceling headphones?"

Yep, it was going to be one heck of a ride.

• • •

I was up early the next morning and let Augusta know that there had been no calls from Nate or Marshall. We agreed that if either of us heard anything, we'd contact each other. Then I was off to grab a coffee from Starbucks and head over to get my mother and Streetman.

When I arrived at her house, she was already out front with the dog. She'd packed a small travel case for herself and a larger bag for her "precious little man." I stashed the suitcases in the trunk and explained that Aunt Ina needed to sit up front. Thankfully, my mother didn't mind since the backseats gave her and the dog more room.

"So where's this hotsy-totsy spa, Ina?" my mother asked as soon as my aunt settled into her seat.

"It's nestled into the Catalina Mountains. Phee has the directions."

I turned around and gave my mom a nod. "Yep. We're all set. All you need to do is sit back and relax. It should take us about three hours at most."

"You're not taking that dreadful Interstate Ten to Route Seventeen, are you, Phee?"

"No, Mother. I'm going crosstown and then through the Indian reservation before I have to get on the highway."

That seemed to pacify her and for the first fifteen minutes or so, everything was fine. Then Streetman discovered my aunt's long braids complete with frilly ribbons. He immediately began to gnaw on them before my aunt realized what was happening.

"Can't you do something about that dog, Harriet? Give him a bone or a toy."

My mother groaned. "I can't help it if your hair looks like one of those rope toys. You may want to consider a new style. Or haircut, for that matter."

"Just move your braids to the front, Aunt Ina," I said. "Streetman isn't about to jump over the seat to get to them." *I hope.*

My aunt did as I requested while my mother handed the dog a few little chewy treats. Surprisingly, he settled in and the remainder of the drive was uneventful. Unlike the rest of the weekend.

The Soulful Serenity Spa looked like an ancient Roman villa set high above Tucson. We could see the city skyline in the distance and groves of orange and lemon trees. My aunt had reserved the Flora suite, a three-bedroom, three-bath suite complete with its own atrium and dining area. I doubted the ancient Romans had it that good.

After a late lunch, the three of us decompressed in one of the soaking rooms while Streetman enjoyed a long walk and playtime with one of the canine attendants. It was times like this that I thanked the gods my uncle Louis was such a good gambler. Otherwise this place would have been unaffordable, even with my aunt's handsome income.

At a little past four, I returned to my room and used one of the two burner phones I'd taken with me to call Rolo.

"Have you heard anything more?" I asked.

"Got the locations of the ham radio operators. If those trail horses and their riders show up anywhere near there, Nate and Marshall will have a way to contact the sheriff's office."

"And if not?"

"They better have a lot of bullets."

"Not funny, Rolo."

"Look, cell phone service is spotty, but not dead. Your guys know how to move around, with any luck they'll be able to pick up a signal. But my money's on those radios."

"I'll call you in the morning," I said. "Meanwhile, you have the number for this phone if anything comes up."

This time I was the one who ended the call. I'd been suppressing the nervous anxiety that was gradually building in my system and all the herbal soaps and aromatherapies into the world wouldn't help. Not until I knew Nate and Marshall were safe.

I'd put Billie's situation on hold since, well, the woman *was* dead after all, and I didn't think anyone was about to go after Louise. Heck, one look at her bodyguards, Shirley and Lucinda, and even the most seasoned criminal would hold off. And as far as the Bye Bye Birdie event was concerned, black balloons and all, my mother would just have to come to grips with the fact that she wouldn't be making a guest appearance on *Sonoran Living*. She'd get over it. *I* might not ever hear the end of it, but I was willing to take that chance. Right now I had a more pressing situation to deal with.

CHAPTER 33

That evening the three of us dined on assorted cheeses, some of which I'd never heard of, grilled pear and candied walnut salad, mussels with leeks and paprika, sautéed kale with currants, cauliflower gnocchi, pan-seared cod, and roasted chicken with asparagus.

Not to be outdone, my mother had the chef prepare a special meal for the dog—braised beef tips with brown rice, which she promptly served to him the minute we returned to our suite.

While my mother fussed with Streetman, I pulled my aunt aside and asked, "When are we going to break the news about tomorrow's venture to Nicksville?"

"I was hoping she'd eat an enormous breakfast in the morning and fall asleep in the car so she wouldn't notice."

"Aargh. One of us has to tell her. I suppose it better be me since this was my idea, after all."

"Shh. Here she comes. The dog must have finished eating. That didn't take too long."

I laughed. "Too long? Streetman can inhale his food in thirty seconds. Twenty if it's something he likes."

"What are you two chatting about?" my mother asked as soon as she stepped into the grand living/entertainment room.

"Um, maybe you should have a seat. Aunt Ina and I need to tell you something."

My mother took the nearest wing chair and sat. "Oh, no. Someone died. Who?"

"No one died," I said. "And we want to keep it that way. Tomorrow, instead of driving straight back to Sun City West, we need to go south. Nate and Marshall are tracking those stolen horses and they've got a lead. The horses are being used to traffic wealthy clientele over the border from Mexico into this country."

"Illegally?"

"Um, yeah. And Billie was involved. For all we know she might have been the mastermind. And that's what may have gotten her killed."

My mother clasped her hands together and let out a long breath. "So you want to get us killed next? Driving south to some godforsaken place where everyone carries a gun and pops it off as if they're opening a bottle of champagne?"

"We're not going right to the border, if that's what you're implying.

Aunt Ina's Wiccan friends are in the area. Three or more covens. They're going to be celebrating Beltane tomorrow evening, their annual summer welcome festival, and—"

"Witchcraft? You're getting them to conjure up some witchcraft to catch those horse thieves? And what are we supposed to do? Dig around for newts and salamanders?"

"I think you're going to the extreme, Harriet," my aunt said. "The Wiccans have agreed to keep an eye out for anyone in the area on horseback but Phee and I felt we should be there as well. In case we have to drive to the nearest sheriff's office if Phee can't reach her boss or her fiancé. True, my friends want to help but I can't expect them to stop their annual celebration on our account."

My mother clenched her teeth. "No. I suppose not."

"Good," my aunt went on, "it's all settled. We'll enjoy a leisurely morning here tomorrow and then drive to Nicksville, where the covens will be gathering. It's spitting distance from Naco."

I moved closer to my mother and sat in the chair opposite hers. "All we're going to do is watch for any movement in the surrounding area. If we see trail horses, we take it from there."

"I'm not liking this, Phee. Not one little bit. And what about poor Streetman? All that chanting and hoo-hahing from those witches could set him back. And just when his socialization skills were improving."

"I'm sure the dog will be fine. The both of you can stay in the car." *As if that's going to happen.*

"No sense trying to talk the two of you out of it. I can see you have your minds made up. A Beltane festival, huh? Please don't tell me I'm expected to wear a black cape, or worse yet, put some hideous head covering on."

"No, we're guests. We're fine dressed as we are."

My mother shot her sister a look that all but said, "You're going to owe me." Then, she stood and walked to her room. "I'm calling the front desk for another massage. It's the only way I'll be able to sleep through the night."

Too bad a massage didn't do the trick for me. Thoughts of gun-toting criminals on stolen horses made for a fitful night. And while I told myself all we would be doing was surveillance, I wasn't so sure. First thing in the morning, I called Augusta on the off chance she'd heard something. She hadn't.

Thanks to my mother's call to the front office, room service arrived with assorted fruits, jams, butters, croissants, juice, and coffee. It was surprising how ravenous we all were considering the huge meal we'd consumed the night before. And that included the dog, who was given small bites of the buttery croissants.

"There's an early morning meditation yoga class," my aunt announced. "It might be just the right thing to have our minds and bodies begin the day in a tranquil state."

"You and Phee go," my mom replied. "I intend to take a long shower and watch *Face the Nation*."

And while my mother caught up on the national and global problems, my aunt and I stretched our bodies into positions that, under ordinary circumstances, I would have relegated to highly paid circus contortionists. At a little before noon, we met in the resort's grand dining area for lunch—tomato, feta, and egg omelet for me, smoked salmon and sable salad for my mother, and some sort of a frittata for my aunt. My mother ordered a plain scrambled egg for the dog and fed him as soon as we got back to our suite.

"Did your aunt happen to mention where we're staying tonight?" my mother asked. "It's too far a drive back to this spa from that Belt Train or whatever you call it."

"It's Beltane, and yes, Aunt Ina did mention it. Some sort of little B and B outside of Sierra Vista. Billowing Breeze or something like that."

"She didn't use the words *cozy* or *rustic*, did she?"

I shook my head. "No. I think she called it *homey*."

"God help us. That's even worse than *quaint*."

Forty minutes later, we checked out of the spa and were on our way to Nicksville. According to my GPS, it was a two-hour drive. But the GPS didn't take into account how many stops we had to make for Streetman. Thankfully, Aunt Ina had gotten good directions from Tersee and I had no problem making it to the large clearing on a hill nine point eight miles southeast of Nicksville.

A field, just past the clearing, served as the parking area for numerous vans, SUVs, and sedans. Streetman immediately watered the ground as soon as we exited the car. I stared at the dozen or so large white tents but it was the sight of a tall maypole, complete with bright ribbons, that caught my eye. It stood in the center of the clearing and it was spectacular to behold. A number of children were chasing each other around the maypole while others blew bubbles into the air. Someone was playing the flute, or maybe even a lute, but I wasn't sure where the music came from.

"This is not what I expected," my mother announced. "Where's the cauldron? I don't see a cauldron. Aren't they supposed to have a cauldron?"

I rolled my eyes and took a quick breath. "You don't see a cauldron because this isn't a filming for *Macbeth*. For heaven's sake, it's a family celebration."

The aroma of grilled food wafted in the air, and as we got closer to the clearing we saw the throng of people lining up at the long tables, just past the tents.

"Come on," my aunt Ina said. "Let's look for Tersee, Serena, or Laurel. I'm starving." Then she turned to my mother. "Make sure that dog of yours stays on his leash. I've seen how he gets around food." With that, my aunt thundered across the lawn, leaving us in her wake.

My mother bent down and gave Streetman a pat on the head. "Harrumph. That's the pot calling the kettle black. Have you ever noticed your aunt at a dessert table? And she says the dog is bad around food."

"Never mind, we'd better catch up to her."

I spied my aunt a few yards away hugging Tersee and another lady. Laurel, perhaps?

"She's over there," I pointed. "Let's go."

Just then, three little girls in pink and purple pinafores raced past us, their floral crowns bouncing on their heads.

"Hmm," my mother muttered. "Maybe this won't be so bad after all."

Seconds later, we were at my aunt's side. Tersee gave me a quick hug, then reached out her hand to my mother and introduced herself. "So glad you could join us. This is Laurel. Serena is around here somewhere, but with all these people, it's hard to say where. I hope you're hungry because we've got quite the spread. All of the vegetables are locally grown and everything is homemade."

"Homemade?"

Oh, no. Please don't tell me my mother is about to make some comment about the ingredients.

"That's wonderful," I said. "We could smell the grill all the way over in the field."

Tersee smiled. "It's not one grill. It's lots of them. We've got roasted pork, and chicken in garlic and herb butter, but it's the salads that are amazing for this festival. Don't be shy around the table. We're not going to run out of food. Grab a plate and find a chair. Lots of time before we start the maypole dance. Then the Celtic dances will begin. Tonight, when the sun goes down, we'll have our bonfire. If you look off to the left, you'll see another clearing with the wood all piled up in the center. It's going to be a huge bonfire. Folks have been gathering wood all morning for it. Got to get the wood early in the day. Too chancy to be in the woods in the afternoon. The light is too dim." Tersee looked around. "Say, we've got a few dogs running here and there if you think yours would like to play with them."

Only if play is defined by making amorous advances.

I shook my head and gave my mother "the eye."

"I'll think I'll keep him here on the leash," she said. "I don't want him to get lost."

As she and my aunt moseyed to the food table, I hung back and motioned for Tersee. "Thanks for agreeing to keep an ear and an eye out for the sound of horses or any trail riders."

She looked around and spoke softly. "Many of our attendees will be taking nature walks in the wooded areas surrounding this place. That's a good thing because all of the covens are on alert. If the people in question could steal horses, some of which are pets, I can't imagine what else they're capable of. Should we see or hear anything, we'll find you right away."

"I just hope I can get a cell signal."

"It's iffy. And that eight- or nine-mile drive to Nicksville is slow going on these roads. But I did see some ham radio towers. Hopefully it won't come to that. Meanwhile, enjoy the festivities."

The sound of bagpipes signaled the start of the maypole dance and I marveled at how the men and women, decked out in colorful attire, wove in and out as they circled the pole, thus wrapping the ribbons they were holding around it. When the dance ended, the pole had been transformed into a glorious braid and smaller circle dances began. I took out my cell phone and tried to reach Marshall but again, only voicemail.

The sun was slowly sinking into the horizon and with it, so was any hope I had of reaching my boss, my fiancé, and those horses.

CHAPTER 34

T hen, the worst happened. A gray poodle with a purple flower attached to her bright yellow collar pranced by Streetman and within seconds he broke free from my mother's grip on the leash. Not only that, but he had managed to break the fastener on the leash as well.

The panic in my mother's voice overpowered the Celtic dance music. "Streetman! You come right back here to Mommy!"

The dog was oblivious to her shouts and instead focused his attention on the gray poodle.

"I think he has selective hearing," I said, bending down to pick up the leash. "Maybe you could wave a chicken leg in the air or something to catch his attention. He's going to be all over that poor dog in a matter of minutes."

My aunt, who had joined a small circle of dancers, suddenly approached us. "Is that Streetman over there? Chasing after the little gray dog? He ran through our dance circle like a maniac."

My mother didn't say a word but her head bobbed up and down.

I bit my lower lip and winced. "Yeah, that's him, all right. In all his glory."

"Can't you do something, Harriet?" my aunt asked.

"Like what? I can't run as fast as that dog." Then she looked directly at me.

"Oh, no. I'm not about to trip and fall over something. He'll come back when he loses interest."

Or if another dog catches his eye. He's the canine version of Herb Garrett.

Ribbons of turquoise, pink, and orange framed the horizon as half the sun disappeared on the skyline. I figured we'd have maybe another half hour—forty minutes tops until dark.

Streetman was now on the edge of the field with the little gray poodle in front of him. I bit harder on my lip, hoping he wouldn't venture into the woods, but it was too late. "I'm on it!" I shouted, thankful I wore a decent pair of Sketchers and not sandals. As I got closer to the woods, I saw the little gray poodle. She ran past me toward the center of the clearing but there was no sign of Streetman.

As if I don't have enough to worry about.

"Phee! Stop! Slow down!" It was Tersee's voice. "I'm not used to running."

I spun around and waited while she caught up. Her voice came in spurts and I was afraid she might hyperventilate. "I thought I'd never reach you. Boy, can you move fast. Listen, two Wiccans from the coven near Sierra Vista were in the woods looking for herbs when they heard the sound of horses. Not a sound you can miss. They said it came from the southwest side of the woods. It could be your horse thieves."

Last thing I needed was to venture into the woods and find myself face-to-face with those thieves, even if it *was* the reason for my trek down here. Locating them was one thing, taking them into custody wasn't. Then again, there was the issue with Streetman. I had to find that little chiweenie or my mother would be beside herself.

I pulled the cell phone from my pocket. "Thanks, Tersee. I'll see if I can get a signal and call the sheriff's office."

"Sounds good. Meanwhile, I'll head back to the coven and get Laurel. We'll drive around until we spot one of those ham operator towers."

"Good plan."

Tersee made a run for it while I entered the pass code on my phone. No sooner did I tap the last digit than the phone vibrated. Marshall! A call was coming in from Marshall.

"Phee? Can you hear me? We're okay. We're north of Naco heading west. Damn good thing Nate carries a burner phone with him. Rolo got through to us but said he'd only talk on a burner. Called him back and he gave us a lead. Also called the Cochise Sheriff's Office but lost the connection. Not sure if they got our info. We're going to—"

And just like that, the call dropped. I phoned his number but all I got was voicemail. As far as Marshall knew, I was back home in Vistancia, not in the general vicinity where he and my boss were.

Like it or not, I had to find that dog, even if it meant going into a wooded area. True, there were a few well-worn paths according to Tersee, but Hansel and Gretel started out in a similar fashion. I tried not to think about it.

"Streetman!" I shouted. "Here, boy! I have yum-yums!"

Either the dog had found something more interesting than food or he was way out of hearing range. If my sense of direction was right, I was on the northeast side of the woods. To verify, I tapped the compass app on my phone, and sure enough, I stood in the exact opposite direction of where those Wiccans had heard the horse sounds.

With any luck, this was the area that Rolo was able to narrow down. Too bad Marshall's call to the Cochise Sheriff's Office failed. That would have meant a professional law enforcement team would be on the scene. Now all I could hope for was that Tersee had better luck finding a ham radio operator who could somehow reach the sheriff's office. But only if the horses were in this spot, as opposed to any number of woods in the Canelo Hills between Sierra Vista and Naco.

I had no way of knowing and the light that filtered into the woods had now become dimmer.

"Streetman! Streetman!" I kept yelling, all the while walking farther down the path. In spite of all the aggravation that dog had given me, I had to admit, I, too, had become attached to him.

The minute I find that dog, I'm going out and buying him one of those GPS collars.

In the distance, I could hear the Beltane celebration music and wondered how long it would be until it got dark and the bonfire started. Given the late hour of day, those horse thieves had most likely found a place to bunk down for the night. No one, no matter how desperate they were, would be cavalier enough to ride trail horses in the dark. Even if those horses were trained to do that very thing.

Scuffling sounds coupled with some rustling in the tree branches above my head were the only noises I heard as I kept following the path. The Beltane music got softer the farther away I walked but it was still light enough for me to scan the area for Streetman. I figured I'd give it another five or ten minutes at most before the impending darkness would force me to turn around.

The sound of a branch cracked and I jumped. Birds maybe, or even a squirrel. I kept walking. And then, a swooshing, clomping sound that overtook the entire wooded area where I stood. Instinctively, I reached for my cell phone.

Like that's going to do me any good.

Then, a soft neigh. At first I thought it was my imagination but the sound grew louder, into that familiar nickering that comprised the soundtrack of every Western I'd seen. And not just one sound. At least two or three more. My God! Those horses the Wiccans heard southeast of where I stood were now headed in my direction.

Poor Streetman. He'd have to find his way out of the woods by himself. I had no choice but to race back to the festival and find out if Tersee managed to get a message out via a ham radio operator. Without wasting another minute, I spun around, intent on leaving as quickly as possible. Unfortunately, that changed in a split second.

I heard a low growl followed by some sort of a snapping sound. The last time I'd heard anything like it was when my mother tried to remove a boneless pork chop from Streetman's mouth. It had fallen off her counter and he'd latched on to it. Never mind it was still raw.

Before I had a chance to shout, two riderless horses roared past me, with Streetman nipping at their heels. I was stunned, speechless, and shocked beyond all belief. I was also frozen in place. They were down the path in a flash when the dog changed direction, charged back in the woods and rounded up two more. This time with two frightened riders clinging on for dear life.

And if that wasn't the end-all, three more horses emerged from the dense woods, but only one of those had someone on it. Someone I thought I recognized as the horse blew past me.

I counted seven horses in all but that didn't mean there weren't more of them in the vicinity. What it did mean, however, was that the missing riders were probably trying to find their way out of the woods. Worse yet, they were most likely armed.

My breath came in spurts as I half walked, half ran down the path and back to the open field. Visions of the seven horses trampling over the Beltane celebrants flashed through my mind, forcing me to move faster.

As I emerged from the woods, I expected the place to look as if a category three tornado had touched down, but instead, what I witnessed was the stuff Hollywood filmmakers spend their entire movie budgets trying to capture. The seven horses, two with their riders still on their saddles, were clumped around the maypole with Streetman running around them in a circle. Most of the Wiccans had moved to the other field for the bonfire so only a few remained in the maypole area. That soon changed when the cavalcade of horses was ushered together by a neurotic chiweenie.

"That dog is herding those trail horses!" someone shouted. "Could be the stolen ones!"

My mother flew toward the maypole, but I managed to stop her before she could shout to the dog.

My voice all but cracked. "Don't call him! Don't do a thing. He's got those horses corralled. If he stops running around them, they might take off." *Or the rider I recognized might pull a gun out.*

"Have you seen Tersee?" I asked. "She left to get word to the sheriff's office."

By now, at least two dozen people had gathered around the spot where my mom and I stood, including my aunt Ina, who made little *tsk-tsk* sounds as she watched the dog continue his circle dance around the horses.

"I didn't know dachshund-Chihuahua mixes were herders," she said to my mother.

My mother looked as if she was witness to a spaceship landing. "I didn't know he could bark, snap, and run at the same time."

My aunt furrowed her brow. "How long can he keep this up? It's getting dark."

Sure enough, Streetman was doing his best running a circle around those horses. But that didn't stop the two riders from trying to get their horses to break with the pack and make a gallop for it. Panic-stricken, I watched as they yanked on the reins, but instead of bending to the will of the riders, both horses reared up, effectively dumping their passengers on the ground.

"Do something, Phee!" my mother shouted. "Before they get away!"

"Who? The horses or those men? Never mind!"

Thankfully, there were quicker minds and bodies on the scene than mine. Three men and a woman charged toward the two men who had fallen from the horses but stopped abruptly.

My aunt moved a palm to her cheek and took a step closer to the ruckus. "Looks like those two got the wind knocked out of them." Then she turned to me. "Which one do you think is Billie's killer?"

I widened my eyes, gave my aunt a shove back, and swallowed hard. "The one walking out of the woods pointing a gun at us."

CHAPTER 35

T *hank you, Arizona Department of Agriculture, for doing absolutely
nothing. Now we're all going to get killed.*

I wiped the perspiration from my eyes and took a closer look to be
sure I'd gotten it right the first time. The man with the gun was the
Boomers very own water volleyball aficionado, Denton, complete with the
Gila monster tattoo on his arm. And maybe, just maybe, *he* was the
mastermind behind the horse thefts and not Billie. Not that it mattered at
the moment.

What mattered was that an armed horse thief/trafficker, aka Denton,
appeared to have the advantage. There was no sign of Tersee, no deputies,
and no Nate or Marshall to come to our rescue. The good Samaritans had
backed away and had now blended into the gathering crowd in front of the
maypole while the others were feeding the bonfire.

Meanwhile, Streetman continued to snap at the horses' hooves, creating
an equine merry-go-round that, under other circumstances, I might have
found hilarious.

"No one make a move," Denton shouted. "And no one will get hurt. All
we're going to do is round up our horses and move out of here."

He motioned to the other men, but what he didn't realize was that
Streetman had stopped nipping at the horses and now stood behind him,
sniffing. Either Denton had eaten something and had wiped the residue on
his jeans, or there was some tasty little tidbit in a pocket. It didn't make a
difference. Streetman had become obsessed with it.

First some gentle sniffs as Denton eyed the crowd, gun pointed straight
ahead. Then, snorting sounds emanating from the dog. And finally, the
pièce de résistance—Streetman sunk his teeth into the guy's rear and
refused to let go. In that instant, Denton dropped the gun, and his
counterpart took off for the woods. The horses whinnied but remained
clumped together around the maypole.

Undaunted, Denton tried to shove the dog off of him, all the while
reaching for the gun that was a few feet from him.

Whatever you do, don't kill the dog!

Luckily, Denton didn't notice that the horse closest to him had become
agitated and stomped its feet. In doing so, he or she managed to kick the
gun farther away, where one of the good Samaritans now stood.

The Samaritan snatched the gun from the ground and emptied the
shells. Then he smiled. "I may be a practicing Wiccan," he said, "but I was

born and raised in Arizona. Held a gun in my hand before I held a rattle."

Just then, someone shouted, "The horses! They're all getting excited."

Suddenly, I was no longer a spectator at the game. With Denton no longer a threat, and the other guys somewhere in the dark woods, I raced toward the horses and at the top of my lungs, I shouted, "Use the maypole ribbons! Tie them to the reins! Hurry!" *And pray they're the strong and durable grosgrain ones.*

I didn't have to shout a second time. The anxious crowd charged to the pole, but tying the horses to the ribbons was next to impossible. The ribbons had formed a braid and would need to be undone.

That's when Serena approached from the bonfire and yelled, "We'll need volunteers to walk backward from the pole with the horses facing forward. The others need to follow along with the ribbons that aren't being tied to the horses." Then she motioned to a stocky gentleman who was holding a bagpipe. "Play some music, Minton."

Had it not been for the fact that there were still armed traffickers somewhere in the woods, it would have been a magical moment. The distant bonfire set off an eerie glow as the parade of Wiccans, accompanied by the seven horses, danced their way backward around the maypole.

"This isn't going to be sacrilegious or anything," I said to Serena.

"If it is, our god and goddess will understand."

Still no word from Nate or Marshall but a frantic Tersee, with Laurel a few feet behind her, arrived on scene. She gasped as she moved toward my mother, my aunt, and me. Both of the women spoke at once and I had to tell them to slow down and take turns.

"Can you believe it?" Tersee's voice cracked. "The ham operator on this side of the hill is a twelve-year-old kid. He was able to contact another radio operator in Casa Grande, who said he'd call the sheriff's office in Cochise County."

I was stunned. "All the way to Casa Grande? He couldn't find a closer contact?"

She shook her head. "I guess that's how it goes with those signals. Anyway, I'm sure once they get word to the sheriff's office, the deputies will be on their way. We gave the kid explicit directions."

Then Laurel spoke. "We saw everything as we drove up. That little dog is incredible. He herded all of those horses. Did you know he was a herder?"

I know he's lots of things but a herder isn't one of them.

"Um, no," I replied.

Laurel pointed to the maypole. "Would you look at him? He's having a field day prancing around everyone."

I eyeballed the scene in front of me and noticed that Denton was off to the side, flanked by three burly men.

Good. He wasn't going anywhere.

On the off chance a signal might go through, I took the cell phone from my pocket and tried Marshall's number. "Marshall! It's Phee. The horses are at the Wiccan field above—" And like that, the call dropped.

Laurel put her hand on my shoulder. "Don't worry. The word is out. Something like this is bound to pull in lots of deputies. Maybe even some border patrol agents."

As long as they can pull in Nate and Marshall, I'll be fine.

I swallowed and nodded.

The blues, pinks, and greens from the fading sunset had now turned to murky mauve and gray. Still, there was sufficient light from the bonfire to illuminate the area.

"How long do you think it will take those deputies to get here?" I asked Tersee.

"The kid was fast on his radio so I imagine his contact in Casa Grande called them right away."

There was nothing any of us could do except listen to the sound of the bagpipes and watch as the Wiccans, the horses, and Streetman continued their reverse circling of the maypole. Then, another sound permeated the air. A buzzing sound that became more intense.

My aunt gave me a nudge and pointed to the sky. "Must be a medical airlift. Some moron probably got stuck on a nearby mountain."

I started to say something when all of sudden, the helicopter dipped lower and flashed a beam into the woods.

"Look!" Laurel shouted. "Two more helicopters are coming. But why are they flashing their beams into the woods? Can't they see we've got the horses corralled over here?"

"They're flying directly over the woods," I said. "And they're moving farther away from us."

I watched in disbelief as the helicopters veered to my right and hovered far enough off that I could barely make out their silhouettes against the now all-gray sky.

Then, another beam illuminated our area, but this one came from a vehicle that had reached the top of the hill and was now headed straight toward us.

"Hallelujah!" my mother exclaimed. "The cavalry's arrived. Took that sheriff long enough."

I squinted to get a better look and grit my teeth. "Not a deputy. It's a truck. A plain old truck."

No sooner did I say the word *truck* than three more appeared. They drove past us and parked a few yards from the horse-chiweenie merry-go-round. I watched, wordless, as men and women quickly got out of the vehicles and began to remove hay bales from the cabs. Not only that, but one of the trucks had water jugs and a few large pails.

"We got word you found the stolen horses," a tall man in a plaid jacket called out. "We figured they'd be thirsty and hungry."

With that, he grabbed a bale of hay and proceeded to spread it around the horses, which were now safely secured to the maypole with their reins attached to the ribbons.

I scurried after the entourage as they loaded up with supplies and began tending to the horses. "How'd you know?" I asked, raising my voice above the sound of the whinnying horses.

A voice in the semi-darkness called back, "There's a network of ham radio operators around here. The kid who called over to Casa Grande kept trying other locations as well. Fortunately, we were in the area. Our house has a decent landline connection and we called friends who had farms or cattle."

"Any sign of the sheriff's guys?" another voice called out.

"They may be too busy with whatever's going down on the other side of the woods. Probably a lost hiker or one hell of an accident," the first voice responded.

"We should go and help with the horses," Laurel said. And with that, she and Tersee walked to where they were tethered. I stood alone and watched the scene in front of me as if I was in an IMAX theater with a front row seat. I watched as people filled the pails with water and offered them to the horses. Streetman had found himself a spot on an open hay bale and proceeded to move the hay around to create a comfortable nest for himself.

Without wasting a second, I rushed over, scooped him up and hurried back to my mother, who stood a few yards away.

"Quick! Get that leash on him." Then I remembered he had broken the fastener. "No, better yet, can you stick him in that tote bag you've been carrying?"

My mother immediately rushed over to the dog and showered him with kisses, muttering things like, "Momma's hero," and "my precious little man." She opened the tote bag, removed two bottles of spring water, and plunked Streetman inside it. Then she reached around the tote. "Almost forgot. I have his collapsible dog bowl in here, too."

Once the dog settled in, she poured the spring water into the bowl and offered it to him. The dog took giant gulps as if he'd crossed the Sahara.

"He must be hungry, too," my mother added. "I'll mosey over to the food table and see what I can find for him. Looks like someone put lanterns on the table so we can find the food."

"Whatever you do, don't let the dog escape."

"Hmm, I could use a bite myself," Aunt Ina said. "All this excitement has gotten me hungry. Come on, Harriet."

While they walked ahead, I kept my eyes on the two-ring circus—the bonfire with all its fanfare, and the stolen trail horses getting the attention they needed. Again, I tried to call Marshall, but this time I got a message across the screen that read "No signal."

CHAPTER 36

Faint beams from the helicopters flashed across the sky and into the woods.

Lost hiker my you-know-what. And it's no accident or there would be sirens.

I took a deep breath and blew it out slowly.

They're looking for the other riders. The ones who didn't get chased out of the woods by Streetman. But how do they know?

When Tersee and Laurel took off to find a ham radio operator, all they knew was that some of their fellow Wiccans had heard the sound of horses in the woods. And that, in and of itself, wouldn't call for a full-fleet helicopter response. Unless it was Nate and Marshall who had somehow managed to get a call through to the sheriff's office. *Oh, my God! A distress call. Those helicopters aren't looking for horses, they're looking for armed killers.*

I tried to talk myself out of the worst-case scenario that had suddenly blown up in my mind, and that was the moment I look leave of my senses and charged over to where Denton was still under house arrest by the three burly men.

He was seated at the base of a tree with one man on each side of him and another off to the side. No need to tie him up. Denton wasn't going anywhere and neither was I.

"How many missing riders are there? And horses? Are there more horses? No sense lying because you know it's over. Those helicopters aren't in the night sky for a joy ride."

Denton's face showed no sign of expression. "Sixteen horses in all. Twelve riders, two guards, two guides. You do the math."

"You don't strike me as a trained guard. That means you're one of the guides."

"You catch on quickly, don't you? Had me fooled. Thought you were another fun-loving, devil-may-care Boomer."

I'm not even in that age group! I'm in my forties, you jerk.

"Well, I'm not. Where are the other horses?"

"Darned if I know. We took two separate trails. If that ankle-biting little dog hadn't showed up, we'd have been out of here by now and no one would have been any the wiser."

I hadn't noticed it before but there was moonlight. Not a full moon, but coupled with the glow from the bonfire, there was enough light for me to see the Gila monster tattoo on his forearm. Only something wasn't right. I hadn't noticed it before while I was in the pool at the water volleyball game, but standing here in close proximity to Denton, I noticed what I should have observed prior—the tattoo of the Gila monster wasn't the original design. That's why it looked three-dimensional. The offset colors and geometric cubes that comprised the Gila monster's skin were originally part of another reptile's body. Whoever enhanced it must have been one heck of a talented artist, but even he or she couldn't undo the faint pattern that comprised the underlying design—a coiled snake.

Then I remembered the pack of Newport cigarettes that I found on the ledge by the library tower. Bowman told me the forensic lab identified a fingerprint on that pack and it belonged to a convicted felon. A bank robber, if I remembered correctly. That might explain the money I found in Billie's condo apartment.

"You killed her. Billie Churl. Because she knew too much. Or she threatened your operation. You're the one who assaulted her in the library tower and sent her hurling down those steps."

"Sorry to disappoint you, but I wasn't the one who tangled with that wretch."

"But you were there, weren't you? And don't lie. The Maricopa County Sheriff's Office has evidence. Too bad you didn't quit smoking sooner."

"I'll admit it. I was at the library the morning of Billie's, shall we say, *unfortunate demise*, but I wasn't the one responsible for it. I was concerned she was getting a bit too cavalier about our operation so I figured I'd have a private word with her before she began that ridiculous exercise routine of hers on the tower stairs."

"And did you?"

"No. I walked through the computer room on my way to the tower when I got this overpowering craving for a cigarette and it wasn't going away. Even though I quit not too long ago, I had an unwrapped emergency pack in my rear pants pocket just in case I fell off the wagon."

"I'm listening."

"I left the building and skirted around the side by the long ledge. No one saw me. I leaned my back against the wall, pulled out a cigarette and was about to light the damn thing when I changed my mind. I didn't come that far to louse things up. I shoved the cigarette back in the pack and tossed the entire thing onto the ledge. Talk about a good throw. I figured with the pack out of the way, I wouldn't be tempted to light up."

"Did you go back inside?"

"I got as far as the computer entrance when those bell chimes went off like mad. I figured one of the maintenance guys must have fallen into them. I opened the door, and as I stepped inside I heard people screaming and shrieking about a dead body. That was my cue to get the hell out of there. Didn't need to get caught up in that situation. I had no idea it was Billie until much later on."

"It will be your word against the evidence and I'm not so sure the sheriff's deputies will believe it. Look, I know who you are and I know what you've done. You're Ted Gillian and you served time in Oregon." *Or was it California? Darn it, I never pay close attention when Deputy Bowman speaks.*

"For robbery, yes. Not murder!"

"Then why brandish a gun?"

"To get the hell out of here."

"Too late for that."

"Too late for that." What on earth am I saying? I have no idea where those deputies are or how much longer Denton's, aka Ted's, security detail can keep him confined.

The Beltane celebration had morphed into two distinct components—the original one as planned with celebrants dancing and singing around the bonfire, and the horse-nurturing one, for lack of a better word, with a steady stream of people making sure the horses stayed calm. The interesting thing was that the celebrants moved seamlessly from one spot to the other, taking turns with the horses and with the festival itself.

My mother and my aunt planted themselves at the large food table, and if my eyes weren't playing tricks on me, I swore I saw a faint red and blue beam coming from behind where they stood. Then the colors faded, only to brighten again off to my right.

My gosh! It's flashers. Red and blue flashers. I couldn't see them in the curve of the road but I do now.

Without wasting a second, I ran in the direction of the vehicle and waited until it had reached a full stop a few yards from the maypole. Then I rushed to the driver's side door and stood still. A slender man with dark hair and equally dark mustache stepped out. I could see the light grayish-beige shirt he wore, complete with a badge and uniform patch on the short sleeve.

"Emilio Ramos," he announced. "Cochise County Sheriff's Office. Got a roundabout call from Maricopa County about some stolen horses but I was pretty sure they were referring to that other situation southeast of here. That's where I was headed until a second call came in to verify."

"You got our call, all right. From a ham radio operator. A kid, no less. He had to reach out to another—oh, never mind. You got the call. That's all that matters. I'm Sophie Kimball. Phee. The woman you spoke with earlier. And look straight ahead. Those are the horses. Seven of them. Tethered to that maypole. They've still got their saddles on. Should be really easy to identify them. And what other situation? The one with the helicopters hovering on the other side of the woods?"

"That would be it. Got an entire fleet of deputies over there. A rancher phoned in to tell our office he rounded up a riderless trail horse on his property with a fancy-dancy saddle from an equestrian riding school near Safford. We looked into it and it seemed that horse was stolen. Then another call came in. From his neighbor. The guy swore up and down he heard gunshots from the woods near his house, and when he went outside to check, he heard the distinct sound of horses neighing. So he took it upon himself to investigate further, and when he and his son followed a path into the woods, they saw a group of rough-looking men on horseback making their way down a little-used trail. Two of the horses were piebald quarter horses and one was a skewbald. Not very common around here. The guy and his son bolted out of there and called our office."

"I don't understand. How was it he was able to call you but none of us on this hill could get through? We had to rely on ham radios. Ham radios! As if we were back in the nineteen forties."

Deputy Ramos shrugged. "Don't know what to tell you except there are dead zones around here. The tower signals don't go through. Look, once we got that call, it wasn't hard to deduce those were the stolen horses we've been tracking. That's when our team kicked into action with the helicopters. Those beams will locate anything and anyone in the woods at dusk. And we've got a half dozen sheriff's cars poised and waiting to ferret them out. What we didn't count on was your call. The one that bounced into Maricopa County and back. So, what can you tell me about the seven horses I'm staring at?"

I bit my lip and winced. "My mother's dog chased them out of the woods. But that's not all. Two had riders who ran back to the woods. But we've got another man cornered. He was on foot. Armed. His name is Ted Gillian. He's a convicted felon and he may have been responsible for the death of a woman in Sun City West. He'll deny it but you can still arrest him, can't you? For horse theft? He pretty much admitted that part to me."

"Yeah, I'll take him into custody, all right, but that's not my real concern at the moment. Five of the horses that dog rounded up had riders at one point. Riders who most likely are armed. Add the horse from that equestrian stable and that makes six possible gun-toting criminals in those woods. Not to mention the little trail-riding ensemble that's making its way out the other end. Who knows how many guns they've got?"

"You said you had deputies on the other side of the woods. What about the two private investigators who've been tracking the movement of those horses since the thefts began?"

"Yep, they're imbedded with our team."

"So they're okay?"

"Last I heard."

"Keep it that way. One of them is my boss and the other is my fiancé."

"Got it. Right now, stay as far away from the woods as possible. Make sure no one goes near there. I'm headed to the other area, but once I get a cell signal, I'll send deputies this way."

"What about Ted Gillian?"

Deputy Ramos glanced at the base of the tree where Ted sat.

"Doesn't look as if he's going anywhere. By the way, those horses can't stay tethered to a pole all night."

"We can't let them loose."

"I wasn't suggesting that. When I reach my deputies, I'll have one of them contact the local ranchers and see if any of them can swing by here with horse trailers. There's a large barn that's not being used by the local grain and feed store in Nicksville. The horses can bunk down there for the night."

"What about the ones on the other side of the woods?"

"Guess they'll have to share the space as well, but only if we can catch their riders first."

Deputy Ramos turned and started for his car. Then he looked back at me. "Nice work, Miss Kimball. Oh, and brace yourself. It could turn out to be a long night."

"Wait!" I shouted as he hustled to his car. "Would you please give a message to Nate Williams and Marshall Gregory? It's important. Tell them I'll be at the Billowing Breeze B and B in Sierra Vista sometime tonight." Then I swept my arm across my body and pointed to the maypole and bonfire areas. "Feel free to fill in the rest."

"Understood."

CHAPTER 37

"**D**on't expect to be getting to that homey little B and B anytime soon," I said to my mother and Aunt Ina as soon as Deputy Ramos drove off. "I'll explain later but right now I need to find Tersee, Laurel, or Serena to let them know what's going on. By the way, I think Nate and Marshall are okay."

My aunt had just finished a bite of Green Man Cake, a Beltane favorite, while my mother continued to stuff small crudités into her mouth. As I hurried off to find one of the three ladies, I thought about Deputy Ramos's remark.

I'd had long nights before. After all, who didn't pull an all-nighter when cramming for a college final, or staying up all hours with a sick child? Not to mention waiting in airport terminals due to a canceled flight and a rebooking that meant flying to the other side of the globe before connecting to a homeward-bound flight. But something told me those experiences would pale in comparison to what Deputy Ramos expected.

I spotted Laurel taking in the bonfire from a short distance. She tilted her head back and stretched as I approached. "I can't thank you enough," I said. "One of the deputies stopped by to let us know that more stolen horses are on the other side of the woods. That's why there are so many helicopters in the area. They're flushing out the riders but they may be armed. We need to keep a good distance away from the woods."

"I don't think that will be a problem. No one wants to creep around the woods at night. And some of us don't even like going there in broad daylight."

I laughed and she continued to speak. "The bonfire will be ending soon. It's down to embers. Most of our celebrants will head home but a few will remain and camp out to make sure the fire is completely out. Our volunteer cleanup committee will be here first thing in the morning to pick up the trash and drive it to a transfer station. Not like we have garbage pickup around here. But what about the horses?"

"The deputy is arranging for some ranchers to drive up here with trailers. They should be here in a little while. There's a barn they can use in Nicksville."

"And the horse thieves? What about them?"

"I think it may turn into a cat-and-mouse game until daybreak, but the sheriff's office has a substantial backup force. If you see Serena or Tersee before I do, will you let them know?"

"Absolutely."

"I'd better go back and find my mother and my aunt before they consume all of your perishables."

This time it was Laurel who laughed.

. . .

Thank goodness Deputy Ramos kept his word. As the bonfire festivities waned and the crowd thinned out, three horse trailers arrived. Two small ones and one that looked as if it could carry the lineup for the Kentucky Derby. Four ranchers, with help from the Wiccans, loaded the stolen horses onto the trailers and drove off.

I watched as the trailers eased their way down the road. Only a handful of people remained, three of whom were still guarding Denton/Ted, and three, namely Tersee, Laurel, and Serena, who kept my mother and my aunt company. Fortunately, none of us had to wait much longer. A sheriff's deputy car with its flashers on cruised up the hill and stopped at the edge of the maypole's circle. This time two men got out. Both in uniform.

"It's about time," my mother called out from where she and my aunt stood. "Arrest that man by the tree so we can all go home."

No sooner did she finish her sentence than the helicopters returned to our area. Three of them hovered over the woods, their high-intensity beams focused in one area. At the same time, two more sheriff's cars arrived.

One of the deputies from the first car approached us and spoke. "This is an active crime scene. Return to your vehicles and stay there. Keep your car doors locked and your windows rolled up. We've got the road blocked so you'll have to ride it out."

I almost burst out laughing when he said "ride it out," but I kept still and watched as he and his partner approached Denton/Ted while two more deputies circled, conversing with the remaining celebrants. I imagined those folks were told to get in their cars as well.

"Let's not waste time," I said to my mother and my aunt. "Better get in the car and wait."

My mother opened a napkin and tossed in a few more crudités while my aunt did the same. I cringed. "Come on, we've eaten enough." Streetman was still tucked into the tote.

Once we were back in the car, I turned on the low beams so we could see what was happening. Sure enough, Denton/Ted was handcuffed and escorted to one of the sheriff's deputy cars. I was sorry I didn't get to thank the three folks who kept him under watch until law enforcement could take over. I figured I'd let Tersee, Laurel, or Serena know once this fiasco was over.

The helicopter beams weren't the only ones illuminating the woods. Two of the sheriff's cars were now stationed a few yards away with their high beams directed there as well. We watched the scene in front of us but there was nothing to see.

It was quiet, too. Only the sound from the helicopters combined with the soft moans coming from Streetman, who was fast asleep in my mother's lap. But Streetman did more than whimper and snort in his sleep.

"My God, Mom! What did you feed him? I don't care if we're supposed to keep the windows up, I've got to air out this car!"

"Phee's right, Harriet," my aunt added. "This is an assault on my nostrils."

I turned around in my seat to watch my mother gently stroke the dog's head. "He's had a very traumatic experience. It affects his digestion."

"Give me a break," I said. "Your dog had the time of his life herding up those horses and eating all sorts of people food."

My aunt waved her hand in the air and nearly bumped my head. "It's almost eleven. The illumination on my watch is wonderful. I never noticed it before. How long do you think we're going to be stuck here?"

"Until the sheriff's deputies have cleared out the woods. Look, I've got to open a window."

I started the car and rolled the driver's side window down about four or five inches when I heard gunshots.

"Roll that window back up," my mother shouted. "And duck for cover."

"The gunshots came from the woods. I need to let some air in here."

Then more gunshots bounced around the woods.

"Fine. I'm rolling it back up."

The next sound we heard was a siren as another sheriff's car made its way up the hill.

My aunt sat up in her seat. "They're bringing reinforcements. Harriet, do you have any more of those cheesy biscuits?"

"Sorry, I gave the last one to Streetman."

As if on cue, my aunt and I groaned at once.

Time moved at a snail's pace, and in spite of the intermittent gunfire, I still found myself dozing on and off.

"Now what time is it, Ina?" my mother asked.

"A few minutes before midnight."

My aunt moved around in her seat, making worse noises than the dog. "This is taking its toll on my sciatica."

I rolled my eyes and leaned back. When I looked toward the woods again, I saw two men being escorted to the sheriff's vehicles. The men were already handcuffed. I glanced at my aunt, then turned my head to face my mother. "Looks like the deputies caught more riders. Gee, I hope this ends soon."

It didn't. It was one thirtyish when we finally got the all-clear from one of the deputies that we could be on our way. I asked if he had any word about the situation on the other side of the woods but he didn't.

"I hope we can get into that Billowing Breeze at this late hour," I said as I drove down the hill in the direction of Nicksville. "It's about a nine-mile drive from here to Nicksville and another nine or ten to Sierra Vista."

"That's not so far," my aunt said.

"It is when I'm driving in the dark with no visible markings. And these hilly roads don't have guardrails. Ugh."

An hour later I pulled into the circular driveway in front of the Billowing Breeze B and B. From what I could make out, the place was a large clapboard cottage complete with a white picket fence.

"Now what?" I asked.

"Now we knock on the door and hope the proprietor is a light sleeper," Aunt Ina replied.

My mother gave my shoulder a nudge from the backseat. "Don't think you need to worry about that. The lights just came on in front."

Before I could say a word, a heavyset woman opened the front door and motioned for us to come inside. Her voice echoed in the stillness of the night. "I'm so glad you finally made it. That very nice Deputy Ramos called me hours ago to tell me you'd most likely be very late. Come on in. Are you hungry?"

I whispered to my mother, "Don't you dare. You and Aunt Ina ate enough for an army."

"We're fine," my mother called back. And with that, we grabbed our overnight bags and walked to the front door. Streetman quickly watered a bush before being ushered into the cottage and down the hallway to where my mother's room was located.

My head hit the pillow twenty minutes later and I didn't see daylight again until eight. I took a quick shower and got to the guest dining area while breakfast was still being served, but instead of my mother and my aunt Ina at the front table near the window, it was Nate and Marshall.

CHAPTER 38

Both men had five o'clock shadows and circles under their eyes. Their shirts were wrinkled and their shoes were coated in dust. I don't know who spoke first but it didn't matter. Marshall and I hugged each other so tight and so long that Nate finally called out, "Give each other some breathing room before one of you has to be resuscitated."

The words tumbled out of my mouth, and for a minute I wasn't sure if any of it made any sense. "How did you know—What are you doing—When did you—"

"Slow down," Marshall said. "Maybe have some of their chamomile and pomegranate tea instead of coffee."

I hugged him again. "I thought I'd never reach you. You can't believe how worried I was."

"It's okay, hon. We know. You might not have been able to reach us by phone but Augusta was able to get a call through. That's how we knew you were in the area yesterday. She explained everything except where you'd be staying. Got Deputy Ramos to thank for that. He delivered your message sometime around midnight. Said it was a regular circus parade and that Streetman rounded up the horses. Unbelievable. Our end of things probably went a tad smoother. The Cochise Sheriff's Office, in conjunction with some border patrol agents, nabbed the rest of those horse thieves."

"I don't suppose you and Nate were bystanders in that operation. Were you?"

Nate chuckled. "What? And miss out on all the fun? Nah, we were part of it, too. But I imagine you figured out that much already."

"Guilty as charged. I couldn't stay in the office. I had to get down here. And when I found out my aunt's friends were celebrating their holiday in the vicinity of those horses, I had no choice. Augusta said she could manage without me tomorrow. And speaking of which, I'll make up all the lost time."

"Relax. That's the last thing I'm concerned with." Nate gave my shoulder a squeeze and smiled.

"You have no idea how relieved I am to see you both in one piece," I said. "Does this mean you'll be able to drive back home today?"

Nate and Marshall looked at each other and finally Marshall spoke. "We'd love, too. Trust us. Our clothes smell worse than those horses. But we've got to deal with the aftermath, beginning with reuniting the horses and their owners. Perry Gaynes is already on his way down here along with his neighbor. They've got to ID the horses and fill out more paperwork than you can imagine. Oh, and Martin Winston-Featherly is on his way here as well. Don't think he appreciated the early morning wake-up call from Deputy Ramos."

"And the arrests?"

Nate rubbed his chin. "Quite the gang, I'll say. Beginning with someone who already made your acquaintance, I believe."

"Yeah. Denton. Who's really Ted Gillian. Boy, is this a mess. But at least we can put Billie Churl's assault to rest. He had to have been the one who wrestled with her on the top of those stairs, even though he denied it."

"Not only did he deny it, but he says he can prove it. Bowman and Ranston are looking into his alibi. Yep, another early morning call that those two didn't appreciate. Meanwhile, this Gillian character is under arrest for possession of stolen property and he's not going anywhere soon. According to Deputy Ramos, horse theft is not taken lightly in these parts and bail is usually denied."

"That's a relief. At least until his alibi falls short."

Nate and Marshall didn't say a word.

I grabbed Marshall's wrist and shook it. "His alibi *will* fall short, won't it? I mean, who else could have tangled with Billie? Denton had motive and opportunity. And he was at the right place at the right time."

"Hard to say, but if his alibi doesn't check out, Bowman and Ranston will work with the Cochise Sheriff's Office to add assault-resulting-in-death to the charges against the guy. Meanwhile, the best thing you can do is enjoy your breakfast and take a nice, slow drive home. Cell phone service is fine in this part of the state. I'll call you later today." Then he gave me another hug. "Don't worry. Nate and I plan to be back tomorrow. Stock up on laundry detergent."

"Can you stick around a few more minutes until my mother and Aunt Ina show up for breakfast?"

The panicked look on Nate's face answered the question for me, but it was Marshall who spoke. "Give them our best and tell them we'll catch up another time. We told Deputy Ramos we'd meet him at the barn where those horses are being stabled. And once Martin Winston-Featherly arrives, heaven knows how much paperwork he'll bring."

"I'll meet you in the car," Nate said to Marshall. Then winked.

We were the only two people in the dining room and took advantage of the few seconds of alone time by enjoying a long, lingering kiss before Marshall hurried off to join his partner. A minute or so later, the B and B waitress arrived with a steaming cup of coffee and some scones. She handed me a menu and asked how many people were in my party. Before I could reply, my mother showed up with Streetman in his tote, followed by Aunt Ina, who hadn't braided her hair yet.

"My God, Ina!" my mother shrieked. "Are you trying out for *Hair*?"

I had to admit, my aunt resembled the profile on the 1967 album cover for the rock musical. I tried not to laugh and told them Nate and Marshall had been here a few minutes ago and were off to finalize their case with Deputy Ramos.

"At least Louise Munson will be able to get a good night's sleep," my mother said. "And so will the rest of us. Thank goodness we don't have to put up with that parrot of hers anymore."

I bit into the cranberry scone and winced. "Denton, aka Ted, may have an alibi. He said he wasn't the one who fought with Billie in the library tower."

My aunt tore off a large chuck of her scone. "If he could lie about his name, he could lie about anything. I say we tell Louise the good news and keep our fingers crossed it stays that way."

Six hours later, more or less, I dropped my aunt off at her house.

"This jaunt has been so exhaustive, both physically and emotionally, that Louis and I will need to get away for a few days to unwind," she said as she got out of the car. "But I'm glad we were able to find those horses."

My mother sat up in her seat. *"We?* It was Streetman. And if they offer a reward, it should go to him."

"Thank Tersee, Laurel, and Serena for me," I called out to my aunt. "I'll talk to you later this week."

"When we get to my house, do you want to stop in for something to eat?" my mom asked.

"We ate lunch in Casa Grande. I'm fine. But I'll help you in with your bag and the dog."

When I finally got home, I dumped my overnight bag on the floor, grabbed a Coke from the fridge and plopped myself on the couch for twenty minutes of uninterrupted bliss. Then I called Augusta and Lyndy to tell them about the events north of Naco.

"I know," Lyndy said. "It's been on the news. Some field agent by the name of Feathery or something like that is being hailed as a hero for breaking the case."

"What? Martin Winston-Featherly? That weasel! I can't believe it. Usually Bowman and Ranston take all the credit when Nate and Marshall solve the MCSO cases, but this is outrageous."

"Hey, as long as those horses were found, who cares?"

"My mother, for one. If she could find a way to get that dog of hers to receive a congressional medal of honor, she would. Aargh."

"Take a breath. At least no one has to worry about some maniac tossing people down stairwells. Guess it was an inside job, huh?"

"Looks that way. Our office should know more later this week."

• • •

I got to work earlier than usual the next morning to make up for lost time. Two hours earlier, in fact. Marshall phoned and said they'd be back by early evening and not to worry about dinner. He'd be too tired to eat.

By Wednesday, our full crew was back at Williams Investigations with Augusta going nuts rebooking all of the appointments she had to change in the past week. Still, she was elated Nate and Marshall were no longer on the road. The horse theft cases were put to rest, as was the break-in at Tula's. Turned out those thieves were the guilty parties after all. The good news was that Perry Gaynes and his neighbors were finally reunited with their horses, as were the other owners who went through that ordeal. I thought about Brandon and Robyn Marionette from Wickenburg and almost welled up.

Back in Sun City West, the book club ladies were reasonably sure Denton/Ted was the tower culprit and Louise finally began to sleep without a babysitter in her house. That's when Bowman and Ranston delivered the disturbing news to our office.

It was Thursday afternoon and Augusta had just finished replacing the toner in the copier when the call came in from Deputy Bowman for Nate or Marshall.

"Get one of your investigators on the line," he told her. "The Billie Churl case is still open."

Augusta immediately transferred the call to Nate's office and raced into mine to tell me what Bowman said.

"Shh! Keep your voice down," she said. "Bowman's on the phone with Mr. Williams. The Billie Churl case is still open. Means Denton isn't your guy."

"Oh, no. We're back to where we started. Only worse. Denton and his crew were the only ones with a decent motive to wrangle with her. I hope those deputies don't go blabbing this all over the place. I'll be forced to have Streetman as an overnight guest when it's my mother's turn to stay with Louise. This can't be happening."

Unfortunately, it was, and it did. Nate gave Marshall, Augusta, and me the rundown when he got off the phone with Bowman, but I could have just as easily caught it on any of the local TV stations that aired the news that night, the same way Louise and everyone else in my mother's book club did. Especially when the news anchors mentioned the "special witness" who recognized the distinct odor in the library tower.

Too bad Denton/Ted had an alibi. An ironclad, not-to-be-tampered-with alibi. He was seen on not one but two video surveillance cameras, both time-stamped, from two of the three places of worship across the street from the library. Evidently the sheriff's office had neglected to review those at the time of the investigation, focusing instead on the library's incomplete video.

Augusta patted her hair in place when Nate explained. "Harrumph. Looks like Bowman and Ranston stepped into it this time," she said. "Now they'll be reviewing protocol with their office for the next month."

I winced. "Uh, speaking of stepping into it, I'm afraid my mother's going to send me back to the dog park to see what else I can find out."

Marshall patted my shoulder. "At least it's a nice, safe place."

CHAPTER 39

A s luck would have it, my mother didn't ask me to take Streetman to the dog park. Instead, she came up with something far worse—another impromptu meeting of the book club ladies, this time at Bagels 'n More the following night. And if that wasn't bad enough, she also invited Herb, who, in turn, asked his pinochle cronies to join him. There was no escaping it. Given my involvement in the case, I had no choice but to attend.

"Six thirty, Phee. We scheduled it early so you can drive over right after work," she said when she phoned our office later that Thursday. "Louise is on the edge of hysteria. Remember, she was tossed into a moving car the last time those news anchors mentioned her conversation with the deputies."

I took a breath. "They didn't mention her name. And besides, it was after a bingo game. It could have been any disgruntled player."

"Highly doubtful. And the news media didn't have to mention her name. You should know how this community works by now."

"Fine. Six thirty tomorrow."

• • •

Early Friday evening at Bagels 'n More was to a senior community like a sports bar was to a multigenerational one. The place was filled to capacity with the usual crew at its reserved table in the center of the room. There were thirteen of us in all and that meant lots of shouting in order to be heard. Miraculously, the ordering process went smoother than I expected, although the waitress grimaced when Myrna told her we all wanted separate checks.

Herb, who wound up seated next to me, gave my elbow a poke. "Heard you had quite the roundup on the border. Guess that little ankle biter of your mother's earned his keep this time."

"If you're referring to Streetman," my mother said, "his skills far surpassed anything those deputies could have pulled off."

Then Kenny spoke, "Enough with Harriet's dog. I thought we agreed to meet here in order to figure out who might be after Louise."

My aunt retied one of the large burgundy tassels on a braid and leaned into the table. "There's only one thing that can help Louise at this point. She needs to be hypnotized. Once under the deep hypnotic spell, she'd be able to recall the events of that morning with clarity. And that includes remembering exactly what she smelled in the library tower."

"I'm not going to be hypnotized!" Louise shouted from her place at the far end of the table. "What if I don't come out of that spell? Then what?"

"She makes a good point," Wayne said. "Don't need another person walking around in a fog. Or worse yet, driving in one. Got enough of those in Sun City West."

I stifled a laugh and took a bite of my BLT. Then I spoke. "It's an open case and the sheriff's office is taking it seriously. I'm confident they'll find out who was in that tower with Billie." *I may be collecting Social Security by then, but I'll be darned if I say that.* "Best thing any of us can do is report anything we hear to their office."

"What about your office, Phee?" Cecilia asked. "Are Nate and Marshall looking into it?"

I shook my head. "No, they're not consulting on this one. They just finished up that statewide horse theft ring and need to catch up on their other cases. Everything was pushed back a few weeks."

Bill reached across the table for the pepper shaker and proceeded to cover his lox until no visible signs of pink could be seen. "Talk about a shocker. One would have thought it was one of those guys in that ring who was responsible for what happened to Billie. After all, they were the ones with the motive."

"Maybe that wasn't the only motive," Lucinda said. "Could Billie have been having an affair and some jealous wife got into it with her?"

Here we go again. Someone save me now. We're back to my mother's usual theory about jealousy and rage.

I started to say something but I was vocally overpowered by Myrna, Shirley, and my mother, who spouted off every Danielle Steele and Sidney Sheldon plot they could remember. As I darted my eyes from one woman to the next, something occurred to me. Something I'd forgotten about all together. Thank goodness I wasn't collecting a paycheck for investigative work.

"Um, as much as I'd like to stay here and commiserate with everyone, I really need to get home. I have to be at work tomorrow. It's one of my Saturday work mornings."

"Call me if you hear anything," my mother said. "Meanwhile, we'll stay here a bit longer in case we have a brainstorm."

I did a mental eye roll, said good night to the crew and raced to the cashier before anyone tried to detain me. I had been so fixated on the horse thefts and Marshall's safety I had neglected to follow up on another lead.

It was still early and I had plenty of time to make a quick stop at Jimmy John's subs. With any luck, Richie Salisbury would be working the evening shift and Marshall and I would either have a late, late snack or subs for lunch tomorrow.

When I stepped inside the sub shop, two workers were behind the counter. A girl with curly reddish hair and her male counterpart, also with red hair and a fair share of freckles.

"Hi!" I said, before either of them asked me what I wanted. "I'm looking for Richie Salisbury."

"Uh-oh, Richie," the girl said and giggled. "What have you done now?"

I looked directly at Richie. "I work for an investigative agency and I wondered if I could ask you a few questions. Meanwhile, your friend can make up two ham and Swiss subs with all the fixings on wheat bread rolls."

Richie gave the redhead a nod and walked out from behind the counter. "Let's talk over there by the soda machine."

"I won't take up much of your time," I said. "I understand your aunt, who lives in Sun City West, was scammed out of her jewelry. She may not be the only one. Unfortunately, we weren't able to get her name in order to chat with her."

"It's Adelaide Sasher. She volunteers in the library. She used to be on the water volleyball team if you can believe it, but her arthritis got really bad. She's still pretty close with the players, especially Julia Ornstern. I can give you my aunt's phone number if you'd like. She's not the greatest when it comes to email."

Adelaide Sasher and Julia Ornstern. Right under my nose. "That would be great."

"Do you think there's a chance she'll ever see her missing jewelry again?"

"I hope so."

Wonderful. Now this kid thinks I'll be able to find his aunt's family heirlooms. Aargh. One more thing to add to my list because I'm such a sucker.

Marshall was thrilled that I picked up a sub for him because he had to drive to Goodyear in the morning to meet with a client and didn't feel like stopping anywhere for lunch. I told him about Richie and he said something about me sharing that info with Bowman and Ranston. But thirty seconds later, he turned away from the TV and gave me a wide grin.

"You're going to track down that lead yourself, aren't you?"

I grinned back and crinkled my nose. "You bet your life I am!"

• • •

Julia Ornstern. Of all people. It made sense, though. She was a dear friend of Adelaide's and when Adelaide got duped by Billie, maybe Julia thought she could recover the stolen jewelry when something went wrong. I finally had a viable suspect, but getting her to admit it would be tricky at best.

I needed to eke the truth out of Julia without finger-pointing, and what better way to go about that than to practice what I intended to say, using Augusta as my listener and coach. I waited until our break time the next day and got Augusta to play along with me.

"We've been through this five times already, Phee," she said. "Now my coffee's cold and my break time is over. Stop trying to sugarcoat the whole thing. It won't work. Just tell this Julia woman that you know she was responsible for sending Billie down that stairwell and leave it at that."

"I don't want to sound accusatory."

"As opposed to what? Just spit it out. You'll feel much better once you do."

Suffice it to say, I didn't.

Julia had agreed to chat with me over coffee at the Starbucks across Grand Avenue from Sun City West later that afternoon. By the time I arrived, I was a bundle of nerves and prayed I wouldn't lose mine.

"Um, I suppose you're wondering why I asked to meet with you this afternoon," I said. "I'm afraid you may have gotten the wrong idea. It's not about water volleyball. Well, maybe a little bit. Because only a seasoned volleyball player would have the strength and dexterity to use a hand strike maneuver on another person."

Oh, my God! Talk about hitting someone over the head with a sledgehammer. I didn't even lead into it. At least Augusta would be proud.

Julia set her coffee cup down and clasped her hands. "Billie. I don't know how you were able to reach that conclusion but I'll save you some time. I didn't kill her. But I may have set something in motion that did."

"So you admit to being in the library tower with her the morning of her death?"

"It'll come out somehow and there's no use denying it any longer. Yeah, I was there. Long story, but if you got this far, you probably figured out the rest. Billie stole some valuable jewelry from a good friend of mine. A lady who was too embarrassed to report the incident to the sheriff's office for fear they'd think she was one of those old senile seniors who got taken in by every scam artist. And in this case, they were right. About the scam artist. Not the rest. My friend was very trusting. Too trusting. And Billie was the worst kind of grifter."

"Hmm. You thought you could have it out with Billie and recover the jewelry."

Julia nodded. "I knew she exercised on that stairwell and I made it a point to learn her schedule. On the day of the incident, I got there very early and waited at the top of the stairs by the bell, hoping to take her by surprise, and it worked. However, someone else came into the tower before Billie arrived. When Billie got there, she called that person a fossil and then I heard the door open and close. Whoever it was, left. Billie didn't know I was in the tower until she reached the spire, but I didn't push her. Not at first. I tried to reason with her about those family heirlooms and you know what that little witch did?"

I shook my head.

"She replied, 'Tough noogies,' and gave me a poke in the shoulder. Then she added, 'Get out of my way or you'll be sorry.' When I told her I wasn't going anywhere and that I would file a report with the posse, she said, 'You are now!' and gave me a shove. That's when I shoved back. I must have really had some momentum on my side because that heavy bell started swinging and chiming like crazy. Billie lost her footing and tumbled down the stairs. But not all the way. About halfway down, she was able to use the guardrail and stand."

I took a sip of my coffee and motioned for her to continue.

"'I'm on my way down,' I called out to her. 'Try anything and next time I'll really show you how a volleyball feels when it's going over the net.'"

"Did she—"

Julia shook her head. "She let me pass and didn't say a word. I left the tower figuring I'd report the incident to the posse along with the jewelry theft so they could follow it up with my friend."

"But you didn't."

"No. Because once I left the tower, I had to use the ladies' room, and when I got out everyone was screaming that there was a dead body at the foot of the stairs. I was petrified I'd be accused of murder so I blended into the crowd for a few seconds and then exited the building before the deputies arrived to take statements."

Julia reached across the table and grasped my wrist. "I'm telling you the truth. I didn't kill her."

CHAPTER 40

"Someone had to have killed her between the time you left the tower and the time you exited the ladies' room," I said. "Julia, think back. The other person in the tower was Louise Munson and she said there was a cloying smell in there mixed in with the usual stale, smoky smells. Do you recall anything?"

"Huh. Now that you mention it, I do. It smelled like someone eating a garlic bologna sandwich in a perfumery. I figured the odor wafted in from outside."

"Are you sure you were the only one in there?"

"I'm sure. Unless someone was outside on that top ledge that surrounds the bell portion of the tower. I never thought of that."

And so far up that it's not in the video surveillance from those houses of worship. Drat.

"I'm thinking that's what happened. You weren't the only person familiar with Billie's exercise schedule. Her killer was. Given what you told me, I have a pretty good idea who it is. If we hurry, we can catch up to him at the supermarket deli in Vistancia. Are you willing to do that?"

Julia slugged the last of her coffee. "Might as well. I can't have this hanging over my head indefinitely."

"Um, you may need to stretch the truth a bit in order to get him to confess."

"At this point I'll do anything to get it over with."

"Meet me in front of the supermarket on ninety-ninth and Lake Pleasant Road. We'll go inside together."

With that, we left Starbucks, got on Route 60 and onto the 303 to Lake Pleasant Road. I could see Julia's car in my rearview mirror all the way to the parking lot in front of the shopping complex.

It was a little past four when we walked to the deli but no Eddie Krome in sight. I turned to Julia and shrugged. "I probably should have called first."

Just then, Eddie appeared from the back and placed a large ham on the rear counter. "There you go, folks. I'm punched out for the day."

"Wait!" I shouted. "Remember me? Phee Kimball. I need to speak with you. Can we talk outside?"

"Gimme a sec. Be right with you."

"Follow my lead," I whispered to Julia. "And feel free to improvise."

As we got to the exit, I reached in my bag for my cell phone and made sure to set the Voice Memos, something I learned not too long ago. Eddie was already seated and motioned us over.

"This is Julia, a friend of mine," I said. "And the key witness to Billie Churl's murder. But you probably know that already."

Eddie started to stand but I motioned for him to sit. "I think you need to hear what she has to say before you bolt out of here. But you won't get far. We already called the sheriff's office."

Eddie took out a cigarette and lit it. "I have no idea where you're going with this."

"Then allow me to explain," Julia said. "I was the one who had the altercation with Billie at the top of the tower, but you already knew that because you watched us from a vantage point on the ledge that surrounds the bell. You knew Billie was alive, albeit bruised up, when she fell down the stairs. That's when you made sure she'd never get up."

"You're lying. Billie and I were the only ones on that stairwell."

"True, but once I left, I opened the door slightly and peered in. That's when I saw what you did."

Oh, my gosh! Julia lies better than I do.

Eddie slammed his fist on the table. "That hellcat had it coming. Yeah, you were right. I was waiting for her at the top of the tower but not to kill her. I only wanted to ruffle her up a bit to get her to stop spreading lies about me. Lies that could have cost me my job."

The sexual harassment, according to Rashida.

"When I heard the door open below, I knew I had to get out of there so I crawled onto the ledge by the bell. And yeah, I did see you get into it with her. When she tumbled down the stairs and you made a run for it, I knew I had my opportunity to set her straight, only it didn't go like that."

"What do you mean?" I asked.

"Even half seated on the stairs, that damn shrew punched me in the groin and told me I'd be on report with HR. That's when I lost it completely. I yanked her up and shoved her so hard I could hear her bones hitting the stairs."

I winced and saw a similar expression on Julia's face.

"Didn't waste any time," Eddie continued. "I got the hell out of there." Then he looked at Julia. "Guess you hightailed it, too."

"Did you stay in the library?" I asked.

"Sat myself on the crapper and waited it out. When I heard the commotion, I joined the crowd. That was the story I gave that deputy—that I was in the john taking a—"

"We get it," I said, trying not to shudder.

"Look, it's your word against mine, so let's forget this whole deal and move on. Billie deserved what she got."

I bit my lip and took a breath. "Maybe so, but that's not our choice."

"I'll deny everything when those deputies get here, you know."

"That's up to you."

"Come on, Julia," I said. "We're done here."

When we were out of earshot, Julia looked back at Eddie. "He's still sitting there. I wonder why he didn't bolt."

"Because those deputies would have found him no matter what. Yikes! I almost forgot—I need to call them."

Bowman's grumbling sound when I told him what Julia and I had done escalated and then stopped. "Lake Pleasant Road, you said?" he asked.

"Uh-huh. And I have the entire conversation recorded on my iPhone. It won't be admissible in court but it's enough to eke out a full confession."

"I don't know whether or not to thank you or admonish you for putting yourself in danger, so I'll leave it at that. Stop by the posse office with that phone, will you?"

"I need to get home first, but Marshall and I will be in later."

Then, I remembered something and knew I had to deal with it. Danger or no danger. I thanked Julia, said goodbye to her and raced back to where Eddie was seated.

"I need to ask you something else," I said. "Did you shove a short, stocky woman with grayish frizzy hair in front of a car after a recent bingo game in Sun City West?"

"After a bingo game, you said? Why on earth would I do that? Those people are maniacs when they get out of there. I avoid those games like the plague. What happened with Billie was personal. Not a public spectacle like bingo. Why? Did someone accuse me of that, too?"

"Uh, no. Just clarifying a matter."

I could hear Eddie moan as I walked back to my car.

Marshall gave me the biggest hug when I told him what Julia and I pulled off. "We have to stop by the posse station with my phone," I said when I got home, "and then maybe we should do the same with my mother. Now at least she'll be able to focus on that Bye Bye Birdie event. Black balloons and all. Meanwhile, I need to call Nate, Augusta, Aunt Ina, Lyndy . . ."

"I'll give Nate a buzz and save you a call."

"Great. I'll start with Augusta."

"You owe me tacos for a month," she said when I got her on the line.

"Huh?"

"My theory. Remember? I told you someone had a seething rage and made it look like an accident."

"Beef, carnitas or chicken?"

"As long as they're not bean."

Both of us laughed and I moved on to my other calls.

• • •

News of Eddie Krome's arrest hit the airwaves and the TV the next morning with Bowman and Ranston getting credit for solving "one of the community's most perplexing cases." To add insult to injury, that lab report on Billie's wounds cinched the case. Too bad it was after the fact. The bite marks were from a horse. A horse! Most likely one of them bit her when she tried to halter it. Had I known that sooner, it would have saved me lots of trouble.

Lyndy phoned as soon as she caught the segment. "Can you believe it? You did all the grunt work and those two got the credit. Aren't you even a teeny-weeny bit upset?"

I laughed. "Nah. Let them bask in their glory. I'm glad it's over with. Truth is, I need Bowman and Ranston on my side."

I didn't know how prophetic that statement was until the next morning, when Julia called to tell me Adelaide's family jewelry had been recovered in Billie's house and Adelaide was ecstatic. Like the money stash, the jewelry was hidden in a pair of old boots under the bed. Yuck!

The only mystery left was the one surrounding Louise, but a few days later that, too, was solved. Louise had filed a report at the posse station and they had recently taken the time to pursue it further. That meant they sought out and reviewed footage from the social hall's video camera that faced the parking lot.

The camera caught a clear facial shot of Louise's assailant when the woman turned away from the parking lot and walked back toward the social hall. From there, the deputies were able to make a positive identification, and the attack had nothing whatsoever to do with Billie.

"Can you imagine that?" my mother asked when she phoned me at work on Wednesday to tell me what she heard from Louise. "That crazy woman shoved poor Louise in front of a car because Louise had purchased the last big chocolate chunk cookie at the refreshment stand and the woman wanted it. I'm telling you, Phee, some of these people are not well-balanced at all."

Gee, you think?

"By the way, I'm having Shirley make a little cowboy outfit for Streetman. It's quite fitting considering his rodeo skills."

Rodeo skills? Chasing horses around and biting at their heels? Yikes.

"Um, great idea. But you're not going to have him wear it at the wedding ceremony, are you? I thought we agreed on the cummerbund and a simple little dance after our vows."

"Yes, yes. The cummerbund. Meanwhile, I need to call Herb and get moving on Bye Bye Birdie. We can launch those balloons from the tower and give those snowbirds the farewell they deserve."

"And vie for a spot on *Sonoran Living*?"

"If anyone deserves that spot, your mother does," she said.

I rolled my eyes. "Good luck."

EPILOGUE

The Bye Bye Birdie event went off without a hitch and my mother was able to juggle the Broadcast club, the clay club, and the Booked 4 Murder book club booths while ensuring that "Herb didn't mess things up" with the balloon launch. The proverbial icing on top of the cake came when ABC's *Sonoran Living* hostess approached the event coordinators and told them how impressed she was with the black balloons with their handwritten silver messages.

"I must say," Suzanne Casperini said, "the balloons aren't the usual bold color choices. Did you select the black and silver theme to reflect how saddened you were to see the snowbirds leave for the summer months?"

"It's not the same without them," my mother announced into the microphone.

That simple comment prompted the hostess to invite my mother and the book club ladies to appear on *Sonoran Living* as a testimonial to how welcoming the Sun City West community was.

"What was I supposed to say?" my mother asked when I chatted with her later in the day. "That we're celebrating less traffic on the roads and no long waiting lines at the restaurants or movie theaters? I couldn't very well tell them the truth in front of a zillion viewers."

"I suppose not. Do you have any idea what the show's theme will be when you and the ladies make a guest appearance?"

"Yes. It's about pets that brighten our lives."

"Please don't tell me—"

"Louise is bringing that parrot of hers so Streetman will need to stay home. He'll be terrified if that thing starts squawking. Anyway, he needs time to prepare for your wedding. We're practicing a new dance routine. Your uncle Louis was able to get us the soundtrack from *Rawhide.*"

"Be sure to thank him for me." *And tell the guests to remain seated.*

ABOUT THE AUTHOR

 J. C. Eaton is the pen name of husband-and-wife writing team Ann I. Goldfarb and James E. Clapp.

A New York native, Ann spent most of her life in education, first as a classroom teacher and later as a middle school principal and professional staff developer. Writing as J. C. Eaton, she and James have authored the Sophie Kimball Mysteries, the first book of which, *Booked 4* Murder, took first place in the 2018 New Mexico-Arizona Book Awards in the Cozy Mystery category. They are also the authors of the Wine Trail Mysteries and the Marcie Rayner Mysteries. In addition, Ann has published nine YA time travel mysteries under her own name.

When James E. Clapp retired as the tasting room manager for a large upstate New York winery, he never imagined he'd be co-authoring cozy mysteries with his wife. Nonfiction in the form of informational brochures and workshop materials treating the winery industry were his forte, along with an extensive background and experience in construction that started with his service in the U.S. Navy and included vocational school classroom teaching.

You can visit Ann and James at www.jceatonmysteries.com, www.jceatonauthor.com, www.facebook.com/JCEatonauthor/, and www.timetravelmysteries.com.